A PERILOUS JOURNEY OF DANGER & MAYHEM

BOOK 1: 'A DASTARDLY PLOT'

Christopher Healy

WALDEN POND PRESS
An Imprint of HarperCollinsPublishers

Walden Pond Press is an imprint of HarperCollins Publishers.
Walden Pond Press and the skipping stone logo are trademarks and registered
trademarks of Walden Media, LLC.

A Perilous Journey of Danger & Mayhem: A Dastardly Plot
Copyright © 2018 by Christopher Healy
Library of Congress Control Number: 2018021260
ISBN 978-0-06-234198-3

Typography by Joel Tippie
19 20 21 22 23   PC/BRR   10 9 8 7 6 5 4 3 2 1
❖
First paperback edition, 2019

For William Picchioni

Uncovering the Mysteries of the Inventors' Guild

A *New York Sun* Exclusive

by Sherwin St. Smithens,
high society and technology columnist

NEW YORK—Towering marble columns, golden-wreathed windows, chubby naked angel babies tootling on trumpets overhead: Where could we be, loyal readers, but the world-famous Inventors' Guild Hall right here on Manhattan's Madison Square? This is a building so grand, I couldn't fault an unwitting tourist for thinking it a palace or cathedral. And it might as well be! Because this, ladies and gentlemen, is where our national treasures, the magnificent men of the Inventors' Guild, put their stylishly coiffed heads together to work mechanical miracles daily—men like George Eastman, who crafts photographic cameras small enough to be held in human hands, and Alexander Graham Bell, whose incredible "telephone" allows us to carry on conversations with folks all the way on *the other side* of Manhattan Island. These are giants among men who harness the raw powers of combustion, steam, and electricity to serve up tidbits of the future as easily as if they were tiny cheese cubes on a cocktail platter. Remember when, only a short time ago, women had to sew shirts by hand and the only way a man could open a can of soup was by stabbing it with a screwdriver? This reporter certainly doesn't. Because I'm too busy living in our modern Age of Wonders! And we have the men of the Guild to thank for it.

It's no wonder that every journalist in the country has been clamoring for a sneak peek behind the scenes at the Guild Hall. But it certainly is quite a feat for this reporter to have nabbed just such an exclusive tour. How did I manage it? I'll never tell. But you, lucky readers, get to join me in my walk among the intellectual elite! Shall we?

My host, Guild clerk Oswald Lemmington, meets me on the steps outside the hall and ushers me in. Our first stop: the clockwork carnival that is the hall's Grand Entry Chamber. It is truly a sight to behold. But it's open to the public, so I'm not going to waste precious space talking about it here. Get down to the hall and see it for yourself! No, the second floor is where the real action is. So what are we waiting for, Lemmington! Take us up that gilded staircase!

When I step from that upper landing into the winding, gorgeously wallpapered upper-level corridors, I feel as though I've wandered into the digestive tract of a snake, a big beautiful snake that eats geniuses— because they are *everywhere*! Brash, bold men of science pop in and out of offices trading witty banter about fuses and batteries. The atmosphere is electric!

And speaking of electricity, why, there's Mr. Thomas Edison himself, co-chair of the Guild and the man who gave us the light bulb! Thank you, Mr. Edison! Now I can see in the dark without a candle flame lighting my ascot on fire!

And who do we see chatting with Edison? Why, it's none other than our swankiest president, Chester A. Arthur, clad in a fur-collared coat that would make Alice Vanderbilt blush. Now, if you are wondering what the president of the United States is doing at the Inventors' Guild, well, you haven't been reading my column! President Arthur has positioned himself as the Innovation President. A powerful friend to the Guild, this style icon is determined to unite the powers of government and technology to make America the most advanced nation on Earth. There is far more to Chester A. Arthur than just the country's most envied sideburns. Perhaps that is why his nickname around the Guild is President Dream-Maker! (And perhaps that is why Thomas Edison has hinted at a run for office of his own.)

So here I am, dear readers, already feeling like I've struck gold with sightings of both Thomas Edison and President Arthur, when who should pop in from across the hall but Edison's co-chair, Alexander Graham

Bell. Turns out this trio of titans needs to discuss the marching order for the Brooklyn Bridge dedication parade. All three will be on hand as, in a few days, New York celebrates the opening of the world's longest bridge with a spectacular fireworks show.

While the three pose for some photographs, I try to get them to spill some tantalizing secrets about the upcoming Event of the Century: the 1883 World's Fair & Cultural Exhibition. When the Fair opens its gates on May 30 in Central Park, the miracle makers of the Inventors' Guild will be the stars of the show. It was the Guild, of course, that was instrumental in bringing this global celebration to New York City (thereby fulfilling the lifelong dream of the late, great Guild founder, Johann Rector). So, while the Fair will be home to pavilions and showcases from forty different nations, "Inventors' Alley" is sure to be *the* hotspot of the entire affair. Where else can you see fifty of the globe's finest minds demonstrating their latest creations? And don't forget the big lighting ceremony at 6:00 p.m. on opening night, when Thomas Edison will officially flip the switch on his new citywide power grid and turn this World's Fair into a day-*and*-night event. World's *Fair*? More like World's *Amazing*!

Sadly, Edison, Bell, and Arthur are all mum about the Fair—don't want to spoil the surprise and all that. And, believe me, I understand. No need to school this reporter on the need for a little drama! Enough about next week anyway—let's talk about *now*! After all, we have so many more geniuses to meet.

We move down the hall and there's James Ritty, who is revolutionizing retail shopping with his "cash registers." And there's Levi Strauss, who is revolutionizing the art of pants-wearing with his "blue jeans." And now we come to Serbian heartthrob Nikola Tesla, who greets us with a fork that is literally shooting lightning from its tines. What is it for? This reporter couldn't begin to guess. But we have no doubt it will soon change the world. For this is the age in which we live—when any one person's blip of ingenuity can fuel the spark that changes history.

And look who's in the next office—it's Byron Edgerton, showing off his solid gold necktie and ruby-buckled (continued on p. 6)

PART I

1

The Age of Invention
New York City, 1883

IT WASN'T EASY, being the child of a genius inventor. There was the rooting through trash bins to find scrap metal, the misplaced wrenches winding up under your pillow, the constant cleaning of spilled pickle juice. But the job certainly had its perks too, such as front row seats to the moment your mother changed the world. For newly twelve-year-old Molly Pepper, that last bit was going to happen in exactly eight days. And everything she'd sacrificed would finally pay off.

One week from tomorrow, the World's Fair would open its gates and Cassandra Pepper would present her Icarus Chariot—the very first personal flying machine—to the public. A hundred thousand people would crane their necks to see Molly and Cassandra soar among the clouds overhead. The crowd would be so awestruck they'd need medical assistance just to get their jaws shut again (and Cassandra could no doubt invent a Mechanical Mandible Clamper to do just that).

Molly wished she could've been there for the Icarus Chariot's maiden flight, but, for the sake of secrecy, her mother had insisted upon a late-night test, and after a long day of sanding boards and fetching tools, Molly had dozed off before the big moment. She only learned of her mother's historic achievement when Cassandra woke her up, yelling, "Molls! Molls! Guess what? Mr. Tortellini has a chicken living in his apartment upstairs! Oh, and the Icarus Chariot works. That's how I saw into Mr. Tortellini's apartment."

There was no way Molly was going to miss it tomorrow, though, when her mother demonstrated her flying machine before the World's Fair Planning & Preparatory Committee. Until then, her main focus was putting finishing touches on the Icarus Chariot. The vehicle might have been ready to take to the air, but it was not ready to take to the Fair. To put it bluntly, it looked like trash. Which was mostly what it was made from.

The Peppers didn't have piles of cash to spend on building supplies, so all of Cassandra's creations were constructed from secondhand parts. Cassandra never fretted about how her inventions looked: "If it works, it works," she'd say. And while Molly agreed in theory, she was also savvy enough to know that a sleek, freshly painted flying machine would earn more admirers than a mildewed, splintery one with anchovy labels still stuck to its rudder. It was to that end that the Peppers began clearing space in Cassandra's workshop. Which also happened to be a pickle store.

For the most part, Pepper's Pickles looked like any of the other specialty food establishments along the bustling thoroughfare that was Thompson Street. Upon entering, customers would see barrels of fermenting cucumbers and a wooden counter stacked with murky jars of dill spears. They would smell a tang in the air from the canisters of salt and flasks of vinegar crammed onto shelves. But few took note of the tall folding screen that protected the rear half of the store from prying eyes.

If a customer were to peek behind that screen, however—which none did without feeling the sting of a shot from Molly's Thimble Cannon—they would see a long worktable littered with springs, screws, bolts, gears, and tools of every type. And they'd see two thin beds, a stovetop, and a clothesline drooping with damp bloomers. Because the Peppers also *lived* in their pickle shop.

Most of Cassandra's inventions—like the Self-Propelled Mop, the Quick-Crank Corn De-Cobber, and the Astounding Automated Secretary, to name a few—were small enough to stow under and among the furniture. The Icarus Chariot, however, was her greatest work in more ways than one. It didn't fit behind the screen. Normally, they stored it in pieces, but in order to assemble it for painting, varnishing, and (if Molly had her way) a little glittering, they would need use of the full store space.

Cassandra bolted the door and began moving heavy jars of garlic dills from the counter to the floor. "As long as the pickles are safely behind the counter," she assured her daughter, "I think we can avoid another incident."

"Good thinking," Molly said. "And I'll handle the windows." Floor-to-ceiling shop windows might be good for luring in hungry customers, but they didn't do much for privacy. Molly stuffed five sticks of licorice gum in her mouth and began chewing as she grabbed the pile of *New York Sun*s that sat on a barrel of brine. She'd been collecting newspapers for weeks, trading defective pickles to the newsboy down on Bleecker Street in exchange for day-old copies. She'd already read every article, but far be it from the Peppers to use something only once. Molly held the clump of gum between her crooked front teeth, pulled away a fingertip's worth, and stuck the dark goop onto the glass. She then peeled the front page from the top copy of the *Sun* and smushed it—*voilà!*—onto the gum. One twelve-by-twenty-inch section of window was successfully covered. Twenty or so more and they'd have all the privacy they needed.

While Molly continued her chewing, spitting, and sticking, her mother hummed "Polly Wolly Doodle" and dragged the preconstructed segments of her flying machine from the rear of the store. The more of the window Molly covered, the dimmer it got, so she struck a match and lit one of their oil lamps.

By the flickering lamplight, Molly scanned the headlines she'd pasted up. Almost all of them were about inventors. But not just any inventors—the members of the illustrious Inventors' Guild.

IS HYATT'S "PLASTIC" REALLY BETTER THAN STEEL?

EASTMAN TO AMERICA:
ANYONE CAN BE A PHOTOGRAPHER

WILL SERBIAN UPSTART TESLA OUTDO EDISON
WITH HIS HANDHELD GENERATORS?

Molly huffed. Even if she couldn't deny her fascination with these modern-day Merlins who were using their magic to shape the future, she still held a grudge against the Guild. She had lost count of the number of times Cassandra had taken one of her brilliant creations to the grand Guild Hall, only to be turned away because of the Guild's longstanding rule against admitting women.

Molly had hoped for a change after the Guild's founder, coal magnate Johann Rector, passed away. A big deal had been made of the Guild's leadership being taken over by two of its most famous members: Thomas Alva Edison and Alexander Graham Bell. Bell, the mild-mannered Scotsman, had transformed the field of communication with his telephone. And Edison, always the dapper showman, had given the world the electric light bulb. And the phonograph. And the kinetoscope motion picture viewer. And about a thousand other things. From his lab across the river in Menlo Park, New Jersey, Edison pumped out inventions on a weekly basis. (Nearly as many as Cassandra.) Together, Edison and Bell had promised to "lead the Guild in bold new directions!"

But that was two years ago, and the Guild's roster didn't look much different than it had before.

Adding to Molly's anger was that the Inventors' Guild had come incredibly close to stealing Cassandra Pepper's chance to enter the World's Fair. Six months earlier, on the very first day the Planning & Preparatory Committee was to accept applications for exhibition spaces in the Fair's Inventors' Alley, the Peppers woke at 5:00 a.m. to ensure they'd be at the head of the queue. They were told, however, that the Guild had already scooped up every single slot for its members. The Guild, it seemed, had been instrumental in bringing the World's Fair to New York, so they got first pick at, well, everything. The best Cassandra could do was put her name on the waiting list and hope that some Guildsman would drop out. But what inventor worth his monkey wrench would give up a shot at the World's Fair?

And then, just yesterday, the postman delivered a gift from on high—a letter from the P&P Committee informing Cassandra that one of the Guildsmen had fallen into a vat of shellac! Unfortunate for him, yes, but great for the Peppers; Cassandra was formally invited to present her work for consideration. It wasn't a done deal yet, but Molly knew that once the planners saw her mother's flying machine—not to mention all her other astonishing inventions—that exhibition slot was as good as hers.

"I love what you've done with the place, Molls," Cassandra said, looking at the windows. "I'd consider keeping it like this, but I can't imagine those gum wads look very appetizing from outside."

"No matter," said Molly. "We won't need the pickle business come next week when we're living off flying-machine money!"

"Can't argue with that. Now, let's get these clothes off and get to work." An added bonus of covering the windows was that the Peppers could safely shed their long, stiff, black dresses. Fastened with a line of buttons that ran from chin to ankle, the dresses barely allowed for bending at the waist, let alone crouching to tighten a bolt on the underside of an experimental aircraft. The feminine wardrobe, Cassandra often said, was not designed for engineering.

Molly watched as her mother, in her one-piece, full-body bloomers, began clamping canvas-covered wings to the old rowboat that made up the body of her flying machine. She didn't mind having to help her mother show off her inventions at the World's Fair—so long as it didn't mean she had to miss out on seeing all the other amazing exhibits there.

"So, I know we'll be busy at our booth," Molly said, "but can we still ride the Ferris Wheel?"

"Absolutely!" Cassandra said cheerfully. "What's a Ferris Wheel?"

"It's a big wheel," Molly said. "Built by some guy named Ferris."

"And people can ride on it?"

"So they say," Molly replied.

"In that case, we wouldn't dare miss it." Cassandra began strapping wooden chairs to a mast in the center of the boat.

"Ooh, and can we try some candy corn? It's a new sugary treat they're gonna have at the Fair."

"That's always been the problem with candy: not enough vegetables involved. Put us down for two buckets' worth." Cassandra hammered a foot pedal into its slot.

"Oh," Molly continued. "And we're definitely going to see the lighting ceremony on opening night, right?"

Cassandra paused. "You mean Mr. Edison turning on his electric grid? Frankly, Molls, I don't think we'd be able to avoid it. His men have been installing those light poles all over the city for weeks. We'd see it from here."

"I know," Molly said, hardly able to keep the excitement from her voice. "But wouldn't it be a thrill to be there and see him throw the switch?"

"Whatever you want, dear," Cassandra muttered. She went back to hammering, noticeably louder than before.

"Easy, Mother," Molly warned. She didn't want a repeat of the Crumpled Clock Episode two weeks earlier. "Just remember, soon it's not gonna matter whether the Guild lets you in. Once the world sees your inventions, you'll be just as big and famous as those guys. Oh! And I have just the thing to remind us." She squeezed past piles of tools and shuffled through an envelope of papers by her bed until she found a photograph she'd clipped from the newspaper weeks ago.

The picture had originally shown Alexander Graham Bell and Thomas Edison shaking hands with other Guildsmen lined up behind them. But Molly had drawn a picture of her mother over Edison, Cassandra's long black dress and high-piled bun neatly covering up Edison's checkered suit and derby. Molly had sketched her mother into that scene because Cassandra Pepper deserved to be in these news articles as much as any Guildsman.

She'd also drawn an eye patch and pirate hat on Bell, because why not?

11

Molly used her last bit of gum to stick this creatively altered photo in the window, where it was illuminated by the afternoon sun. "Eight days, Mother." Molly grabbed two cans of paint. "Eight days and you will upstage all of them."

And then, Molly added to herself, *we can stop living pickle-to-pickle and start changing the world.*

Dreams Take Flight

MOLLY HADN'T ALWAYS been her mother's assistant. There was a time when her father, Nathaniel Pepper, had been Cassandra's right hand, her biggest supporter— and all while on his way to becoming the Pickle King of New York City. People from all over the neighborhood would stop by Pepper's Pickles not just for a jar of Hungarian Half-Sours, but also for a laugh or an "Oho!" or a "You don't say!" because Nathaniel Pepper was a man who knew how to tell a good story.

But that was before the tuberculosis. Before the sallow cheeks, the coughing jags, the customers who refused to make eye contact even as they apologized for taking their business elsewhere. It was before the rain-soaked funeral, at which Molly angrily counted the mourners and decided there weren't nearly enough.

Afterward, Molly did what she could to ease the burden on her mother. She told herself not to be sad as Cassandra sold her beloved clamps and wrenches at the pawnshop, and not to be scared as her only remaining parent stood night after night in their apartment doorway arguing with black-suited bank men. She taught herself to cook beans and eggs, and to fall asleep without hearing the next chapter of her bedtime book. She swept and straightened, and made a corny pun whenever she saw the telltale glint of a teardrop in her mother's eye. But eventually, the Peppers had to admit they could no longer afford rent on both an apartment *and* a store. That was when Molly quit school and took over business at the pickle shop. She did it because dusting and joke-telling weren't bringing back the joyful mother she'd always loved. And because her usual As and Bs had already begun turning into distracted Cs and Ds. But mostly, she did it because she vividly remembered the night, many years earlier, when Nathaniel Pepper had promised his beloved Cassandra she would never have to give up on her dream—and Molly refused to let her father become a liar.

Tired, sweaty, and just a tad dizzy from the paint fumes, Molly dipped a thin brush into the royal blue and raised it to the bow of the boat. She paused. "Before I do this," she said gently, "are we a hundred percent sure about the name?"

"Icarus Chariot?" Cassandra asked, accidentally drawing a purple stream down her nose as she scratched an itch. "What's wrong with it? In Greek mythology, Icarus was the first human to fly."

"He was also the first human to crash," Molly said. "Is that the connection we want people to make with your flying machine?"

Cassandra shook her head. "Our flying machine will *redeem* the name of Icarus. Icarus was a dreamer. He thought big, Molls. He didn't take no for an answer."

"And it killed him."

"Not this time! This time, Icarus will soar. 'Icarus' it will be." She stepped away to view her creation from a distance. "Although now I'm not sure about the 'chariot' part."

Cassandra Pepper's flying vehicle looked like a boat, except its "sails" stretched out horizontally to either side. Four non-matching chairs were arranged in a circle, facing outward from the mast they encircled. The front-most seat featured foot pedals, which, when cranked, powered a small combustion engine that, in turn, operated a propeller atop the mast. Once in the air, the pilot could steer the vehicle with two tall levers that raised and lowered the wings. During their demonstration tomorrow, Cassandra would be in the pilot's chair, but Molly would get to ride in the rear seat, waving down to the gawking members of the Planning & Preparatory

15

Committee, who would be shouting things like, "How is this brilliant woman not a member of the Guild?" and "How is she not *running* the Guild?" and "I bet that girl in the back deserves a lot of the credit!"

Molly finished painting ICARUS CHARIOT on the side of the vehicle and plopped her brush back into the can. Tomorrow, she'd get to experience true human flight. But for now, they had the exciting evening activity of watching paint dry. "Might as well take off the parts that aren't wet," Molly said. They planned to borrow the cucumber deliveryman's wagon in the morning to haul the disassembled chariot uptown to show the committee how easily it could be put together. Molly unlocked the right wing from its casing.

"Actually, Molls," Cassandra said with a devilish gleam in her eye. "I think you should try it out first."

Molly stared, perplexed.

"I feel bad you weren't there to see me make liftoff last week," Cassandra continued. "So I want you to be our pilot for the committee tomorrow."

Molly didn't know what to say. Her mother never let her do any of the important stuff. "Wow, um, thank you. But . . . I don't think I know how."

"You've heard me talk it out a gazillion times. It's easy," Cassandra scoffed. "Give it a try now. Don't look at me like that—not through the roof or anything! Just a few inches, so you know you can get it off the ground."

On the one hand, this sounded to Molly like a wholly inadvisable idea, but on the other hand—*flying machine!* She flashed a licorice-blackened smile at her mother and leapt into the pilot's seat. Not having inherited her mother's height, she had to stretch a bit to reach the pedals, but she was ready. And then came a knock at the door.

Cassandra scurried to toss a tarp over the Icarus Chariot, while Molly, grumbling, hopped down and opened the door a crack. "We're closed," she said to the stumpy man outside.

"But it's only 6:20," the man said, checking his pocket watch. "And the sign says—"

Molly grabbed her paintbrush, reached her arm outside, and slapped a swath of blue across the posted business hours.

"Says nothing," she said.

The man frowned. "But I want some pickles."

Molly turned to Cassandra. "Pickle me!"

Cassandra plucked three fat dills from a jar and tossed them across the room to Molly. She caught two of them.

"Here." Molly shoved the wet pickles into the man's hand. "Five cents."

"Is there . . . something I can put them in?"

"Try your mouth. That's what most people do." Molly plucked a nickel from the man's coin purse and slammed the door. She then opened it again and added, "Thank you, don't forget Pepper's for all your pickle needs!"

17

"Hurry, Molls," urged her mother. "I want to see you do this!"

Molly climbed onto the chariot just in time for another knock. "Aargh!"

"Stay, dear," said Cassandra. She cracked the door.

"Hello," said a man's voice. "I thought you were closed, but then I saw that man get—"

Cassandra picked up the pickle her daughter had missed, slapped it into the man's hand, and opened her palm for payment. "You, pickle. Me, nickel."

"Um . . . but," the man stammered. "This isn't what I want—"

"Keep it, it was on the floor anyway." Cassandra slammed the door and turned back to Molly. "Okay, pedal fast! Because apparently all of Manhattan has chosen this very moment to have a pickle craving."

Molly pumped her legs until she heard the pop and rumble of the engine kicking over.

"Faster, Molls, faster!"

Molly pedaled harder. Puffs of smoke sputtered behind her as the rotor began spinning rapidly. Soon, a breeze was stirred up within the store. The vehicle began to feel unsteady beneath her—was she rising? She pushed harder and the breeze became a genuine wind. The pages of newsprint on the windows began to flutter, and several tore free, leaving open spots through which the street was visible. Molly panicked. She was using her mother's top secret invention in clear view of everyone. In her underwear.

"Shut it down, Molls!" Cassandra grasped frantically at flying papers. "Pedal backward!"

But Molly's feet slipped from the pedals and the motor continued to churn. Trying to regain her footing, she grabbed the tall levers to her sides—and both wings flapped upward. The right wing—which Molly had unlatched—flew off completely. Twelve feet of wooden pole and stretched canvas crashed behind the counter, spilling a whole line of pickle jars. Molly finally managed to pedal backward and the whirring engine wound down.

All was silent, save the *plip-plip* of dripping brine. "Well," Cassandra eventually said, "I would call that a semi-successful test run."

"Semi-successful?" Molly sputtered. Her mother's optimism only frustrated her further. To Molly, this was a full-fledged disaster. And it was her full-fledged fault. She was never meant to be an inventor's assistant. She didn't feel at ease with machines the way her mother did; carpentry and engineering didn't come naturally to her. Her mother deserved better.

"Well, you know how to work the pedals," Cassandra said, mopping up pickle juice with handfuls of newspaper.

"Mother, I didn't properly re-clamp the wing, and now look! We'll lose hours cleaning up this mess, I've got to re-cover the windows, the paint's already scuffed, the wing looks broken, and we've only got till tomorrow! How could this get any—" There was a knock at the door. "Flaming flapjacks!" Molly leapt from the lopsided aircraft and threw open the door. "We're closed!"

The postman, quivering slightly, passed a handful of mail to the red-faced girl. Molly slammed the door, then reopened it. "Thank you, don't forget pickles for all your Pepper needs!"

She flipped through the envelopes. A bill from the cucumber farm, a bill from the salt deliveryman, a bill from the glassblower for the jars Molly had just broken. And one letter in a glossy envelope sealed with a globe-shaped wax stamp.

"It's from the World's Fair Committee!" Molly shouted. She tore open the envelope and ran to join her mother in a vinegary puddle behind the counter.

> *Dear Mrs. Nathaniel Pepper,*
>
> *This letter is to inform you there is no need to visit our offices tomorrow for a demonstration of your "work." The Inventors' Guild has reclaimed the exhibition space for which you intended to be considered.*
>
> *Cordially yours,*
>
> *Ulysses S. Grant*
>
> *Chairman, World's Fair Planning & Preparatory Committee*

"Oh my," Cassandra said. "That's . . . the president's autograph!"

Molly shot her mother an incredulous glare.

"Okay, *former* president," Cassandra said.

"Mother," Molly said sharply. "Have you read the letter?"

"Not yet. I always read the signature first so I know what kind of voice to use in my head." Cassandra scanned the body of the note. "Why? Is it— What! Unbelievable! Unfair! Un . . . Un . . . Un-*everything!*"

"They can't do this to you!" Molly returned. She marched around the messy store, her cheeks hot and her fists clenched. "They promised you a chance, and now they're not even going to *look* at your inventions? They can't get away with that!"

She expected her mother to join in, but Cassandra only took a seat on the edge of the Icarus Chariot and put her head in her hands. *Oh, no,* Molly thought. Her mother was going back to the Dark, Sad Place.

"Mother, we won't stand for this," she said.

"That's why I'm sitting." Cassandra looked up at her daughter and sighed. "I had so much celebrating planned for us. I was going to take you for ice-cream floats. And chocolates. And maybe some of that corn candy you were mentioning."

"Candy corn."

"Sure, that too. And books, Molls. I was going to take

you to Zimiles Booksellers and let you pick out as many books as we could afford with all that money we were going to make." She looked up. "I was going to buy us tickets to that show with that Italian actor you're always mentioning."

"Sergio Vittorini?" Molly asked with a flicker of hope, as if it might still actually happen. "The Man of a Thousand and Twelve Faces?"

"That's the one," Cassandra said. "A thousand and twelve faces. It's very impressive. Though oddly specific. Oh, and you and I were going to go to the Brooklyn Bridge parade!"

For her entire life, Molly had watched the massive bridge come into being, marveling as—bit by bit, over months and years—immense granite towers rose up from the swells of the East River and steel-cable webs were stretched from the shores of Manhattan to the neighboring city of Brooklyn. In two days, the bridge was finally going to be opened to the public with a gala ceremony that included fireworks and a parade led by President Chester A. Arthur (whose fabulous winglike sideburns were among Molly's favorite things ever).

Cassandra's head dropped again. "Oh, Molls. I thought I'd be able to do all those things, because I thought I was finally going to get my chance. All I've ever needed was a chance."

"The fireworks are free," Molly said as a silver lining.

"We can still see those." She sat down next to her mother on the side of the Icarus. The whole vehicle tipped over. "I guess I'll get the mop," she said, and pulled herself from a pool of blue paint on the floor.

3

Great Moments in Bad Ideas

MOLLY WATCHED HER mother mournfully toss the detachable parts of her flying machine into a pile and then struggle back into her long, stifling dress (because, as Cassandra said, "What's the sense of staying in your undergarments when there's no work to do?"). But they'd bounced back from defeats before. Cassandra's entire career was one long list of rejections: the manager at Haughwout's Fashionable Emporium who insisted— without a demonstration—that no one would buy her Bread Loaf Slice-ifier; the registrar at Columbia College who laughed away the mere thought of her attending an engineering class; the dozens of clerks at Inventors' Guild Hall who pointed her to the door the moment she said she wasn't there for a tour. Yet she never stopped creating.

"Why do you do it, Mother? Your inventions?"

Cassandra, slumped at her worktable, shrugged. "I don't know."

"Yes, you do," Molly said sternly.

"Then why are you asking me?"

"I want to hear you say it."

Cassandra huffed. "Because we're living in the Age of Invention," she said flatly, reciting the line like a bored child forced to memorize a poem for school. "A time of progress and innovation, where any one person's blip of ingenuity may be the spark that changes the world." She sat up, passion returning to her voice. "Yet half the population is too busy dusting windowsills and boiling roasts and wiping baby bottoms to devote more than a few seconds to anything creative. I have been blessed with a family that has given me time, and I will use it to pass on that gift to others, to create time-sparing devices that provide the nation's housekeepers and child-minders and such with the ability to exercise their own inventiveness. *That* is how I will change the world."

Cassandra stood up, hand on her heart, and Molly applauded.

"Excellent speech, Mother. Very inspiring! Although I'm pretty sure people don't boil roasts—that's why they're called roasts. Not boils."

"And that is why *you're* the cook in the family," Cassandra replied.

Molly might not be the world's best inventor's assistant, but world's best daughter? That was something she could aim for. "Peppers never quit. Father always said it, you always used to say it, let's not forget it." She began squeezing back into her button-down frock. "So, what's our next step? Do you think we have any hope of changing the Planning Committee's mind?"

"Not if it means going up against the Guild," Cassandra said. "They're the real mayors of this town. What the Guild wants, the Guild gets."

"But why does the Guild even want that exhibition spot?"

"Who knows? I can't imagine that man in the shellac has recovered well enough in one day. Maybe they're giving Edison two spots."

Molly looked at the few newspaper pages still dangling from gooey strands in the window. "Everything the Guild does is big news," she said, an idea striking her. "Let's see what the *Sun* can tell us." She wrapped a pickle in wax paper and ran outside.

"You'd better hurry," Cassandra called to her. "I'm pretty sure it's beginning to set."

"Not the sun I was talking about," Molly shouted back. "But I'm gonna hurry anyway!"

Molly was hit by the thickness of the air the moment she stepped outside. The stench of horse manure wasn't as strong as usual—a sign that the city had been working to clean its streets before the World's Fair. But what the air lacked in animal stink, it made up for in human body odor. Many tourists had arrived in advance of the Fair to attend the Brooklyn Bridge ceremony. Molly rushed through the crowds and rounded the corner onto Bleecker Street, where a stocky kid in a newsboy cap was stepping down from an apple crate and shoving a small stack of papers under his arm.

"Skiff!" Molly called. "Wait!"

"Well, if it isn't Mittsy," the boy said, flashing something that was halfway between a sneer and a grin. "Don't usually see you this time o' day. Always figgered you was off hangin' in your cave once the sun went down."

"Yeah, bats are nocturnal, so even as insults go, that makes no sense," Molly replied coolly. "You got any evening editions left?"

"Few," Skiff said, scratching his nose and leaving an ink smudge across its tip. "Come back tomorrow morning and we can trade 'em like usual."

"Just give me one now," Molly said.

"No can do, Mitts. I'll get busted if I give you anything other than old papers."

"I didn't come empty-handed. Here's a pickle. Full-sized. Not even a runt."

She waggled the pickle before his eyes until he took it and handed her a paper in return. "Fine, Mittsy. But just this once."

"Pleasure doing business with you, Skiff."

Skiff squinted at her. "You know I call ya Mittsy on account o' you got big ears like baseball mitts, right?"

"Yup," Molly said, heading homeward. "And someday, when you least expect it, I'm gonna pound you for it."

Back inside Pepper's Pickles, Molly found her mother sitting at her worktable with a pile of loose pickles. She crunched loudly into one as Molly entered.

"Mother, are those the pickles that spilled on the floor?"

"I was hungry."

"Well, slide them aside." She took a seat beside Cassandra, began flipping pages, and quickly came upon the information they were seeking.

INVENTORS' GUILD WELCOMES NEWEST MEMBER

by Sherwin St. Smithens,
high society and technology columnist

NEW YORK—The Inventors' Guild, pride of New York and the nation, has added another budding young genius to its ranks. Though only 17 years of age and not yet graduated from Buckminster's Preparatory Academy uptown, Thaddeus Edgerton looked quite at home among the Guild's luminaries as he addressed reporters from his new office in the grand Guild Hall on Madison Square. "My father [Guild member Byron Edgerton, inventor of Tiny Hats for Fancy Cats™] didn't want me to join until school was finished," said the junior Edgerton. "But then I would have missed the chance to fulfill my most recent dream of presenting at the World's Fair."

And just what is this sparkling new talent planning to dazzle us with at the Fair? "You know when you're at a cocktail party or debutante ball?" said Edgerton. "One of the Astors' affairs, say, or the Rockefellers'? And you get stuck talking to a sadly unattractive person? Well, I'm working on a pair of special spectacles with fake eyes on the front, so it looks as if you're paying attention to the hideous beast, while secretly you can glance about for a more appealing conversation partner."

This reporter, for one, smells a hit.

Molly slammed her palms onto the table. This was Problem Number Two with the Inventors' Guild. While many of its members produced work that was actually beneficial to humanity, several were simply rich men who liked to tinker with machines and so bought themselves a place at the world's most prestigious worktable. Perhaps this was to be expected, since the entire organization was founded by a super-wealthy coal-mining tycoon. But whatever happened to that "new direction"

Edison and Bell had promised?

"I can't believe I lost my spot to this hoity-toity rich boy," Cassandra said.

"No," Molly said, pacing around the room. "Your spot was *stolen* by this hoity-toity rich boy! His moneybags father just *made* him a Guildsman. It's obvious he's not even a real inventor!" She waved her arms wildly. "We need to get your spot back! We need to do . . . something! We should . . . should . . . I don't know! We should . . . break into the Guild Hall and smash Hoity-Toity Boy's stuff!"

Molly let herself flop against the wall and slide to the floor, where she took a few slow breaths and waited for her hot cheeks to cool down. It felt good to have let out all that built-up anger and frustration. Perhaps after a good night's sleep, she and her mother would be able to put their heads together and figure out what they could actually do in order to—

"That's genius, Molls!" Cassandra said.

Huh? Molly looked up.

"If young Master Edgerton's awful Eyeglasses-for-Stinkards are destroyed, his exhibition spot will be useless to him," Cassandra said gleefully. "Then I, the rightful owner of that spot, can take it back."

"Um," Molly began.

"It's a perfect plan," Cassandra continued. "Let's hop to it!" Before Molly could respond, Cassandra picked up a crowbar and marched out into the night.

Entering and Breaking

MOLLY WAS HAVING second thoughts about this "genius" idea of hers.

What they were doing was illegal, but she reminded herself they were doing it to right a terrible wrong. She tried to imagine herself as a Robin Hood type, a hero who wasn't afraid to break a few rules in the name of fighting injustice.

She was pretty sure, though, that Robin Hood never found himself flopped over a second-story windowsill with his legs flailing in the night air like spaghetti noodles in a hurricane.

"If we're to succeed, Molls," her mother called from below, "you should probably be more *inside* the building."

"I can't make it over the sill," Molly whispered

between clenched teeth. "The buttons on my dress are stuck. Buttons are evil."

To be honest, she had enjoyed their little adventure up until this point: skulking through a lamplit labyrinth of cobblestone streets, ducking into the shadowy alley between the majestic Inventors' Guild Hall and the ominously dark Madison Square Theatre, stacking empty crates so Cassandra could boost Molly up to an open window. It was all rather like something out of an adventure novel.

Until she got stuck.

"Don't move," said Cassandra.

"Not a problem," Molly replied.

With her crowbar, Cassandra reached up and shoved the soles of her daughter's boots. Molly slid chin-first to the hardwood floor, each successive button snagging the windowsill along the way. Molly cursed every one of them: *evil, evil, evil, evil, evil, evil, evil . . .* The feminine wardrobe, she thought as she struggled to her feet, was not designed for burglary either.

But her clothing troubles were forgotten soon enough. Molly Pepper was now standing in the hallowed halls of the Inventors' Guild. For as long as she could remember, she'd been mesmerized by the Guild Hall's towering columns, its golden laurels, its front door sized for giants. When she was younger, she used to think that if New York had gods like ancient Greece, they would live at the Inventors' Guild.

The hall was no less stunning from the inside, even with only the dim glow of moonbeams to illuminate its wonders: flowered wallpaper that recalled a fairy garden, stained-glass lamps that looked to have been constructed from shattered rainbows, doors with gilded nameplates that probably cost more than Pepper's Pickles earned in a year. Molly felt almost as if she hadn't broken into an office building, but a magical fortress ripped from one of her storybooks.

"Molls?"

Molly poked her head back out. "Hush! Someone will hear!"

"Who?" Cassandra said. She was still balanced on the stack of crates below the window. "It's well past ten. The Guild ends business at seven. And the theater is dark on Tuesdays—no chance of your Sergio Vittorini popping out the stage door and catching us. Although . . . *Ooh*, we should come back sometime when we're not committing a crime and get his autograph. But enough dilly-dallying, Molls! You're in, now let's get me in. Throw down some rope!"

Molly blinked. "What rope?"

Cassandra snapped her fingers. "Rope would have been a good thing to bring. No worries. One of these supposed inventors must have rope in their workshops."

"You didn't happen to bring a lockpick, I suppose?" said Molly.

"Next best thing." Cassandra handed up the crowbar.

Molly tested the weight of the heavy iron tool in her hands. "I suppose this *would* do the trick."

"You look concerned," Cassandra said. She held out her arms. "Hop down and boost me up. We'll trade places. I'll find some rope in there and come back for you."

Molly looked out. Her mother was twice her size and wearing a dress that, thanks to the corset underneath, was even stiffer than her own. Even if Molly somehow mustered the strength to heft her mother to the window, there was zero chance of getting her over the sill.

"It's okay," Molly said. "I'll do it."

"I am your mother, young lady," Cassandra replied sternly. "It is my job to keep you safe. Now jump out that window."

"As much as I'd love to test your daughter-catching skills, I can handle this," Molly said.

She crept down the dim corridor, scanning the names on the doors—GEORGE EASTMAN, NIKOLA TESLA, LEVI STRAUSS. Hmm . . . If she couldn't find Edgerton's office, maybe she could sabotage Levi Strauss instead—all he did was make pants.

The hallway grew dimmer and dimmer the farther she moved from the window. She squinted in the darkness. JOHN WESLEY HYATT. GEORGE WEST-INGHOUSE. THADDEUS EDGERTON. *Found it!* She hoisted her crowbar, then paused. There *had* to be a better way. Something less . . . destructive.

She started back toward the window. She would tell her mother the offices were simply impenetrable and they would have to give up and go home. But as soon as she stepped back into the moonlit end of the corridor, she noticed a bronze plaque on the wall.

THE NATIONAL INVENTORS' GUILD,
A PROFESSIONAL SOCIETY FOR GENTLEMEN
OF CREATIVE AND SCIENTIFIC BRAIN

For gentlemen. The fury was back. She marched straight to Edgerton's office and lodged her crowbar into the narrow space between the door and the jamb. She leaned on the tool with all of her weight until she heard a splintering crack. She grunted and pushed even harder. *Prepare yourself for the wrath of Molly Pepper, Mr. . . .* Thomas Edison? Her breath caught in her throat. She leaned in so close that her eyelashes brushed the gold nameplate.

THOMAS EDISON

Thomas Edison? Thomas Edison! She could have sworn it had said Edgerton! Flaming flapjacks, it was the wrong door. She couldn't break into Thomas "King of the World" Edison's office. Molly yanked her crowbar free. With a splintering snap, the tool flew off into the darkness and Molly stumbled backward into the door across the hall—a door that swung easily open when she hit it.

Well, this is unexpected, she thought as she caught her balance. *I don't suppose I'd be so lucky as for* this *one to be Edgerton's office....* She looked at the nameplate.

ALEXANDER GRAHAM BELL

Wonderful. She'd broken into the offices of *both* the Guild's leaders. But how was she able to read Bell's nameplate so easily? Then she saw the light. It was stark and bright, radiating from an open doorway behind Bell's big, cedar desk: *electric* light.

She stepped cautiously through Bell's office, into the workroom. Long tables were littered with coils of wire and scattered tools; gears were stacked willy-nilly; long, rolled papers jutted from barrels and boxes in every corner. There was a glorious chaos to it all—still a storybook world, but less Cinderella's castle and more Geppetto's Workshop.

Molly edged along the workbench to the lamp. Its bare bulb was like a tiny sun captured in a bottle. It hurt her eyes to stare. But it was so hard not to. She'd never seen one up close. Or felt one. *Whoa! Hot!*

Did Bell leave this lamp on all night? That seemed dangerous. Maybe if they waited long enough, a fire would break out and—*presto!*—the entire World's Fair would belong to Cassandra Pepper.

Molly glanced at the half-constructed contraptions that lay around. Would any of them become something as miraculous as Bell's telephone? She and her mother had joked about how they'd never need a telephone, because there would never be a time when the two of them didn't live in the same room. But they wondered what it would be like to talk through one just the same. They even tried to fashion one of their own by stringing a wire between two cans. It didn't work very well, but Cassandra was convinced that with the right tools and materials, she could create a communication device even better than Bell's. Because hers wouldn't need wires.

A rolled paper sat on a table before Molly. She took a deep breath. She was never going to get an opportunity like this again. She carefully rolled back the corner and saw the word "WORLD'S" by the beginning of a diagram.

She let the paper curl up again. The World's Fair! These were the plans for whatever Alexander Graham Bell was going to present at the Fair. They had to be valuable. She grabbed the roll. They could hold Bell's plans for ransom, tell him to let Cassandra Pepper into the Fair or they'd destroy his papers. No, publish them! They could threaten to sell Bell's plans to the *Sun*. That's the last thing any inventor would want.

She took a step away from the table.

But was this who she wanted to be? An extortionist? Blackmailing a man whose work she respected? She turned to put the paper back and heard a voice.

"Stop!"

An Alarming Coincidence

"I suggest you drop those plans and make a hasty retreat before I am forced to take drastic measures." The stranger's voice cracked on the word "drastic" and he winced, red-cheeked.

He was just a boy, Molly realized, no older than she. A skinny boy in a white undershirt and suspenders. He looked Chinese, maybe. And just as disappointed to see Molly as she was to see him.

"Drastic measures, huh?" Molly asked, both testing and taunting the boy. "That sounds pretty serious. What're you gonna do?"

The boy paused long enough for Molly to know he had no plan. "I'll shout for the police," he finally said, trying to keep his eyes locked with hers.

Molly stared right back. "No, you won't."

"Yes, I will."

"You're a burglar. You don't want the police here any more than I do."

"I am not a burglar." The boy sounded offended.

"So you're *supposed* to be here?"

The boy said nothing.

"You're a burglar," Molly taunted. "You're here to burgle. Burgle, burgle, burgle. Why else would a kid be skulking around the Guild Hall after hours?"

"Just because *you're* a burglar doesn't mean—"

"*I'm* not a burglar," Molly said. It was her turn to be offended. "I'm a . . ." What was she? "I'm a saboteur," she said. "That's someone who—"

"I know what a saboteur is. And it's not any better! You broke in here to tamper with Mr. Bell's work? Who sent you? One of the other Guildsmen? Mr. Bell is always paranoid about someone finding his— *Hey!*"

Molly darted for the door, the rolled paper under her arm. If someone was going to steal those plans anyway, it might as well be her.

"I'm serious," the boy said, taking the opposite path around the table to block the workshop door. "Give me those." He lurched for the roll, but Molly took a quick hop out of reach.

"A thousand nifty thingamajigs to steal and you're hung up on one silly paper," Molly said, climbing onto a table, the bustle of her dress knocking a shower of loose screws to the floor. "Go burgle something else. That rolling chair looks like a lark and a half."

"For the last time," the boy said, cautiously joining her on the tabletop, "I am *not* a burglar."

"Then why are you here?" Molly asked, shuffling backward and scattering tools. "Are you an inventor?"

"In a manner of speaking," the boy replied, stepping with care among the gadgetry at his feet. "Assistant to one, anyway."

"Well, gee willikers. You and I have so much in common."

"I seriously doubt that." He took another swipe, slipped on a screwdriver, and crashed to the tabletop. Molly hopped off the table and was surprised to land on a pile of blankets.

She dashed out past Bell's desk into the hallway. But the boy caught up and got his hands around the paper roll. He and Molly faced off in the corridor, caught in a tug-of-war with the parchment.

"Do you understand who Alexander Graham Bell is?" the boy said impatiently. "The plans you're trying to pilfer could change the world."

"That's why I can't let you burgle them!"

"But *you're* burgling them!"

"For the greater good!" Molly shot back. "Like Robin of Locksley!"

"You're comparing yourself to Robin Hood?" The boy raised an eyebrow.

"How do you know Robin Hood's real name?"

"I read."

Molly eased up and the boy responded with a sudden yank. The paper ripped in half. Molly stumbled backward and slammed into Thomas Edison's already damaged office door. It burst inward, and Molly went tumbling. The next thing she knew, there was a wire tangled around her left ankle, her right foot was jammed in a wastebasket, and her elbow had flattened a half-eaten pastrami sandwich. Glass tubes shattered, a globe was sent rolling, an ink bottle spilled across Edison's desk, and a veritable snowstorm of papers was launched into the air.

Then came the bells.

"What's that ringing?" the boy asked, running into Edison's office. "What did you do?"

Molly looked up. There were round, brass bells clanging ceaselessly in every corner of the room. "I guess Edison invented an electric burglar alarm," she said. "Impressive."

The boy picked up a thin cord running past the doorway. "And *you* set it off. So who's the burglar now?"

"Yeah, well . . ." Molly abandoned her snappy comeback as panic suddenly set in. Based on the boy's frozen, wide-eyed stare, he'd just had the same realization. There was an *alarm* going off.

"This is the police!" came a cry from downstairs. "Nobody move!"

"I can't be found here," the boy blurted.

42

"Aha! I was right!" Molly crowed. "You *don't* belong here!"

The boy attempted to open the nearest window, but it didn't budge.

"The one at the end of the hall!" Molly said, taking him by the arm. She didn't owe this boy anything, but whatever his reason for breaking into the Guild Hall, he was probably just as desperate as she was. Plus, she was a thief now, and Molly distinctly remembered reading something somewhere about honor among thieves. "C'mon, my mother will help us!"

"We're *us* now?" the boy asked as Molly dragged him from the office. But as soon as they heard pounding footsteps on the stairs, the pair ducked back in. They frantically scanned the wrecked workshop. The boy slapped on a pair of safety goggles and tossed a second set to Molly. "Disguises," he whispered. Molly put hers on and grabbed an electric lamp that sat on a small table by the door. "Weapon," she said.

Making sure the cord was long enough, she stepped back into the hall, raised the lamp to adult eye level, and waited at the top of the dark stairwell.

"I hear someone up there," they heard a police officer say. As soon as the silhouette of his head came into view, Molly flicked on the lamp. The bulb burst to life an inch from the man's nose. "*Aagh!*"

As the startled cop tumbled to the next landing, the

masked children sprinted for the window. On the way, Molly spotted a torn shred of curled paper. *Bell's blueprints!* She slipped it up her sleeve as her mother's head popped up outside the window. "I think it's time to leave," Cassandra said.

"No argument from me," Molly replied as she realized her mother was standing on a ladder. "Where'd this come from?"

"I built it," Cassandra said. "From those crates."

"You didn't have any tools," Molly said as she climbed out and scrambled to the alley floor.

"Oh, look," said Cassandra, "there's a boy here."

"Yeah, it's basically his fault we're in this mess," Molly called up. "We should help him."

"Thank you, ma'am," the boy said, and gestured for Cassandra to descend first. Their feet hit the cobblestones and a scowling policeman appeared in the window above. "Burglars in dresses?" he wondered aloud.

"He'll follow us!" Molly said.

"I think not." Cassandra slid one slat out of a notch near the bottom rung and the entire ladder collapsed into pieces. Fuming, the policeman ducked back inside. Molly and Cassandra took off down the alley toward Broadway. Molly glanced back long enough to see the boy watch them for a moment, then flee in the opposite direction.

She considered going after him, but decided she'd already pursued enough bad ideas for one night.

The Dastardly Plot

"SO AFTER ALL that, you didn't destroy anything?" Cassandra said as she locked the pickle shop door behind them.

"Oh, we wrecked a whole bunch of stuff," Molly replied as she lit a lamp. "Just none of it was Hoity-Toity Boy's."

"Because you couldn't read the doorplates? I should make you a pair of spectacles."

"It was dark, Mother! I do not need spectacles." In adventure books, the heroes never wore eyeglasses. Only professors and old people wore eyeglasses. And Molly was neither.

Cassandra grabbed a full jar of pickles from the counter. "It's all right," she said. "It was still a cracking good plan."

Molly held her tongue. She had let herself get carried

away by her anger, and now look what she'd gotten them into. The best outcome they could hope for from this escapade was that the crime would not be traced back to them. Molly needed to remember: her mother was unmatched when it came to book smarts, but the nuts and bolts of daily survival were not Cassandra Pepper's strong suit. Making good choices was Molly's responsibility.

"We have more than a week," Cassandra said, crunching into a pickle. "I'm sure I can think up a new way to get into the Fair. I can invent some sort of . . . mind-control machine and . . . persuade . . . some . . . I'm ready for bed." Cassandra flopped onto her mattress, fully dressed. She pulled the blanket up to her neck and took another bite of her pickle.

"No bed pickles," Molly scolded.

"What's wrong with bed pickles?"

"They mean you're giving up. And Peppers don't give up." As Molly reached for the pickle, she felt a crinkle along her arm and remembered what was up her sleeve. She pulled the torn piece of paper from her cuff. "I almost forgot," she said hesitantly. "I don't really know why I took this; I wish I hadn't. It's just gonna be more trouble for us. It's part of Alexander Graham Bell's plans for the World's Fair and—"

Cassandra tossed back the covers and grabbed the paper. "Well, damage is done, right?" she said. She stepped the six inches from her bed to the worktable and unrolled the paper. "I mean, stealing is wrong, don't do it again, et cetera, et cetera—but having this here in our hands, it feels foolish not to take a gander, no?"

By flickering lantern light, mother and daughter examined the stolen plans—or at least the corner they had in their possession. Most of the paper was covered by a map—a winding maze of paths, running between dozens of oddly shaped buildings, with a large plaza in the center.

"That's the World's Fairgrounds," Molly said. "Just like in the article." She looked up and pointed to the big window but saw only gooey splotches of gray gum. "Wherever it blew to."

"But what has Bell added to it?" Cassandra asked. She grabbed a magnifying glass from a tool pile and bent closer, her nose nearly touching the paper.

There were handwritten notes all over the diagram. The first few were labels: *electric lines, generator, ignition switch.* Or notations on timing: 12:00—*gates open*, 3:30—*assistants in place.* But the more the Peppers read, the more troubling the notes became:

4:30—*take out guards.* Take them out to dinner? Probably not. But "take out" could mean so many things.

5:30—*block exits.* Maybe "block" was being used as a noun, like the exits were made of colorful children's blocks. That sounded like the kind of whimsical thing

47

they would do at a World's Fair.

5:45—top targets take stage. Okay, hard to put a good spin on "targets."

6:00—switch is flipped, NY is mi— The rest of the word disappeared off the jagged edge of the paper, but Molly had seen all she needed. Molly knew from news articles that 6:00 on opening night of the World's Fair was when Thomas Edison was to make history by powering on the first citywide electrical grid. And the "targets" scheduled to be onstage for that ceremony included New York governor Grover Cleveland, President Chester A. Arthur, former president Ulysses S. Grant, and, of course, Edison himself.

But Bell was apparently choosing that moment to do something big of his own.

Sweat beaded on Molly's brow as she scanned down to the crowd of figures sketched into the plaza around the stage, and saw a disturbing bit of editing: *audience* crossed out and replaced with *victims.* What was Bell planning to do to all those people at the Fair?

Only two more partial words were visible by the diagonally ripped bottom of the page:

DEA

MAC

Molly's mind raced through combinations that might fit. "Dealing mackerels . . . deacon's macaroons . . . death—"

"Death machine!" Cassandra leapt to her feet. "That's it! Bell has built a death machine. I bet you anything it's electric. That's probably why he's timed it to the moment Edison's system gets turned on. He's going to trick Edison into triggering his own demise!"

"Mother, you sound almost . . . impressed," said Molly. "You do realize this is bad, right? Very, very bad?"

"Oh, well, naturally, a death machine is bad," Cassandra said. "Bad for Edison and President Arthur, obviously. And terribly bad for those poor people at the Fair. But potentially good for us."

Molly looked at her askance. "How can Alexander Graham Bell attacking the World's Fair with a death machine possibly be good for us?"

"Because *we* have the chance to stop him," Cassandra said, an arch gleam in her eye. "And *that* is going to earn us a spot at the World's Fair."

Peppers in a Pickle

"COFFEE'S ON, MOLLS," Cassandra shouted as her Brew-Master 1900 rattled, gurgled, and puffed steam from its forest of copper pipes. She held a tin cup by the contraption's spout to catch the gush of aromatic coffee that spewed forth.

Molly sat up on her bed and shielded her eyes from the sunlight that streamed in through the storefront windows. A small boy stared in, his face smushed against the window, until his mother finally yanked him away. "We forgot to put the screen up last night," Molly mumbled.

"We had more important things on our minds," Cassandra said, handing her daughter a mug. "Now fire up the secretary, my darling. We need to get all our thoughts down on paper."

Molly sipped coffee between yawns, and pulled shut

the folding screen. "I can just write them down myself, you know."

"If you're going to write things down yourself," Cassandra said, "what's the point in having an Astounding Automated Secretary?"

With a sigh, Molly stepped over the Self-Propelled Mop and squeezed past the Rotating Shoe Tree to the steam-powered secretary, one of her mother's newest inventions: a mostly unrusted barrel with a wide-mouthed cone protruding from one side and a mechanical arm from the other. She scooped some coal into a hatch on the back and used a long match to ignite it—more of her annoying little "assistant" duties. But today it was all in the service of thwarting the secret schemes of a diabolical genius. Which, danger aside, sounded like a grand adventure.

In books, it was always orphans who got to go on adventures. And if Molly were to find any sort of meaning in her father's passing, perhaps it was this. Perhaps his final gift to her was the chance to have an honest-to-goodness adventure. Or at least half of one. Since she was, thankfully, only half an orphan. And she wanted to keep it that way. Because the only thing Molly could imagine worse than failing her mother would be losing her altogether.

"Do you think the boy has anything to do with Bell's plan?" Molly asked.

"What boy?" Cassandra replied.

"The boy from last night. The one I fought with in Bell's office? We helped him escape from the police?"

"Oh, *that* boy! Yes, he's most probably involved," Cassandra said, stirring her coffee with a screwdriver.

Molly slipped a pencil between the tin-tube fingers of the automated secretary and positioned its hand over a piece of blank paper atop the barrel. She flipped several switches, and with a cough of black smoke, the machine rumbled to life.

Coffee sloshing from her cup, Cassandra climbed over her worktable and sat down next to the secretary. She cleared her throat and spoke into the cone. "Begin dictation. The Pepper Ladies and the Dastardly Plot of One Mr. Alexander Graham Bell. Option A . . ."

The mechanical arm slowly jerked back and forth as shaky but legible letters began to appear on the paper. Three minutes later, they had a full sentence. Of sorts.

BEGIN DIKTASHUN THA PEPER LADEEZ END THA DASTERDLEE PLOT OV WUN MISTER ALEKZANDER GRAM BEL OPSHUN AY

"Takes a while, doesn't it?" Cassandra said, squinching up her nose.

"Don't be hard on yourself, Mother." Molly peeked inside the secretary at the complex collage of churning gears and wires. "You taught a machine to write!"

"And now I need to teach it to spell." The machine had just finished writing:

TAKS A WYL DUZINT IT

"Some punctuation wouldn't hurt either," Molly said with a shrug. She powered down the secretary and grabbed the pencil herself. "Okay, Mother, what've we got?"

"Option A," Cassandra repeated as she rose and began the long, arduous process of dressing for the day. "We take this torn portion of Bell's plan to the police. Option B, we go to Bell himself, tell him what we know, and use that leverage to get ourselves a space at the Fair. Or C, we figure out where Bell's keeping his death ray or whatever it is and we destroy it.

"A is out," Cassandra continued, "because what would we tell the police when they ask how the evidence came into our possession?"

"And B is out because that would be a completely bad-guy thing to do," Molly said. "And we're the good guys."

"Right. Which leaves—*errk!* Give me a hand with these laces, Molls? Which leaves us being saboteurs again."

"Except we don't even know if it's safe for us to leave the shop," Molly said. "What if that cop saw your face last night? What if the entire New York Police Department is scouring the streets for the five-foot-ten, brown-haired, hazel-eyed Guild Hall Bandit and her slightly-large-eared-but-otherwise-appealing miniature sidekick?"

"Hmm." Cassandra tapped her lips. "I *am* rather memorable."

"We need to find out. Time to visit the *Sun* again." Molly threw her father's old overcoat on over her nightgown, popped a piece of licorice gum into her mouth, and headed for the door. "If I'm not back in five minutes, devote the rest of your life to avenging me."

Cassandra sipped her coffee. "Naturally, dear."

Extra! Extra!

"I NEED A paper, Skiff."

The newsboy, standing on his crate with a fresh stack of morning editions, scoffed at Molly. "I knew I never shoulda gave you that copy last night. Now you come here thinkin' you can get a same-day paper in the morning? Ain't gonna happen, Mittsy."

"I got something better than pickles today," she said. "Chewing gum."

Skiff absentmindedly rubbed an ink beard onto his chin as he considered her proposal. "What kind?"

"Licorice."

"*Ewww*, licorice is gross."

"I know," said Molly, chewing loudly. "But it's still gum."

Skiff rubbed his chin again. "Okay, but you gotta read

it here and give it back so's I can still sell it after."

"Deal." Molly handed him the wad of gum from her mouth and took a paper. The newsboy shrugged, tossed the gum into his own mouth, and continued hawking his wares to passersby while Molly scanned the day's headlines.

PRESIDENT ARTHUR ARRIVES FOR BRIDGE GALA

"ORPHAN TRAINS" PROVIDE NEW HOPE
FOR CITY'S TROUBLED YOUTH

VITTORINI'S NEW SHOW EARNS RAVES

She flipped furiously through the pages for anything about the Guild. Not a word about last night. Molly felt she should have been relieved, but she wasn't. The Guild Hall was one of the most famous buildings in New York; how could a break-in there not make news? Was the Guild trying to hide something? Were some of the other inventors in on Bell's plan? Was the whole Guild?

"Cheese it, Mittsy! We got a badge comin'!"

The newsboy fled, leaving a trail of flying pages behind him. Molly turned to see a man in a black derby heading her way. The shield pinned to his long coat glinted in the sun. He wasn't a cop, but he was trouble—a Jäger-man. An agent of the Jäger Society for the Prevention of

Cruelty to Children. And while the organization's stated mission was to keep orphaned and neglected children off dangerous city streets, lots of Jägermen were known to get overzealous in their work, harassing and punishing kids for even the slightest offenses. Any New Yorker under sixteen knew to avoid Jägermen at all costs.

"Don't even think about running!" the Jägerman shouted.

"Too late! I've already thought about it!" Molly was so pleased with her comeback that she didn't look when she turned to flee and slipped on a discarded newspaper. Thick fingers clamped around her wrist.

"You all right, lass?" the agent asked as he pulled her to her feet. But Molly thought he should be more worried about himself. This man was not a runner. From that little sprint alone, his face had turned redder than his ginger mustache. "It's best you come with me," the Jägerman said. "There are men in this town'll take advantage of poor orphans like yourself."

"I'm not an orphan," Molly said, trying to pull her arm free.

"Not an orphan, eh?" The Jägerman held her wrist tight. "You're on a street corner by yourself, on a school day, wearing nothing but a nightshirt and an old man's coat. You got bare feet and your hair looks like you brushed it with an eggbeater. Also, you smell like coffee and pickles."

"I'm not an orphan," Molly repeated. She considered simply taking the man to meet her mother, but knowing Cassandra's parenting style, that could potentially make things worse. Instead, she coughed. "I'm . . . I'm not in school today because I'm sick," she said in her feeblest voice. "I threw on my father's coat to go get medicine. I think it's—*cough! cough!*—the typhoid."

The Jägerman held firm, but Molly could see a glint of concern in his eye.

"My parents have it too," she wheezed. "It's incredibly—*cough!*—contagious."

The Jägerman pulled his hand from the flecks of licorice-tinted spittle. "Pigs and whistles! Your tongue's gone black!"

The moment she was free, Molly ran as fast as her legs could carry her. She dodged street vendors, ducked between the legs of a tall grocer carrying a crate of apples, and leapt over a small dog before pivoting onto Thompson Street and jogging until she reached that familiar sign: PICK A PECK OF PEPPER'S PICKLES!

"I'm back," she called as she opened the front door of the shop.

Seconds later, the door opened again and the Jägerman clambered inside, panting. He bent over, hands on his knees, as beads of sweat dripped from beneath his hat.

"You, lass," he grumbled between breaths, "do *not* have typhoid."

Molly shrugged. "It comes and goes?"

"I oughta take you straight to Blackwell's Island," the Jägerman said, straightening up. "They tame wild orphans over there."

"I'll have you know *I* am that wild orphan's mother!" Cassandra threw open the folding screen with such vigor that it fell over. Molly ran to her.

"Well, ma'am, I'm Agent Muldoon with the Jäger Society." The agent flashed his badge. "We look to the welfare of *all* children, orphans or no. Why is your daughter not in school?"

Cassandra eyed the man cautiously. "Because she—"

Molly coughed loudly.

"She's sick," Cassandra said. "So I kept her home."

The agent's eyebrows shot up. "The girl *lives* in a pickle store?"

"What? Ha! No." Cassandra faked a laugh. "Of course not. Who would live in a . . . ha!"

Clearly visible behind her were beds, blankets, a half-cooked breakfast, and several pairs of bloomers hanging from a clothesline. Not to mention the cluttered heaps of tools and bizarre machinery.

"Mrs. . . . Pepper, I assume?" the Jägerman said. "This is clearly not a safe environment for a child. I can see three dozen Jäger Society violations just from where I'm standing. And I don't even want to ask why that teakettle is holding a knife."

"It's buttering our toast," Cassandra said.

"My point is that it would be in my rights to take your girl away from here this minute," Muldoon continued. "I'd like to speak to *Mr.* Pepper."

"Certainly," Cassandra replied, her jaw suddenly tight. "You'll find him at St. Mark's Cemetery, plot 16B. Tell him I'm sorry I haven't visited in a while."

The Jägerman sighed. "Look, I'm not heartless. I'll give you a chance to fix this. But when I return—with the district supervisor—we'll want to see this place clean and safe. And the girl properly dressed and back in school."

Cassandra's hands were balled up, her lips tight. Molly figured her mother was working very hard to avoid saying something she might regret, so she stepped in, and despite her own growing anger, said, "Thank you, sir."

"But understand," Muldoon warned, "if everything is not to our satisfaction, we *will* remove the girl and see that she's placed in a home that can handle her."

Molly was no longer faking that sick feeling.

The Jägerman tipped his hat as he walked out. "See you tomorrow."

"Tomorrow?" Molly sputtered as soon as the door was shut again. "This is outrageous! They can't—" She stopped when she saw her mother flopped along the countertop like a wet rag, arms dangling over the sides.

"I've failed you, Molls," Cassandra mumbled.

Molly tilted her head to be aligned with her mother's. "You're doing your best, Mother. I'm the one who messed up. I let him follow me."

"I thought I could change the world," Cassandra said, lifting her head. "I wanted to make history. And I wanted to do it for you. For us."

"That's why you're my hero," Molly said. "So what if we've had a few setbacks? We're Peppers, right? Peppers don't give up. And when your name does end up in the papers, it will all have been worth it. Now get up, because I'm pretty sure you're lying on the pepper grinder. That cannot be comfortable."

"But twenty-four hours, Molls?" Cassandra said as her daughter helped her down. "How are we going to turn this into a respectable home by then?"

"We're not," Molly said as she grabbed a slice from the Crust-o-Matic Toastinator. She took a bite, then held it out for Cassandra to chomp into.

"We're not?" Cassandra repeated with her mouth full. "I mean, some curtains might help."

"No, Mother. We're sticking to our original plan," Molly said. "The Jägermen aren't going to take away the daughter of the woman who saved the World's Fair, right? We still need to foil Alexander Graham Bell's dastardly plot. We just need to do it faster."

"How are we going to do that?"

"We're going back to the Guild."

Return to the Palace of Wonders

MOLLY WOULD HAVE been happier had they worn disguises on their return trip to the Guild Hall, but her mother insisted nobody would so much as glance in their direction. It turned out Cassandra was right. Though the vast cathedral-like entry chamber was packed wall-to-wall with people, every eye in the place was cast upward. There would have been spectacle enough with the towering marble pillars, mosaic tiles, and the kind of gold-railed staircases you'd expect to see a princess glide down on her way to the ball. But there was also the ceiling, which could have given the Sistine Chapel an inferiority complex. As gears spun and pistons churned, mechanical dolls waltzed with one another, swung on teensy trapezes, rode clockwork horses, and pounded the scenery with miniature hammers as if repairing the endless machine they themselves were part of. A tiny tin fairy "flew" around on wires, setting electrical stars aglow.

"I used to think all this clockwork hoo-ha-ha was the Guild's gift to the people of New York," Cassandra said. "Now I'm certain. it's a distraction—to keep anybody from giving too much thought to what goes on upstairs. So let's not allow ourselves to be delayed for one more— oh, look! A chicken rowing a boat!"

"To the Welcome Desk, Mother. And take your invention," Molly whispered. She forced the wicker basket she'd been carrying into Cassandra's hand. "We need to talk our way back into Bell's office." *And hopefully find some clues to the whereabouts of his death machine,* she thought.

As Molly pulled Cassandra across the immense room, a band of tin angels tooted out a fanfare on their trumpets and the crowd parted as a man strode into the building like royalty. Molly had seen enough photos to recognize that crisp checkered suit, the trademark bow tie, the eyebrows like startled caterpillars: it was Thomas Edison.

Molly froze, unsure of what to do. Should she try to approach Edison directly and tell him what was going on? Or did he already know? Edison and Bell worked together on so much—what if this World's Fair plot was another of their collaborations?

But the crowd made Molly's decision for her. She and

Cassandra were engulfed as scores of cheering fans swarmed the famed inventor. Security guards swooped in to hold back the whooping spectators.

"Thank you, thank you!" Edison called out. "Now, *that's* the kind of reception a man likes to get on his way to work! All right, all right—who wants an autograph?"

Dignified men in top hats and elegant women in gowns bounced like delighted toddlers. Several people surged forward, waving autograph pads over their heads. Cassandra was bumped in the rush and Molly saw a folded piece of paper fly from her basket. The secret plans! Molly dove forward and snatched up the parchment a fraction of a second before it would have been impaled by a high-heeled boot.

"Whew." Molly struggled to her feet, but quickly realized her mother was forging on without her. "Wait!" She waved to get Cassandra's attention and yelped as someone plucked the folder paper from her fingers. She turned to see Thomas Edison scribbling his signature across the back of Bell's secret plans. Molly yanked the paper back.

"Hey, I wasn't fin—" the inventor began.

"How about a dance, Mr. Edison?" Molly shouted.

"Yeah, a dance!" cried another woman in the crowd.

"Give us a show, Tommy!" a third fan called out. And soon dozens joined in.

"Oh, you people are terrible!" Edison joked as the

guards cleared a space for him at the foot of a grand spiral staircase. "But you also know I can't say no to my fans!"

With a flourish, Edison tossed his hat high into the air and a tiny spinning propeller emerged. A bright light erupted from beneath the brim, turning the derby into a hovering spotlight. And then, Edison began to dance.

With the crowd occupied, Molly darted to join her mother at the Welcome Desk. "We are here to see Alexander Graham Bell," Cassandra announced.

"Mr. Bell regrets that he needs to cancel all his appointments for today," said the clerk.

"That's no problem," said Cassandra. "We don't have an appointment."

The man, whose long nose and twiggish arms made him look more marionette than human, stared at her for a few seconds before clarifying. "You can't see him."

Behind them, the crowd applauded as Edison finished his dance routine and headed upstairs. "Let us see Edison, then," Molly said. She and Cassandra needed to snoop around Bell's office, but a "consultation" with any of the inventors should get them to the second floor. "He's definitely here."

"And he just said how busy he is." The clerk's instant frown told her that he was an adult of the children-should-be-seen-and-not-heard persuasion.

"Look, we don't need a lot of time with Bell," Cassandra said.

The clerk's patience seemed to be wearing as thin as his hair. "Mr. Bell," he sneered, "like all of our scientists, is working on a big surprise for the Fair."

"Bigger than you know," Cassandra muttered.

"Excuse me?" said the clerk.

"The surprise," Molly interjected. "It's bigger than *you* . . . no?"

The man rolled his eyes.

"Well, speaking of surprises," said Cassandra, mimicking Edison's showy manner. "I'm sure Mr. Bell will make room in his schedule when he sees . . . this!" From her wicker basket, she produced a helmet (crafted from the kitchen strainer Molly used to wear to play King Arthur) fitted with a network of knobs, coils, and gears.

The clerk stared. "Are you planning to cook him some beans?"

"This, my good man, is the amazing Automated Sneeze Shield," Cassandra continued. "Now, you look like the hustle-bustle man-about-town type. Wouldn't it be wonderful if you didn't have to put your gadfly lifestyle on hold every time you came down with a head cold? 'But,' you ask, 'how can I protect my fellow socialites from the icky business that shoots from my face when I sneeze?' That, my friend, is where the sneeze shield comes in. You wear it like so." She plopped the device onto the startled clerk's head. "It reacts to the sound of an oncoming sneeze. It would, of course, be too late if the machine waited until the 'choo' part of the sneeze, so the helmet has been designed to lower its shield the moment it hears a loud 'ah!'" And with that—*boing!*—a curved sheet of tin sprang down from within the helmet.

It should have covered the man's entire face, as it had done for Cassandra and Molly during their test runs. But the Peppers had much smaller noses than the clerk. The man howled in pain. "You cut off my node!" With a struggle, he slid the shield back up to reveal a large, red welt on his ample nose (which was, thank goodness, still attached to his face).

"Okay, I apologize for that bit," Cassandra said. "But as you can see, the device works. Your nose just isn't supposed to be that big."

The clerk seethed.

"Sooo," said Cassandra. "Can we see Mr. Bell now?"

The clerk slammed his hands on his desk and shouted, "Absolutely not!" But most of his shout was muffled, since, after the first syllable, the shield slammed down on his nose again. Yowling, the man tossed the sneeze shield from his head. The Peppers gasped as it hit the floor and broke apart.

"You, woman, are a dangerous loon!" the clerk yelled. "Take your obnoxious girl and that ridiculous nasal guillotine back home and tell your husband that if he's too embarrassed to demonstrate his own inventions, he should keep them to himself instead of sending his flibbertigibbet of a wife in here with them!"

"Husband?" Cassandra's gaze went dark. She leaned over the desk, close enough to make Molly wonder if she might bite the man. "*I* am the inventor! And back when my husband still walked this earth, he assured me that, someday, each and every person in this building would know my name. And they will. Even those high-and-mighty hoop-de-hoos upstairs. So don't think for a moment that you and that farcically oversized beak of yours have stopped me. You haven't heard the last of Cassandra Pe— Molly, what?"

Molly was tugging her mother toward the exit. "Strategic retreat," she muttered. They had gathered almost as big a crowd as Edison.

"Detain them," the clerk snapped at the guards who materialized out of the crowd. "I'll call the police."

Call the police? That meant he had a telephone! And Molly wasn't going to get to see it. Of all the rotten luck.

"Operator, get me the police," they heard the clerk say behind them. "There's a woman causing a disturbance at the Inventors' Guild! Her name is Cassandra something . . . Cassandra Pemollywot!"

Molly heard the guards shouting behind her as she and her mother ran for the doors. But then— *"Oof!"* And—*thud!* And, "Excuse me! I'm so sorry, gentlemen!"

Molly glanced over her shoulder to see the two guards in a jumble on the floor, having just tripped over an older woman's parasol.

"Outta the way, lady," one guard barked.

But the woman in the funny little knit cap didn't budge. "Oh, dear," she said. "I think you've broken my umbrella. Look at it—oh, I'm sorry again! Was that your ear? I really should wear my glasses."

Molly could have sworn the woman winked at her.

Outside, the Peppers ducked under the marquee of the Madison Square Theatre next door. From behind the box office booth, Molly watched as the guards poked out from the Guild Hall entrance—one with a blue parasol jammed down the back of his coat—and peered around before grumpily heading back inside. Molly sighed—a mix of relief and frustration. If they were going to succeed in thwarting Bell's wicked plot, outbursts like the one her mother had just had were not going to help. But how could she express this gently? "Mother," she began. "I think we might need— Flaming flapjacks! Look behind you!"

The boy from Bell's workshop had just stepped out of the Guild Hall.

10

Molly's Archnemesis

THE MYSTERY BOY looked very different than he had the night before. In a tweed suit, cap, and tie, he looked surprisingly professional for an eleven-year-old. And he was carrying an unusual twine-wrapped box. Could it be that he actually *did* work for Bell? If so, why had he been sneaking around the Guild after hours? Why had he fought so hard for that roll of paper? Had he been trying to protect his boss's plans—or swipe them? Maybe so he could turn Bell in himself? One thing was certain: the boy was nervous now. His eyes were darting every which way. This was someone who clearly did not want to be followed.

"We have to follow him," Molly said to her mother. "I don't know if he's delivering that package for Bell or if he stole it from him, but either way, we need to find out where he's taking it."

Cassandra nodded. "Let's move."

Molly paused. Stealthily trailing her archnemesis was going to be challenging enough without her mother tagging along. "Actually, maybe we should split up? We can meet back at the shop."

"Don't be silly, Molls," Cassandra said. "The more Peppers, the better."

"But . . ." Molly was at a loss until she spotted her third surprising face of the day—a face surrounded by the same curly hair and braided beard as the faces on the theater posters all around them. "Look, Mother! Heading to the stage door—it's Sergio Vittorini! This is your chance to get an autograph!" She reached into the basket and pulled out Bell's plans. "But not on this." She tucked the paper down her collar, patted her mother on the back, and raced off after the mystery boy before Cassandra had a chance to object.

Her quarry kept glancing over his shoulder, so Molly took to using taller, wider pedestrians as camouflage, peering out from behind a puffy skirt or under the elbow of a pointing tourist. When the boy turned to walk under the elevated Bowery rail line, the wealth of shadows, hanging clouds of soot, and forest of iron beams provided ample hiding spots. Molly had been giving a lot of thought as to what type of career she should pursue once she'd helped her mother achieve fame and they could leave the pickle shop behind. Right now, spy was moving to the top of that list.

Twenty-five blocks later, though, the boy and his box took a hard left onto East Broadway, leaving the cover of the train tracks and heading into a quieter part of town that held mostly warehouses and stables. Aside from Molly and a man in black suspenders, the street was empty. She hustled up close behind the man for cover.

"Thought you'd nick my wallet, eh?" the man sneered as he turned around. "A lady pickpocketer? Now I've seen everything."

"No," Molly sputtered. The boy turned a corner. There was no one else in sight. "I just—" She looked around. Still nobody.

"It's a shameful world we live in, when even the thieving's left to females." He grabbed Molly's wrist. "You'll come along with me now, missy. The Jägermen'll—*OW!*"

Molly bit his hand and ran.

In an alley around the corner, she crouched behind a row of dented trash cans and bowed her head. Chasing the mystery boy across Manhattan all by herself, she'd felt elated. And proud. And free. But when Suspenders Man grabbed her, she fully expected her mother to pop up and save the day. Now she was disappointed in herself for feeling disappointed.

"Why are you following me?" The boy from Bell's lab was standing by the alley wall.

Molly leapt to her feet. "Aargh, stupid Suspenders

Guy ruined everything!" she snarled. "If he hadn't given me away, you'd never have spotted me."

"I've known you were behind me since we were a block away from the Guild Hall," said the boy.

"Impossible." Molly crossed her arms defiantly. "I move like the wind."

"If you mean that you knock people's hats off as you go by, then, yes, you do."

"I knocked off *one* hat," Molly said. "It was big and I couldn't see past it."

"Why are you following me?" the boy asked again.

Molly poked her finger into his chest. "I think a better question is, Why are *you* so afraid of being followed?"

"That is not a better question," he said, backing away. "Mine was a perfectly reasonable question. I'm just trying to do my job."

"And what job is that?" She cornered him against the alley wall. "Burglary?"

"Don't start that again."

"If you didn't steal whatever's in that box, why've you been so skittish?"

"Maybe because I was being followed by a crazy girl?"

"Don't call me crazy."

"Don't call me a burglar."

"Then tell me what your real job is!"

"I told you last night!" the boy snapped back. "I'm an inventor's assistant! I'm delivering a package for my boss. That's a perfectly normal thing for an assistant to do. You're the one doing all the suspicious stuff."

Molly shook her head. "Don't try to turn this back on me. If what you're doing is so innocent, why have you been looking so goosey from the moment you stepped out of the Guild Hall?"

The boy broke eye contact and peered toward the end of the alley, then down at the package he gripped tightly. "I just . . . I don't like being made to deliver something when I don't know what it is," the boy said. "That can lead to trouble."

"Trouble, eh?" Molly touched a fingertip to the box and the boy yanked it away. "Wow, you are *extra* goosey," she said. "What's in there? A bomb?"

"I don't *know* what's in there!" he blurted. And he peeked down the alley again. "But it's not a bomb. Obviously. Why would you think it was a bomb?"

"No reason," said Molly.

"It's not a bomb," the boy repeated. He sounded like he was trying to convince himself as much as Molly.

"It *could* be a bomb," Molly rebutted. "If you don't know what it is, then you don't know what it's not."

"It's *not* a bomb. Alexander Graham Bell doesn't make bombs!"

Molly practically jumped out of her skin. "You *work* for Bell?"

"I told you! I'm a lab assistant, not a burglar!"

74

"But if you work at the Guild, why were you so afraid of the police seeing you there?" Molly asked.

"Because I *work* there. I'm not supposed to be *living* there."

Molly remembered the blankets in Bell's workshop. One mystery solved. But if this boy was Bell's assistant, did that mean he was involved in the World's Fair plot? Of course, he was also keeping his own secrets from Bell, so maybe the two weren't so buddy-buddy. Maybe he—

The boy's eyes darted once more toward the alley's entryway.

"Why do you keep looking down there?" Molly asked. "Is someone coming? Is this a trap? Aw, man, did I fall into a trap? I am going to be so ticked at myself if I walked into a trap."

"If anyone walked into a trap here, it's me," the boy said. "There's not a person in New York who would assume *you* were the one to pin *me* back here. I'm Chinese. We don't have the best reputation around here."

Molly had heard people make awful, hateful comments about Chinese immigrants, read them in newspapers even. She'd never believed the horrible generalizations or understood why people said such things, but she'd also never thought about what it would feel like to hear them if you *were* Chinese. She suddenly felt guilty about all her burglar comments. "Well, I'm happy to meet a Chinese person," she said, trying to feel less guilty. "There aren't too many of you around here." The boy's face flattened and she immediately regretted her words. She'd forgotten about the Chinese Exclusion Act, a law that had been passed the previous year banning Chinese people from entering the United States. Chinese immigrants who were already in the country were allowed to stay, but they were in constant risk of deportation. "Anyway," Molly said, hoping to fix the downward course this conversation had taken, "your English is better than most of the boys I know."

"I've been in America since I was two months old!" the boy snapped.

Molly had to make this better. "Hey, come back behind these barrels," she said. "No one will see us there. We can talk more."

"Why would I want to talk more with you?" the boy asked. "I have no idea who you are! Give me one good reason why I should go into a hidden nook for a secret chitchat with a girl who has attacked me, spied on me, and insulted me?"

Molly didn't even stop walking. "Because you may not be a criminal, but your boss is."

The Mysterious Package

"ALEXANDER GRAHAM BELL is a criminal? That's the craziest thing you've said so far," the boy scoffed as he stepped behind the foul-smelling tar barrels with Molly.

"If it's so crazy, walk away."

His shoulders slumped. "Just tell me what you're talking about. I can't lose two jobs in a row this way."

"Two?" Perhaps this boy was more interesting than Molly thought. "You make a habit of working for criminals?"

"Just Oogie MacDougal."

"Oogie MacDougal?" Molly shouted loud enough to make the boy double-check the alley again. "Sorry," she said more softly. "You worked for Oogie MacDougal? The leader of the Green Onion Boys? The most wanted man in New York?"

"I didn't *know* he was Oogie MacDougal. The guy's got a really thick Scottish accent—I couldn't understand half of what he said. All I knew was I needed a job and he needed a delivery boy."

"Your defense for working for a known mobster is his accent?" Molly said, raising an eyebrow. "That's a pretty nifty excuse to give the cops."

"If you ever meet the guy, you'll see."

"That would be amazing, actually," Molly said, envisioning herself toe-to-toe with a notorious crime lord.

"No, it wouldn't. Look, I only ever handled the one package for him. And as soon as I saw what was in it—"

"Guns?" Molly asked. "Money? Opium? Ransom notes? Poisonous snakes?"

"Um, yes," the boy said. "Well, guns and money—not the rest. But I don't want any part of that stuff. So when another kid told me who it was who'd handed me that bag, I peeked inside and then dumped the whole thing in the river."

Molly's mouth dropped open wider than she'd thought possible. "You *stole* from Oogie MacDougal?"

"It's not stealing if I didn't keep it."

Molly raised her other eyebrow.

The boy sighed. "I know, I'm as good as dead if he ever finds me again. But people would have been hurt with those guns. I . . . I probably saved lives by dumping them."

Molly smirked. "So you didn't just do it 'cause you got scared?"

"I don't think the reason makes a difference."

"Well, at least I understand why you're so itchy about delivering another mystery package."

"Yeah, but I can't have made the same mistake again. I got a job working for *Alexander Graham Bell* this time—I mean, he invented the *telephone*! He's not going to send me on illegal errands. He's been . . . He's been decent to me."

Molly saw in the boy's eyes how much he wanted that to be true. "Not everybody's as decent as they might seem," she said. "I'm gonna show you something." She reached into the bodice of her dress and the boy immediately covered his eyes.

"Yeesh! What'd you think I was going to do?" Molly shook her head and laid Bell's paper on the box. "You need to relax, Goosey."

"Please stop calling me that," he pleaded.

"You got a real name?"

"Emmett Lee."

"Emmett, huh?" Molly said. "Not as fun as Goosey, but we can make it work."

"Supposedly, it means 'whole' or 'universal,'" Emmett said, sounding a bit defensive. "My father said he chose it as my American name, because I was his whole world."

"Oh . . . that's actually really sweet," Molly said. "So, what's your original Chinese name?"

Emmett looked down. "I don't know," he mumbled.

Molly feared she had stumbled onto a difficult topic

for Emmett, so she held out her hand. "Nice to meet you, Emmett Lee. I'm Molly Pepper. Now: look at the paper."

Emmett examined the torn parchment. "It's the World's Fairgrounds," he said. "Mr. Bell has diagrams like this around the workshop."

"Keep reading," Molly said.

"Oh," Emmett said as he read. "Oh! *Oh, oh, oh.* Someone is planning something very bad."

"Not *someone*—your boss," Molly said. "This is the rolled-up paper we were fighting over last night. You really didn't know what was on it?"

"I don't look at things I'm not supposed to! But *you*—this is what you snuck into the Guild to steal? How did you know it would be there?"

"I didn't. Like I said, I was going to sabotage Thaddeus Edgerton's Fair exhibit, but I misread Edison's nameplate and tried to break into his office by accident, and that's when I fell into Bell's place and found the plans."

Emmett blinked at her. "Maybe you need spectacles."

"I do not need spectacles! Look, it doesn't matter why I was there—this paper came from Bell's workshop."

"Impossible," Emmett insisted. "Even if the map was Mr. Bell's, anyone could have written all this stuff on it. *You* could have written all this stuff on it."

"Ha. My penmanship's not that good. You work for Bell—is the handwriting familiar?"

Emmett bit his lip. "It's . . . well . . . It's not . . . *un*familiar.

But it's not as if I've spent hours studying Mr. Bell's penmanship. I couldn't swear with complete certainty that he wrote this."

"But you're pretty sure, aren't you?" Molly didn't want to smile at this, because Emmett was clearly distraught, but she couldn't help feeling some pride in being right.

"It doesn't matter who wrote it; we have no way of knowing what this plan really shows, anyway," Emmett said, working hard to convince himself.

"'Targets,' 'victims,' 'New York is mine,'" Molly quoted.

"It's cut off, though. Maybe it says, 'New York is . . . minty fresh,'" Emmett said.

"Nice try," Molly said, wrinkling her nose. "What about 'death machines'?" She pointed to the torn edge:

DEA
MAC

"Oh, now you're really stretching," the boy countered. "That obviously says . . ."

Molly waited.

"Deals on macaroni?" Emmett finally said.

"Yep, you nailed it," Molly deadpanned. "These are Alexander Graham Bell's secret plans to win over New Yorkers with bargain-priced pasta. Look, I understand why you don't want to accept that your boss is up to something sinister, but this plot is real, and whatever's in that box is most likely part of it."

"It's probably just a stack of cogwheels or something," Emmett said.

"One way to find out," Molly said, reaching for the loose end of the twine. Emmett pulled the box away again.

"I could lose my job."

"Your job working for a diabolical fiend?"

"He's an *inventor*. You've got to understand, before Mr. Bell, I had no one. Not since my father . . ."

"Yours too?" Molly asked after a moment. "How? Mine was tuberculosis."

"My father was a ferry pilot," Emmett said. "He took people back and forth from Manhattan to Brooklyn. A few years ago, Alexander Graham Bell and his family were on his boat and there was a storm. The ferry started rocking and my father yelled for everyone to tie themselves down. But Mr. Bell's wife is deaf, and in the confusion, she went overboard. And probably would've drowned if my father hadn't dived in after her."

"Your father drowned saving her?"

"No, but the choice he made that day still led to his death."

Molly waited for him to continue.

"Mr. Bell felt he owed my father," Emmett went on. "And in addition to inventing, Mr. Bell also loves exploring. He was always talking about discovering new lands, new peoples. He wanted to find the South Pole. Or, like a lot of rich people, have someone find it for him. So he sponsored an expedition to Antarctica—and asked my father to captain the ship.

"I don't need to tell you what an honor that was. Chinese folks don't often get the chance to work side by side with men like Mr. Bell. I was never more proud. But . . . that ship never came back."

"I'm sorry," Molly said. "Was your mother—?"

"Died when I was born, back in China. I never knew her. After I lost my father, I tried to make it on my own for a while. Lived out of an old book wagon for longer than I would've thought possible. But I reached a point where I needed money badly. That's how I stumbled into working for Oogie MacDougal. And after that, I was scared to show my face on the streets, so I went to Mr. Bell. I didn't even know if he'd agree to talk to me, but he ended up offering me a job. Said it was the least he could do."

"So you're telling me Bell is some kind of saint who helps orphans." Molly couldn't help sounding disappointed.

"No, I think he mostly helped me out of guilt," Emmett replied. "But he's been pretty nice to me since."

"If Bell's such a generous guy, why not tell him you're camping out in the office?" She hopped up to sit on a tar barrel, not caring if her dress got dirty.

"When I first told him who my father was, he started on about getting me to an orphanage," Emmett replied. "But a call to the Jäger Society would basically mean a one-way ticket to China for me. I had to cut off that line of thinking fast, so I told him I was living with an aunt. And when he asked me where my aunt lived, I gave him an address in the worst part of town, to make sure he never got the notion to stop by and check on me." He hoisted himself onto another barrel, setting the box down between them. "Why am I telling you this?"

"It's either my irresistible charms," Molly said, "or that you have no other friends."

She thought he'd laugh at that, but he didn't. "You have an interesting definition of friend," Emmett said. "We've known each other for less than twenty-four hours and have spent the majority of that time arguing."

"All friends have fights eventually. We've gotten ours out of the way early. That's just smart planning."

Emmett looked down and shook his head like he was annoyed with her, but Molly could see he was smiling. "*You* have a lot of friends?" he asked.

"I think this is the longest conversation I've had with anybody other than my mother," Molly replied. She shifted closer. "So, the inventor thing? That's what you wanna do with your life?"

Emmett shrugged. "I guess. I like to think I'm pretty good at it. But honestly, you don't spend much time thinking about the future when you're worried about surviving day to day."

Molly nodded. She could relate. But at least she'd had the dream of her mother's success to keep her motivated. A dream that was in danger of being extinguished. "Speaking of surviving," she said, "we ready to find out if there's a bomb in that package?"

"No," Emmett said, putting his hands on the box. "Things might not be perfect for me right now, but they're the best they've been since my father died, and I don't want to mess that up. Besides, I simply cannot believe Mr. Bell is up to something so sinister."

"You yourself said he's acting paranoid," Molly pointed out.

"He *is* trying to hide something," Emmett admitted, running his hands over his face. "But I figured that's just the way it is at the Guild. Those guys are always spying on one another, trying to steal one another's ideas and such. But . . . oh my goodness—it's Mr. Edison."

"Edison's what? His accomplice?" This was more exciting than cake!

"No, his motive," Emmett said. "Mr. Bell and Mr. Edison might look like friends and co-leaders in public. But it's all an act."

Molly leaned in. "Go on."

"Mr. Bell is always complaining about Edison hogging the spotlight and trying to outdo him. Recently he's been even more vocal about it—behind closed doors, anyway—because Mr. Edison gets the whole opening night ceremony to himself. 'Light bulbs, light bulbs,' Mr. Bell says. 'It's just light bulbs again, but more of them.'"

Molly snickered. "Why are you doing that odd voice for Bell?"

"He's Scottish. Or he was born in Scotland, anyway," Emmett said. "Still has a little bit of an accent. But not nearly as strong as Oogie MacDougal's. Really, you have to believe me—I couldn't understand that guy."

"Yeah, yeah, I get it—MacDougal's got an accent," Molly said. "But go back to Bell's rivalry with Edison. That sounds super important. I mean, my mother and I assumed President Arthur was Bell's main target, but what if it's Edison? What if Bell's tired of living in Edison's shadow and it's pushed him over the edge? And now he wants to ruin the biggest moment of Edison's career in order to show him up."

"I don't know. It still hard to believe." Emmett sighed. "Or maybe I just don't want you to be right."

"Then let's prove me wrong." Molly hopped down and grabbed the box. "You know this is the only way to eliminate doubt," she said. "Let's make a deal. If there's nothing scary in here, you win and I won't bother you anymore. If there's some kind of doomsday device, then I win. Or, we blow up."

"Fine," Emmett said. "But the package is my responsibility; I'll do the peeking."

Satisfied, Molly handed the box back. Emmett lifted the corner a bit, and put his eye to the crack.

"What is it?" Molly asked eagerly.

"I'm not sure," Emmett said. "I can't . . . GAH!" He tossed the box in the air, and fell off the barrel.

"What was it?" Molly scrambled to the package.

"Aheadinthebox! Aheadinthebox!" Emmett cried.

"What's ahead in the box?" Molly asked. She lifted the package to her eye.

"There's. A. *Head*. In the box," Emmett repeated.

"GAH!" Molly tossed the package to the ground and leapt away from it. "There was an eye!" she screamed. "An eye eye-to-eye with my eye!"

"I know!" Emmett shouted back. "I just did the same thing!"

"Wow, a head." Molly shuddered. "Maybe Bell is sewing corpse parts together to make some kind of monster, like the doctor in that book, *Frankenstein*. Maybe the plan didn't say 'death machine,' maybe it said . . . 'dead macramé.'"

But Emmett wasn't listening. He pulled at his own hair and kicked a barrel angrily. "Unbelievable! Can't I just once get a job from someone who's not a criminal? What am I going to do now?"

"Take that box to the police," Molly said. "If he's

cutting off people's heads and sending them around in boxes, it doesn't even matter what he's got planned for the Fair."

"I'm not touching that thing again," Emmett said. "And I can't risk the police anyway. You take it."

"*I* can't go to the police," Molly said. "I'm a burglar! And we have no way to prove the head came from Bell. He'd just deny it. Who are the cops gonna believe? Us or one of the most respected men in America?" She thought for a moment, then picked up the box and forced it into Emmett's hands. "Where are you supposed to deliver it?" she asked.

"Mr. Bell has a warehouse on Pike Street. Two blocks down."

"Deliver it," Molly said. "And while we're there, we look for more clues about Bell's death machine. If we can't go to the cops, that's our only option—that's what my mother and I were gonna do and it's still the best plan."

Emmett held the box at arm's length like it was a drippy sack of rancid mutton.

"C'mon, Emmett, you can do this," Molly said. "It's for the greater good. Same as when you tossed the Green Onion Boys' guns into the river in order to save lives."

"Yeah, except I mostly did that because I got scared," Emmett replied.

"Perfect—you're scared now too!" Molly gave him a

playful punch on the arm. "And anyway, this time you've got me with you."

"Wonderful."

"Come on, Goosey, let's go save the world!"

"I thought we were just saving the World's *Fair,*" Emmett said.

"Have you read any Jules Verne?" Molly asked. "No mad genius is going to quit after conquering a big carnival. This is only the beginning of Bell's diabolical schemes. I guarantee it."

Emmett's chin dropped to his chest. "I was supposed to get paid today."

"The righteous feeling you get from performing a brave and noble deed will be your reward," Molly said.

Emmett's shoulders slumped. "I was going to buy ice cream."

"I can get you free pickles," Molly added helpfully. "Well, one free pickle. I've got a business to run."

12

The Hidden Laboratory

ALEXANDER GRAHAM BELL'S secret lair was incredibly disappointing. Molly had been hoping for a moat, perhaps a few cannons—at the very least some gargoyles! Instead she got a standard brick warehouse no different from any other on the block.

"Is it more exciting inside?" she asked.

"I didn't know this place existed until this morning."

They waited for the echoing clip-clops of a passing coal cart to fade, then ran along the side of the warehouse into a yard stacked with lumber and sheets of aluminum. The aroma of corned beef wafted through an open window, reminding Molly how long it had been since she'd eaten. She peered over the sill and saw a sooty-faced man in an apron and goggles finishing a sandwich. No one else entered or walked past the doorway.

"I think it's just the one guy," Molly whispered. "Go up front and deliver your box of horrors like nothing's wrong. But talk to him, keep him busy. I'm gonna pop in here and look around. Go. Skedaddle."

Emmett hesitated. "This doesn't feel right. It's trespassing."

"On *criminals*," Molly said.

Emmett huffed and headed around front. As soon as the doorbell rang and the man rose to answer it, Molly slipped through the window and tiptoed to the doorway—stealing a tidbit of corned beef along the way. She peered into a lantern-lined corridor that dead-ended in a massive steel vault. She was about to head for it when, from behind her . . .

"*Psst!*"

It was Emmett, climbing in through the window. "Get any evidence yet?" he whispered.

"It's been eight seconds! I haven't gotten anything!" she shot back. "Except some corned beef. Which was really good. What are *you* doing here? You were supposed to talk to the man!"

"I did," Emmett replied. "I talk fast when I'm nervous."

"Well, I'm not leaving yet." Molly *really* wished her mother had followed her. But she wasn't giving up. Peppers didn't give up. She pulled Emmett into the hall and pointed to the vault door. "You can either pull down a lantern and come in there with me," she said. "Or run away and feel guilty when I get caught. Or go grab a piece of that corned beef. Seriously, it's delicious."

Emmett stood for a second, his jaw clenched, then wordlessly reached up and unhooked a lit lantern from the wall. Molly hurried to the tantalizingly mysterious iron door and, with two hands, turned its X-shaped crank. *Click, thunk*—the vault cracked open. Together, they pulled back the heavy slab door just enough to squeeze inside.

Molly slapped her hand over her mouth to keep from screaming. Emmett did the same, tossing his lamp to the ground with a clatter. As it rolled, its dancing flame cast flashes of light on glinting metallic claws, spiked iron boots, steel-trap jaws, dagger-point teeth, and cold, dead eyes like the one that had stared at them from Emmett's box. An army of hideous metal men surrounded them. Molly closed her eyes.

"They're not moving," Emmett said breathlessly.

Molly risked a peek. The lantern had come to rest at the feet of a metalloid warrior. The figures were indeed still. For now.

"Marching," Emmett whispered. "On the telephone, I heard Mr. Bell. He told someone he was going to *march* on the Fair. I thought he was speaking figuratively. But this . . . this is an army."

"An army of death machines," Molly said. In the lantern's dim circle of light, it was impossible to ascertain exactly how many automatons there were, but there were easily dozens stretching out into the darkness. Maybe a hundred even. And it wasn't difficult to imagine the havoc these clockwork devils could cause if Bell were to unleash them on an unsuspecting crowd.

"We should go," Emmett whispered. "Corned Beef Man might've heard us."

"We need to destroy them," Molly said with determination.

"How?" Emmett sounded terrified, but Molly inched toward the closest of the metal men, the one with the lantern sitting by its anvil-like feet. The thing's face was still bathed in shadow, but Molly could see a nameplate bolted to its barrel-thick torso. She squinted, trying to read the inscription, when Emmett scooped up the lantern and quickly pulled her out into the hallway.

"No, we—" she started, but Emmett quickly held a finger to his mouth. A man's shadow was growing longer against the wall. Someone was coming. They'd never make it back to the room they'd entered from without being seen, so Emmett pulled open another door, just a few feet from the vault, and they rushed blindly inside.

Among the bolt cutters and welding torches around them, they saw an array of clockwork body parts—arms, ears, feet, fingers. They did not, unfortunately, see any windows.

"What now?" Emmett mouthed, as footsteps sounded

in the hall. "The vault is open. He's checking inside."

Molly spotted a metal panel on the wall and gave it a pull. It was a garbage chute, leading to a trash bin outside. She waved Emmett over. "Easy escape," she said, and jumped through.

She landed in a pile of dented gears and pointy springs (which was only slightly less comfortable than her bed at home). Emmett popped through after her, but didn't make it into the bin. Instead, he dangled from the hatch, upside down, by one leg.

"My shoe's stuck," he hissed frantically. "The lace is hooked on the inside handle."

Molly stood up to help, struggling for balance on the trash mound. It didn't help that the bin was on wheels. Through the hatch, Molly saw the workshop door open.

She grabbed Emmett, set her feet against the wall, and threw her entire body backward until the boy's foot popped out of its shoe. The hatch fell shut with Emmett's shoe still dangling from its handle like the world's worst Christmas ornament. Their momentum started the bin rolling away from the wall, and they quickly hopped over the side before being taken for an unwanted ride. They dashed from the alley and didn't stop running until they were three blocks away, at which point, Molly finally paused and fell over, laughing.

Emmett gaped at her. "What can you possibly find funny right now?"

"I told you the hatch would be an easy escape," she said between giggles. "But I was *pulling your leg*." She laughed some more.

"I can't believe you," said Emmett. "I don't have another shoe. I don't have *any* other clothes. I wouldn't have this suit if Mr. Bell hadn't bought it for me."

"My mother'll build you a new shoe." Molly wiped her tears on her sleeve. "But, hey, we did it, right? We discovered Bell's secret plan! Now that we know we're up against an army of metal maniacs, we can figure out how to stop them, right?"

"Yeah, I suppose," Emmett muttered, staring at his frayed sock.

"C'mon, Goosey, we gotta tell my mother." She turned toward home, but quickly realized Emmett was not beside her. "Emmett."

"What am I gonna do?" he said. "Next person who opens that hatch is going to find my shoe hanging there. Corned Beef Man will tell Mr. Bell I showed up with the box. They'll put two and two together, and . . ." It sounded like he was holding back tears.

"Don't worry. Really. My mother'll figure it out."

"No, I'm done with this," Emmett said. "I'm done with you." He began to walk away.

"Where you gonna go?" Molly scoffed. "Back to the Guild?"

Emmett laughed, but it was a sad laugh. "You're right,

I can't go back to the Guild," he said. "The one good thing I had in my life and you ruined it. No, that's not fair. It's my own fault. I'm the gullible one who keeps letting people talk me into terrible decisions. So now what? I can't go back to the dump."

"Dump? What are you talking about? Emmett, come with me."

He shook his head. "I know how to survive on my own. I'm always on my own." He disappeared around the corner.

Molly wasn't as confident about Emmett's chances. But she couldn't force him to go with her. Could she? She wasn't sure how real friendships worked, just the ones in books. If Emmett were D'Artagnan and she were one of the three musketeers (probably Porthos—he had all the good laugh lines) she'd pretend she was giving him the space he needed, but she'd secretly follow him so she could swoop in to help if he got into trouble. And that was just what she'd decided to do when she heard voices from around the corner.

"Look what we have here! Oh, no! You're not running anywhere. Not sure where the likes of you belongs, but we'll get that sorted out back at the Jäger Society."

Taken!

MOLLY LEANED UP against the corner of a tall, redbrick row house and tried to listen. But they were back by busy East Broadway again, and she struggled to hear over the sounds of the passing horses and wagons.

"—got your papers in order," she heard the Jäger agent saying. "But if not—"

SCRAAAAPE!

A street cleaner was scooping clumps of horse dung from the curb. She glared at the man, who tipped his cap and went about his job.

But "papers"? If the Jägerman was talking to Emmett about adoption papers, maybe this was for the best. Maybe Emmett's fears of deportation were unfounded. She strained to listen harder.

"But I don't even speak the language," Emmett was yelling.

"You're better off with your own kind," the Jägerman replied. "They'll see to it that—"

SCRAAAAPE!

The noise didn't matter. Molly had heard enough. She swiped the shovel from the startled street sweeper, loaded it with a stinking pile of horse droppings, and ran around the corner to where a tall Jägerman in the usual long coat and round hat had Emmett by the wrist. The boy squirmed, trying to wriggle free.

"Help!" Molly yelled in a high-pitched baby voice. "I'm a poor little orphan who can't find my mama!"

The agent looked up and received a heaping helping of manure in his face.

"Goosey, let's go!" Molly shouted, dropping the shovel. As the Jägerman spat and wiped the filth from his eyes, the children hoisted themselves onto a passing chicken wagon. The birds squawked and flapped in their cages, but Molly and Emmett just grinned.

"Thanks for coming back for me," Emmett said. He and Molly walked along Bleecker Street, having hopped off the chicken cart as soon as they'd put a safe distance between themselves and the Jägerman.

"That's what friends are for," she replied.

"This is the first time I'm not going to argue your definition of that word," he said. He put his head down and his shoulders started shaking. Molly thought he was crying, but when he looked up, she realized he was laughing.

"What?" she asked.

"I'm an orphan who can't find my mama!" He mimicked the baby voice Molly had used. "Orphans *don't have* mamas. That's the definition of orphan."

"Hey, I had to improvise!" Molly said, throwing her hands in the air.

"I'm not complaining! I'm thanking you for the laugh," Emmett said. He wiped his eyes. "Believe me, it's not easy for me to laugh about being an orphan. I'm always afraid, you know. That someone will figure out I don't have the right papers to be here. I've been in the US since I was a baby, but I never got the proper documentation after the Exclusion Act went into effect. I had no one to get them for me."

"Wow, yeah," Molly said, reminded once more how thankful she was to still have her mother. "It must be your worst nightmare."

"Basically. Although finding a head in a box is right up there."

"At least we know now it wasn't a real head," Molly said. "New rule: next time we think we have a box with a severed head in it, we look real close to make sure."

"I don't like that rule," Emmett said. He grimaced as he stepped on a rock with his bare foot. "Do you really think your mother can make me new shoes?"

"Ask her yourself." Molly stopped and, with a flourish, opened the door to Pepper's Pickles. "I can't wait to tell her about—"

The business area of the shop was empty, but voices came from behind the folding screen. Molly held a finger to her lips, shushing Emmett. Molly peeked around the screen and saw her mother face-to-face with a woman in an extravagant blue dress. Ostrich feathers wreathed the stranger's collar. She had pearls in her hair and a silver cane in her hand.

"Yes, Mrs. Pepper, we know exactly who you are," the woman said in a crisp British accent. "And we know what you've seen."

14

International Woman of Mystery

THIS WAS A job for the Thimble Cannon! Molly crouched and scanned the room for her favorite of the little "toys" her mother had built for her. Alas, it was sitting on the table right next to the mystery woman. *Drat.* She would have to improvise. What was within reach? The Rotating Shoe Tree . . . the Super Bubble Soap Squirter . . . *Aha!* The Self-Propelled Mop. Molly grabbed the ball of coarse, ropy fibers with a turn key jutting from its side. Molly gave the device a few quick cranks and it rolled out across the floor. The mystery woman barely had time to turn her head toward the whirring sound before she was knocked off her feet. She landed on the Astounding Automated Secretary, which burped a cloud of black soot into her face.

"Molls!" Cassandra gasped.

"Clever," the stranger said. "But I did not come here to be attacked." She pointed her silver cane at Molly, and its head split open into four spinning blades. Molly braced herself, hoping that the sensation of being minced into stew meat would not be as painful as she assumed. But the woman merely used the rotating fan blades to blow the dust from her cheeks. Molly exhaled—just before a net sprang from the cane tip and enveloped her. "Now, as I was saying," the British woman went on.

"Who are you?" Molly snapped. "Mother, who is this?"

"A daughter-trapping villain, obviously," Cassandra said, rushing to free her struggling child. "Which now makes me feel rather awkward about having offered her tea. You don't still want that tea, do you?"

"I'm a civilized woman, and it is the afternoon," said the stranger. "Of course I want the tea." She held out her hand but nobody shook it. "Hertha Marks. Mathematician, electrician, physicist, and inventor. Note that the word 'villain' did not appear on that list."

She looked younger than Molly's mother, but sounded older. It was probably the accent.

"Speaking of names, Miss Marks," Cassandra said, sidling past boxes to the teakettle. "How is it that you know mine?"

"Please, call me Hertha," she said. "I know your name, Cassandra Pepper, because one of my associates saw your little song and dance this morning at the Inventors' Guild."

"Oh, I didn't do the song and dance—that was Edison." Cassandra placed a steaming mug before her uninvited guest. "I mostly just yelled at the clerk."

"It was the woman with the parasol, wasn't it?" Molly said. "The one who tripped up the watchmen."

"Clever again," Hertha said, raising the mug to her lips. "My associate surmised that your last name was not actually Pemollywot, but that it did begin with a 'P.' From what you'd shouted at the clerk, she also divined that you were a widow—sincere condolences—and that you had some connection with pickles. From there it didn't take much to track you down." Hertha turned to Molly. "And you—our young lady so full of dash-fire— you must be Molly. Wot?"

Molly wasn't sure what "dash-fire" was, but it certainly sounded like something she'd be full of. She had no idea whether this Hertha Marks was a potential ally or yet another enemy, but the woman seemed impressed by her, and it was one of Molly's goals in life to have everyone recognize her cleverness, villains included. She held out her hand. "Molly Pepper: lab assistant, pickle seller, saboteur, and spy."

Hertha shook her hand. "I can already attest to those last two."

"Let's make it three. Want a pickle?" Molly turned toward the storefront, and realized, with disappointment, that Emmett was gone.

103

Cassandra cleared her throat and steered her daughter to the table. "So, we know *how* you found us," Cassandra said. "The answer being 'sneaky business.' But I'd still like to know why."

"I represent a secret cabal of women inventors. And we have a proposition for you."

"I didn't even know there *were* other women inventors!" Molly blurted.

"There are," Hertha said. "And we'd like to invite your mother to join our group, the Mothers of Invention."

"You all have children?" Cassandra asked.

"Some, not all. Not I," Hertha answered. "The name is a play on the old saying, 'Necessity is the mother of invention.'"

"And you want my mother?" Molly asked.

"We do," said Hertha. "We in the MOI take a very different approach from the competing, spying, backstabbing boys at the Inventors' Guild. We work as a team to perfect all of our collective projects. Share your ideas with us, Cass, and we will share ours with you. You've obviously got a lot to contribute, like the incredible speech-activated technology in your sneeze shield."

"The sneeze shield?" Cassandra said. "It stops you from spraying boogers on people."

"But it works through the recognition of specific sounds," Hertha said. "That's never been done before."

"Her Astounding Automated Secretary's even better,"

104

Molly added proudly. "It can understand full sentences!"

Hertha's eyebrows shot up. "What else have you made, Cass?"

"Um, there's the Stay-Dry Rain Hat," Molly answered. "If the sun goes behind a cloud, a little umbrella pops out!"

"It senses light levels," Hertha said. "Incredible. What else?"

"The Toastinator will crisp your bread in three seconds!" Molly said.

"Instant heat," said Hertha.

"Oh, and best of all is the Ic—"

Cassandra covered her daughter's mouth.

"The Ick, huh?" Hertha said. "Name needs work. What does it do?"

Molly watched her mother squint warily and drum her fingers. If what this Hertha woman said was true, this could be the greatest opportunity her mother had ever been offered. Then again, if this woman had more sinister motives, an invitation to an elite inventors' club would be the perfect bait to trap Cassandra Pepper.

Cassandra stood tall. "All right, Bertha—if that *is* your real name—"

"It's not," said Hertha.

"How do we know you're not a Guild spy?" Cassandra continued. "That dress of yours is obviously a disguise. How do we know this whole persona you're showing us isn't fake?"

105

Molly considered the possibility. "Yeah, are you really English?" she asked pointedly.

"Do you mean 'really' as in 'actually,' or 'really' as in 'very'?" Hertha replied. "The answer, incidentally, is yes, to both. Look, I can't deny using subterfuge to locate you, but I am no friend of the Guild."

"The Jägermen, then?" Cassandra said. "You'll not be taking my daughter."

"I wish no such thing," Hertha replied. "The only group I work for is the Mothers of Invention. And we want you. Your ideas are brilliant, Cass; you simply need some collaborative input on how they might best be applied. And where else are you going to find that kind of help?

"I'm sure you've experienced firsthand the difficulty a woman has trying to be taken seriously by the scientific establishment. Back in London, when I applied to present my work before the Royal Society, I was told I would need to give my papers to a male colleague so *he* could present them. Molly, you said you were unaware of the mere existence of female inventors. *That* is the reason we created the MOI."

"Ah, this is what you were talking about, isn't it?" said Molly. "When you told my mother, 'We know what you've seen.' You were talking about the obstacles, the rejection."

"Precisely." Hertha brushed some feathers from her face and sipped her tea. "So, have I sparked your interest?"

"Did you invent that nifty cane of yours?" Molly asked.

"This came from a colleague," she replied. "My own work centers around energy. Electric arc lamps, for instance. The ones we used in the university laboratories at Cambridge hissed horribly; 'twas quite distracting. So I made some improvements. I'm also studying the ripple effect, which is rather—"

"No," Cassandra said bluntly.

"Beg pardon?" Hertha asked. Molly was just as surprised.

"We'll not be joining your little club," Cassandra said. "I do not believe, Mertha—"

"Hertha."

"—that my daughter and I are your type of people. Thank you for the invitation, but we are quite fine on our own."

"I'm . . . sorry you feel that way," Hertha said.

"And yet we do," Cassandra replied coolly. "I think it's time for you to go."

Hertha pointed to the mug that was currently at her lips.

Cassandra sighed. "After your tea."

Several awkwardly silent minutes later, Hertha drained the last drop from her cup and, with a nod, took her leave.

"Why did you turn her down?" Molly immediately asked.

"I don't trust her," Cassandra said. She began violently chopping pickles. "The woman comes in here talking as if she and I are kindred spirits, as if she knows what I've been through. 'Allo, I'm called Fertha and I'm from merry ol' England, cheerio and wot-wot! I went to a fancy university and learned science in a big lab with electric lights but it was all fribbledy-frapp because the lamps made icky noises, tally-ho, pip-pip!"

Molly learned two things from that tirade. One was that her mother did the worst British accent of all time. But more important, she now understood her mother's distaste for Hertha Marks. Cassandra hadn't had a day of schooling beyond the eighth grade. The only "laboratory" she'd ever known was a table in a pickle shop. The only lamps she worked by required a match to light. Every amazing machine she built had to be crafted from old parts they found in alleys or garbage bins. Hertha was a woman who'd obviously had unfettered access to the kind of privilege and opportunity Cassandra could only dream of.

But did that mean she and the Mothers of Invention were no better than the Guild?

"Apparently not all celebrities are as appreciative of their fans as Thomas Edison," Cassandra said bitterly. "Sergio Vittorini was completely unwilling to sign my broken sneeze shield."

"Mother."

"What else was I going to offer him—you took our only piece of paper. You know, if you'd let me come with you, nobody would have been here when that horrid Marks woman showed up and we wouldn't be down one cup of tea right now. Did you at least find that boy?"

"Yes!" Molly burst from her seat and squeezed her mother's hands tight. She couldn't believe she'd gotten distracted enough to forget. "Yes, I did! And better yet, we found Bell's death machines!"

"Machines, plural?" Cassandra squeezed back. "What are they? Tell me!"

"Robots."

"Robots?" Cassandra echoed.

Molly nodded. "Robots."

"What's a robot?" Cassandra asked.

"Yeah, what's a robot?" Emmett asked, crawling out from beneath a bench.

Molly's face lit up. "You *didn't* run away!"

"I was hiding," he said sheepishly. "In case you needed . . . just in case."

"Sorry, what's a robot?" Cassandra asked again.

"Bell's death machines," Molly said. "They're metal men. With creepy eyes and pointy fingers."

"The automatons?" Emmett said. "They were automatons, like the clockwork figures at the Guild Hall. Only much bigger."

"So why are you calling them Herthas?" Cassandra asked.

"Robots," Emmett said. "She called them robots."

"That's the one!" Cassandra said, snapping her fingers. "Why are you calling them robots?"

"*I'm* not calling them robots," Molly said. "*Bell* is. That's what he engraved on their chest plates. I got a look right before Emmett pulled me away."

"It does have a nice ring to it," Cassandra agreed. "But I believe we're drifting from the main question." She spun to Emmett. "Who are *you*?"

"Oh! This is Emmett!" Molly threw an arm around Emmett's shoulders and pulled him to her side. Shifting uncomfortably, Emmett gave a weak wave. Cassandra simply stared. "The boy from last night?" Molly tried.

Cassandra stared at him. From a nearby shelf, she grabbed some goggles and held them up to Emmett's face. "Ah, yes! That's him," she said cheerily. She threw the goggles aside and shook his hand. "It's good to meet you, Emmett." Then she bent and whispered in his ear, "*Is* it good to meet you? Are you on our side?"

"Um, yes?"

"Then, sit down, young man," Cassandra said. "I'll make some extra sandwiches. I want to hear all about these doomsday Herthas—*robots!* Doomsday robots."

The Story of Emmett Lee

EMMETT ATE LIKE he'd never had a triple pickle and mustard sandwich before. Which was very likely.

"Thank you, Mrs. Pepper," the boy said for the fourth time.

"You're still welcome, Mr. Lee," Cassandra replied. "How do you normally feed yourself, Emmett? Living on your own?" The children had filled her in on Emmett's history as well as their discovery in Bell's lab.

"For a while, I did odd jobs for food. Sweep a stoop for an apple, tighten a wobbly gate for some biscuits. But Mr. Bell pays me now, so I—uh-oh . . ." Pickle juice ran down Emmett's chin, and he looked as if he might hide under the table out of embarrassment.

"Relax, Goosey," Molly said. "You think we're gonna kick you out for dribbling? We're not much for highfalutin manners here. Watch." She removed the top slice of bread from her sandwich, leaned forward, and planted her face into a layer of mustard. She sat up again with yellow-brown dollops dotting her nose and cheeks like clown makeup.

"Molly!" Cassandra chided. "I expect better from you. Like *this*." She opened her own sandwich and slammed her face into it. She came up with a gherkin jutting from each nostril.

Molly snorted in delight. Which made Cassandra laugh, and the tiny pickles shot from her nose. Emmett looked as if he still hadn't ruled out hiding under the table.

"Is this typical for you two at mealtime?" he asked.

"Only when I want to test out a new invention like the Wipe-Oscillator," Cassandra said. From a nearby shelf, she retrieved what appeared to be a jack-in-the-box. "I put this together yesterday morning," she said. "I have no idea if it works. Want to test it on your face?" Emmett politely declined. "Such a gentleman," Cassandra said. "You're right—I made the best mess, so I get to go first."

She held the box at chin level and turned its crank until the lid popped, releasing a gloved hand that slapped her cheek with a handkerchief.

"I think the Wipe-Oscillator just challenged you to a duel," Molly said.

"Not a problem," Cassandra said, her face no cleaner.

She grabbed some pliers from a nearby shelf. "I just need to adjust the torque on the pinions for better control of the oscillation."

It sounded like a foreign language to Molly. But Emmett perked up. "May I try?"

"By all means." Cassandra handed him the gadget and looked on as he tinkered with its inner workings. "Molly tells me you're headed for a career in inventing."

"Um, maybe," Emmett mumbled. "I don't know." Finished, he held the contraption by his own chin and turned the crank. This time, the mechanical hand gently wiped his mouth with one smooth stroke.

"Crackerjack!" Molly said. "Now put it back like it was, so I can use it as a slapping machine."

"You're a talented young man, Mr. Lee," Cassandra said.

"I've picked up a few tricks from Mr. Bell," Emmett said, blushing. "But honestly, he could probably learn a lot from you, Mrs. Pepper. Molly told me about some of your inventions." He turned in his seat. "Is that the Icarus Chariot?"

"Well, the pieces of it."

"And it really flies?"

"How else would I know that our upstairs neighbor likes to eat turkey legs while trimming her toenails?" Cassandra said.

"Incredible," Emmett said, looking around in awe.

"And you've made all sorts of things with motors, and devices with limbs that move on their own, and machines that understand human speech! Mr. Bell would kill to get his hands on . . ." He got suddenly quiet. "Mr. Bell's probably wondering where I am. Especially if he's heard about my shoe dangling from the trapdoor in his secret workshop." Emmett shut his eyes tightly. "I wanted this to work out so badly."

Cassandra patted him on the back. "And it *did* work out badly."

"No worries, Goosey, you can stay here with us," Molly said, tossing her last morsel of sandwich into her mouth.

"For tonight at least," Cassandra said. "Come morning, none of us can risk being discovered at Pepper's Pickles."

"Oh. The Jägermen," Molly said gloomily.

Cassandra rubbed her daughter's back. "It's just temporary, Molls. A week at most. By the time the World's Fair is over, so too shall our troubles be."

"Where will you go?" Emmett asked.

"I don't know," Molly said glumly. "Where were *you* living before the Guild?"

Emmett shook his head. "I promised myself I'd never go back under the dump."

"What's 'under the dump'?" Cassandra asked.

"Down Rivington, toward the water, where people dump the ash from their furnaces and such," he explained. "Folks without homes hollow out spaces for themselves under the mountains of ash. I didn't have to live in an ash cave, though, 'cause I had Miss Addie's book wagon."

Emmett must have seen the next question coming and went on. "I used to wait around the docks while my father worked his ferry shifts. Every day, Miss Addie would come by with her bookmobile. She never asked me for money, just let me borrow a new one each day, like a library on wheels. I'd find myself a nice spot—in an empty dinghy or one of those big coils of rope—and just read and read. After my father died, Miss Addie took me in for a while. Then she passed on too. She was old. But I still had the bookmobile. So I took it to the ash dump to keep out of sight, made a few alterations, and it became my home."

Molly didn't want to say what she was really thinking—which was that living in a book cart sounded far more exciting than living in a pickle shop—so instead she ran to her own chest of books to show off the stacked titles: *Frankenstein, Oliver Twist, The Count of Monte Cristo, The Age of Fable, The Adventures of Tom Sawyer, Little Women, Legends of King Arthur, From the Earth to the Moon*—and that was only the top layer. Each hardbound volume, read and reread dozens of times, had been a gift from her father—with the exception of her still-glossy copy of *Treasure Island*, which she'd received just one week earlier as a twelfth birthday present. Her mother had sold her favorite socket wrench set in order to buy her that book. Emmett picked it up and ran his finger along the embossed ship on the cover.

"Go 'head, read it," Molly said. "There's useful information in there if we should run into any pirates during this Bell business."

"I hope you can read quickly, though," said Cassandra. "Because tomorrow morning, out the door. All of us. Oh, but at least you can come watch the fireworks with us tomorrow night."

"Mother, you're a genius!"

"That's true," said Cassandra. "But why am I a genius this time?"

"The fireworks! Tomorrow night will be the best time to take care of Bell's metal men!" Molly said. "The whole city will be along the river, focused on the bridge. It'll be noisy, with all the drums and the tubas and the boom-boom-booms. And Bell himself will be in the parade, so we know we won't run into him."

"You're right," Cassandra said. "It's a unique opportunity; we should take advantage. Even if it means missing the fireworks ourselves. Which will be disappointing. I bet they have those big ones where the sparks spread out like a flower."

"So we're saboteurs again." Molly rubbed her hands together.

"Again?" Emmett said, raising an eyebrow. "Last time you attempted to sabotage something, all you did was make a mess for the janitor. Can I ... make a suggestion? There are only three of us—and that's counting me, which I'm not entirely sure we should be doing—so perhaps you could call upon Miss Marks and her friends—"

"Maybe one of them has invented a robot smasher?" Molly said. "I call dibs on riding it!"

"Emmett, I was beginning to grow quite fond of you; don't mess it up by mentioning that feathered crumpet," Cassandra said firmly. "I don't trust her farther than I could throw her—and I say that as someone who has built a catapult. Anyway, I know how we're going to destroy Bell's robot army: explosives!" She stood dramatically with her hands on her hips and mustard on her nose.

"Where are we going to get explosives, Mother?" Molly asked.

"Why, they're lying all over the Brooklyn Bridge."

Goodbye, Pickle Shop

THE NEXT MORNING, after some toast and coffee, the Peppers got dressed and packed their bags—special flat-bottomed carpetbags that Cassandra rigged with hidden shoulder straps for the inevitable moment in which one would need the use of two free hands. Cassandra filled hers with tools and a few of her more destructive inventions: the Double-Ended Hammer, the Self-Propelled Mop, and the Thimble Cannon.

For her part, Molly packed sandwiches and reading material. She agonized for some time over which book to take—so many of them, upon rereading, would conjure her father's voice back into her head. But in the end, she decided on *Treasure Island,* because Emmett had seemed so interested in it.

"Oh, and Mr. Lee," said Cassandra. "Stick your feet into

these." She held out a pair of clunky-looking brown shoes.

"You made these?" Emmett asked, gawking at the shoes as if they were exotic birds. "I mean, thank you, but . . . you *made* these? Overnight?"

"Measuring your feet while you slept wasn't easy," Cassandra said.

Emmett slipped the shoes on and stood up, wobbling a bit. The thick soles made him almost a full inch taller. "They fit."

"That isn't all they do," Cassandra said. "Press down with your big toes. Don't look so frightened—try it."

Emmett wobbled again as dozens of pointy tacks protruded from his soles. Molly put her cheek to the floor to peek under the feet.

"Traction spikes," she said enviously. "You'll be able to climb walls so much easier with these!"

"I'm going to be climbing walls?"

Cassandra marched out onto the quiet, predawn streets, shouting, "Eastward ho, children! We need to be gone before any Jägermen arrive."

"Wait," Emmett said, clicking his toes to retract his shoe spikes. "Let me carry your bags."

"Thank you, but that's quite unnecessary," said Cassandra.

"There, um, aren't a lot of Chinese people around here," Emmett said. "It will attract less attention if people assume I'm working for you."

As much as Molly hated it, she knew Emmett was right. Flashing an apologetic smile, Molly handed over her bag. Cassandra did so as well, looking equally uncomfortable. "Here you are then, Mr. Lee," she said. "But I hope you know I would never *expect*—"

"And I would never have expected you to make me a pair of shoes," Emmett said.

As they walked away, Molly blew a goodbye kiss to Pepper's Pickles—something she often did when leaving the store. This day, however, she wondered if she were doing so for the last time.

The parade across the Brooklyn Bridge was a glorious event. It *sounded* like one, anyway.

Molly could do no more than listen to the distant strains of "Hail to the Chief" from several blocks away. She understood why they couldn't risk being seen, but it still seemed cruelly unfair that the unwitting fopdoodles whose lives she was about to save got to revel in the heavenly glow of President Arthur's sideburns, while she had to spend her day on a slightly damp bench eating slightly soggy sandwiches in a slightly malodorous nook beneath the Broadway rail line.

As afternoon turned to dusk, and the sounds of drums and tubas faded, Emmett began to fidget. Molly would have liked to assume he was just avoiding the cockroaches, but she knew it was more than that.

"She'll be back," Molly said confidently, taking a bite of her supper sandwich (which was no different from her lunch sandwich).

"She's been gone for hours," Emmett replied, his leg shaking anxiously. "The music stopped. That means the parade's in Brooklyn already. It won't be long before the fireworks start. We were supposed to be *in* Bell's lab by then. What if she got caught?"

"We've got plenty of time. They've still got to clear all the spectators off the bridge before they start lighting fuses. Hey, do you remember what my mother said today at lunch?"

"That with the right teacher a monkey could learn to play the ukulele?"

"Not that; the thing she said about you being with us."

"She said I don't need to worry about anything because I'm with the Peppers now and Peppers never give up," Emmett said. "But never giving up is different from never failing."

Molly narrowed her eyes. "You, Emmett, are—" But she swallowed whatever harsh words were about to follow. Because Emmett had a point. Maybe they should rethink the family slogan. For now, though, she needed to stay positive. "—not an optimist," she finished. "My mother is going to be back here any second with loads of exploding rockets, and we're going to destroy Bell's army of killer machines. I bet we finish blowing up those robots fast enough to come back and catch part two of the parade when they march back over to Manhattan after the fireworks. We might even get to see President Arthur."

"I can't say I'm a fan," Emmett said. "He is the one who signed the Exclusion Act."

"Oh . . . wow, I . . . I guess he was," Molly said awkwardly. "I never really thought about that."

"I figured," Emmett said. "That's why I mentioned it."

"Yeah, thanks," Molly said, nodding. She was afraid Emmett was upset with her, but when he nodded back, she saw in his eyes that he was commiserating. She and her mother weren't the only ones who knew what it was like to be on the receiving end of unfair policies. "It's important to remember stuff like that."

Cassandra finally appeared and hurried under the trestle to join them.

"Success, Mother?"

"I've never seen more people jammed into one place," Cassandra said. "The entire populace of New York must be crammed around that bridge."

"So, no success?" Molly asked.

"I'm a Pepper, Molls—we never give up."

Molly gave Emmett a sheepish look.

"The fireworks are set up on the big lower roadway, where carriages and streetcars will normally go," Cassandra explained. "But the paraders are on the pedestrian walkway above that, so while everyone was watching the trumpets and tubas, I was able to grab . . . this!"

From behind her back, she produced a four-foot-long, candy-striped tube with a long dangling fuse at the other end.

"Just the one?" Molly asked, trying not to sound too skeptical.

"Chain reactions, Molls," her mother replied. "One rocket is all we need to get it started. Based on what you told me, there should be plenty of flammable materials in that building. Now, where's my dinner sandwich? I'm famished." She sat down next to Emmett and rooted through Molly's bag. "Mr. Lee, you haven't taken a bite of yours. Eat up; you're going to need energy this evening."

"I'm sorry, Mrs. Pepper. I don't have much of an appetite."

"Understandable," she replied. "Should we relocate to someplace less . . . urine-y?"

"It's not that," Emmett said. "I'm just . . . thinking about Mr. Bell."

"Bell is marching to Brooklyn as we speak," Cassandra said. "You don't need to worry about running into him."

"No," Emmett said sadly. "It's just that . . . I can't believe I was so wrong about the man. He's been good to me."

"You keep saying that," said Molly. "But this is the

man who pretty much killed your . . ." She clamped her lips shut.

"It's okay," Emmett said. "I understand how you could see it that way. But for years, I've been thinking of Mr. Bell as the man who gave my father an incredible opportunity when no one else would, as a man who saw my father's potential. I don't hold him responsible for my father's death any more than I do Ambrose Rector, the man who built the ship. Or Ezra Hopper, the man who charted their course to Antarctica. Or Silas Cotton, the cabin boy. They went down with the *Frost Cleaver* too. So did twenty-one other sailors—twenty-one men who called my father captain before they died. I can name every one. It feels important to remember their names."

The tears running down Emmett's cheeks dampened the ruffles of Cassandra's dress as she pulled the boy in for a hug. "I am so sorry, Emmett."

Molly felt for him too, but couldn't bring herself to say so. Lost fathers were not her favorite topic. And regardless of how Emmett felt, *she* blamed Bell for what happened to Captain Lee. She liked having someone to blame.

Out on the sidewalk, a lamplighter fought his way against the flow of people still heading for the bridge. He used a candle on the end of a long pole to ignite the gas lamps along Broadway. As one particular lamp burst to life, it illuminated a tall, elegantly dressed woman, staring in Molly's direction.

"Someone's watching us!" Molly blurted.

"Where?" Cassandra spun to see. But as soon as Molly pointed, the woman by the lamp rushed off.

"One of Gertha's, no doubt," Cassandra said. "They *are* working with Bell!"

"Not necessarily," Molly said. "Maybe she—"

"—was just a fancy rich lady glaring at us because we'd taken her favorite bench by the rats?" Cassandra shook her head. "Come, we need to go anyway. Boom time."

The three grabbed their things, left the shelter of the trestle, and headed to Bell's secret lab, checking over their shoulders the entire way.

Playing with Fire

THE SUN HAD nearly dipped behind the rooftops when the trio reached the deceptively bland-looking warehouse that held Bell's hidden laboratory.

"You think Corned Beef Man's still in there?" Emmett asked.

"Corned Beef Man." Cassandra chuckled. "That's a silly name."

Molly shushed her mother and led them down the dark alley that ran alongside the building. No light came from within. "Looks deserted," she whispered. "Convert to espionage mode."

Molly and Emmett reached under the flat bottoms of the carpetbags, pulled free the hidden shoulder straps, and them slung the bags onto their backs like mountaineers.

Cassandra looked on admiringly. "Even more dashing than I'd hoped."

"Should we go back in that way?" Emmett pointed to the garbage chute by the big, wheeled trash bin.

Molly figured he was still hoping to find his lost shoe, but she shook her head. "Too risky to enter by a room we can't peek into first." She moved to the rear yard. "Lucky break! That back window's still open." She climbed inside.

"Um, isn't that a little *too* convenient?" Emmett said. "Is it luck or a trap?"

Holding her skirt in one hand, Cassandra shimmied awkwardly over the sill to join her daughter. "If it's a trap," she said, "at least we'll know Bell is onto us. One mystery solved!"

Reluctantly, Emmett followed.

They had only the faintest glow of moonlight to see by, and the rumble of the far-off crowd gave the feeling of a storm closing in. But Molly was undaunted; her mother was with her.

Cassandra unclasped the bag on Molly's back and retrieved one of her Illuma-Sticks, a foot-long metal tube with a glass sphere at one end. With her thumb, she flicked a switch, and a thin flame ignited within the bulb. The light was faint, but enough to ensure that they could make it through the dark room without tripping. Cassandra passed the flickering device to her daughter and said, "Lead the way."

Molly beamed.

She guided the others down to the gleaming vault door,

turned the handle, and heard the hiss of escaping air.

"You two go ahead," Emmett said, heading to the room with the garbage hatch. "I'm gonna check for my shoe."

"Do what you must, Mr. Lee," Cassandra said. "But before you go, if you could kindly give us the incendiary device?" Emmett retrieved the long rocket that had been jammed into his bag. "Thank you," Cassandra said, taking the firework. "You'll also find a second Illuma-Stick in the bag if it's too dark in there."

Emmett took out the light and flicked it on. "Um, since this thing makes fire," he said hesitantly, "should I have been carrying it in the same bag as an explosive rocket?"

"Excellent observation, Mr. Lee," Cassandra replied. "I knew you were a clever one."

Shivering, Emmett stepped into the workroom, while Molly tugged her mother into the vault. The Peppers stood face-to-steely-face with Bell's metallic army.

"So these are *robots*." Cassandra said the word as if it were magic. She and Molly were about to step up for a closer look when they heard Emmett scream.

"He's here!" Emmett burst into the vault.

"Who?" Cassandra asked.

"Corned Beef Man," Emmett said. Molly turned to run, but Emmett grabbed her arm. "No. My . . . my shoe's not there. But Corned Beef Man is. I think he's dead."

"Are you sure?" Cassandra asked. "Did you get a close look?"

"No, I did not get a close look," Emmett said, flustered. "What is it with you Peppers and *getting a close look* every time there might be a corpse?"

"I'll check on this Beef fellow," Cassandra said. "You two gather as many lanterns as you can from the corridor. Spread them among these metal chaps. That will be our chain reaction. We can't get too distracted from our mission." She traded the rocket for Molly's Illuma-Stick and rushed to the workshop.

Molly had so many questions for Emmett: Was there blood? A murder weapon? Why did Bell kill one of his own men? Something didn't add up. But they had to focus on getting their job done quickly.

While Emmett gathered lanterns, Molly approached the robots, brandishing the rocket like a peppermint-striped club. She squinted at the figure nearest her. Funny . . . last time, she could have sworn these things had sharpened fangs, not handlebar mustaches. And the hands looked less clawlike than she'd remembered. She scanned the thing's oil-drum chest. "Hey," she called out. "This one doesn't say 'robot.' It says . . . 'char'?" She envisioned flames spewing from beneath the metal demon's mustache. "Or is that 'chase'?"

"Are you *sure* you don't need spectacles?" Emmett said, carrying in an armful of lanterns.

"I don't need spectacles!" Molly grumbled. "It's dark. Give me the Illuma-Stick." She attempted to pull the handheld torch from Emmett's overburdened arms. But just as she got hold of it—*BOOM!* The children yelped and dropped everything. As glass shattered and oil splattered, Molly and Emmett fled the vault and ran smack into Cassandra in the hall. More explosions sounded. They were distant, blocks away.

"No cause for alarm," Cassandra said. "Just fireworks at the bridge, so . . . ooh, I take it back—*that's* cause for alarm."

She pointed to the rocket, which now lay on the floor of the vault, in a flaming puddle of lamp oil. They barely had time to absorb the danger of that situation before they heard the warehouse door slam.

"And *that's* even more cause." Cassandra pulled both children back into the workroom with her, careful to lead them around the facedown figure slumped on the floor.

"Is he—?" Molly asked.

"Very much so," her mother answered. "Is that the trash chute?"

Cassandra held open the hatch for the children, then quickly dove through after them. The trash cart shifted slightly on its wheels as the trio landed painfully among discarded scrap metal.

"Well, that could have gone better," Cassandra said.

"From where I stand," said a man in a strange mask, "it went perfectly."

Masks!

"THANK YOU FOR doing exactly what I expected," the stranger said. He wore a black suit and a grotesque, crooked-faced mask. Though his expression could not be seen, Molly could tell the man was smiling. His voice had a sinister tone, but also an element of glee, as if he enjoyed sounding scary.

A second masked man—thickset with long, simian arms—arrived from the front end of the alley. "Did it work?"

"Yes, Mr. C," said the first stranger. "As I anticipated, the slamming door did indeed flush them out. We've got them, Mr. T! You can abandon the window." A third masked man, built like a tall scarecrow, ran to join them.

Molly recognized the masks on the two newcomers. They were theatrical masks—one happy, one sad.

Comedy and Tragedy. But the mask worn by the leader was unfamiliar—a half-melted face with angry arched brows, crooked nose, and a mouth contorted into a permanent scream.

"Something tells me you fellows are not police," Cassandra said, huddling the children behind her in the bin.

"No, Mrs. Pepper, we most certainly are not," the leader said. "Though I suppose—"

"Let the children go," Cassandra said. Fireworks continued to rumble like distant thunder.

"Yeah, let us go," Molly joined in. She hacked out a fake cough. "We're sick. I think it's contag—"

"Oh, Molly, you offend me," the leader said. "Trying a trick that didn't even work on that Jäger Society goon?"

Molly gripped the side of the bin. How did he know about that? What else did he know about them?

"I'd hate to think I've overestimated you," the villain continued. "But like the man who loses his left hand to a crocodile, then tries to retrieve it by reaching into the beast's maw with his right, you, dear Molly, do not learn from your mistakes."

"Okay, Ugly, three things!" Molly squeezed in front of her mother and held three defiant fingers in the man's face. "One: my trick *did* work on the Jägerman. He just happened to be a bit more spry than I thought. Two: Who's this guy with the crocodile? 'Cause he sounds like a dolt. And three: next time you see your boss, *Alexander*

132

Graham Bell, tell him he's not the only one capable of spying on his enemies."

The masked man applauded. "Oh, I'll be sure to pass your message on to him." His voice was softer now, with a slight Scottish lilt.

"Mr. Bell?" Emmett whispered.

"Aye, Emmett," Bell replied. "But you knew that already, didn't you? Since you stole those plans from my workshop."

Molly grabbed Emmett's trembling hand.

"So, why the mask, you ask?" Bell went on.

"No, we didn't," Molly said. "We didn't ask."

"You little thieves may have lucked into my secret," Bell said, reverting to his "evil" voice. "But that doesn't mean I want the whole world to know. Not *yet*. But like the spider who spends years weaving a gargantuan web until it is one day vast enough to snare a wild stallion, I too will shock the world with my abilities."

"Your knowledge of spiders is seriously flawed," said Molly.

"Watch yer yap, girl," snarled the man in the comedy mask. "If the boss says there's giant spiders, there's giant spiders."

"Ignoramus," Bell hissed. "It's not the spider that's huge, it's the web."

"But if it's a tiny spider, how's it gonna eat a horse?" asked Tragedy.

"It's a metaphor!" Bell snapped.

"Ah, I heard of them metaphor spiders," Comedy said seriously. "Deadly creatures."

"A metaphor is not a—!" The leader took a long, deep breath through his nose.

"Hey, boss—" said Tragedy.

"Do not ask me about spiders!" Bell snapped. "I will strangle you with my bare hands if you—"

"I just wanted to ask why there ain't been no boom," said Tragedy. "In there." He motioned toward the building.

Bell glared through the eyeholes of his mask. "There has been no . . . *boom*, as you so eloquently put it," he said, "because these supposed saboteurs were apparently unable to set off even a simple—"

BOOM!

Bell's lab exploded.

Rocket's Red Glare

WINDOWS SHATTERED, FLAMES gushed forth, and the garbage hatch was blown violently from its hinges. The force of the blast sent the trash bin—and its three passengers— careening madly down the alleyway. Bell and his goons dove out of the way as the runaway rubbish cart bounced off the curb and rattled along the cobblestone street.

"Stop, stop, stop!" Emmett shouted, crouching amid the trash with Cassandra and Molly. Cassandra reached over the side and dragged a metal pipe along the stones until the bin slowed down. That's when they saw the masked trio climbing onto a horse-drawn wagon.

"Go, go, go!" Emmett shouted.

Cassandra tore open the bag on Emmett's back and pulled out the Self-Propelled Mop. "I knew there was a reason I'd packed you!"

Molly watched in confusion as her mother leaned over the back of the cart and fastened the motorized mophead between the bin's wheels. Outside the burning warehouse, Bell snapped the reins and his open-backed wagon headed their way.

"Mother, I see what you're trying," Molly said with urgency. "But that mop goes about as fast as a tort—"

The mop motor began spinning and the trash cart took off like a runaway streetcar.

"Tornado?" Cassandra asked, sounding very proud of herself. "Is that what you were going to say? Fast as a tornado?"

"How?" Molly shouted.

"When I saw how you used it against Nertha, I realized how much better it could be, so I—*look out!*" Cassandra thrust her pipe out and pushed them away from a dangerously close tree.

As the bin sped along, Cassandra jabbed her pipe out every time an oblivious street musician, clumsy pedestrian, or cat with a death wish crossed into their path. And Molly whooped victoriously every time they avoided a collision. But the farther they went, the more people began clogging their path. The noise of the fireworks was also getting louder—and closer.

"We're going too fast," Emmett said, covering his head.

"It's a clockwork motor," Cassandra said. "It will wind down eventually."

"When's eventually?" Emmett asked.

Molly pointed above the eastern rooftops, where sparks cascaded across the night sky. "We're headed toward the bridge," she said.

"Wonderful," Cassandra replied, steering around a terrified bicyclist. "We can lose our pursuers in the crowds."

Suddenly, Bell was right alongside them. "Impressive motor," he said. "Perhaps you're cleverer than I've given you credit for."

"It's about time somebody realized that!" Cassandra cried.

"Gotcha!" From the rear of Bell's wagon, Comedy reached out and wrapped his meaty fingers over the side of the trash cart, extending himself like a clothesline between the two speeding vehicles.

"Nice idea," said the gangly Tragedy before placing one foot squarely on the small of his partner's back.

"That—*oof!*—was not the idea," Comedy grunted.

Tragedy jumped into the trash cart. "Looks like the hunter has become . . . still the hunter."

Emmett tried to back away from the henchman, kicking out at him, but Tragedy grabbed the boy by the feet. "Aha! Gotch-*YOWWW!* His shoe bit me!" Emmett clicked his toes up and down, repeatedly stabbing his attacker's palms with dozens of tiny pins.

While Tragedy rubbed his aching hands, Molly

clambered onto Comedy's back. "Aw, no," the minion groaned. "You ain't really gonna—*oof!*" Molly crossed the human bridge into Bell's wagon. Emmett followed ("Not again!"). As did her mother ("Enough already!").

"Fools!" Bell hollered at his minions. "Get back into the wagon!"

"Coming, boss!" Tragedy shouted.

"Please no more," Comedy groaned. But Tragedy was already straddling his partner's back. At that moment, however, the mop motor ground to a halt. The trash bin slowed, while Bell's wagon continued flying. Both henchmen flopped into the street.

"That," Cassandra said. "Was *eventually.*"

"Fools!" Bell screamed again.

"You're repeating yourself, Belly-Boy," Molly said. She, Bell, and Cassandra began fighting over the reins, but the horse took their tugging as a signal to turn, and the wagon veered directly toward the Brooklyn Bridge—and a thousand oblivious spectators staring at the fireworks show overhead.

"Move, move, move!" Emmett shouted.

As people shrieked and dove for cover, Molly noticed with horror that the bridge's main roadway was lined with loads of rapidly firing mortars and rockets. She yanked the reins to the right, and the wagon jolted onto the pedestrian walkway, which quickly proved too narrow. The wagon jammed itself tightly between the steel railings, and all four passengers tumbled onto the wood-plank deck as the spooked horse broke free and continued its mad dash to Brooklyn.

With no choice but to run farther onto the bridge, Cassandra and the children darted into a war zone. Molly could feel the shock waves in her chest as mortars boomed below, enshrouding her in wafting clouds of pastel smoke. Her rib cage rattled as rockets zoomed skyward and filled her nostrils with sulfur.

"I think there's a reason they cleared the walkway!" Emmett shouted as he ducked a wayward rocket.

They heard Bell grumbling in the fumes behind them, and then the shouting of police officers. "Stop! You can't be in there!" A group of cops rushed onto the bridge.

"Are they chasing us or Bell?" Emmett asked.

"I'm not sure it will matter, if Bell reaches us first," said Cassandra.

"Then let's make ourselves harder to catch." Molly hopped the railing onto one of the bridge's massive steel cables. Wide as a tree trunk, the cable arced all the way up to the peak of an enormous limestone tower. Imagining she was scaling the back of a mythical serpent, Molly moved cautiously, making hand- and footholds of the gray metal clamps that ringed the cable every yard or so, all while glowing cinders rained down upon her. Halfway along, Molly took the risk of looking down. Bell had abandoned the walkway as well, but he was out on the network of steel girders above the roadway, leaping from beam to beam with a dancer's grace.

"You all right, Emmett?" Molly called. "Got your climbing spikes out?"

"None of this is really happening," she heard the boy mutter. "I am not really clinging to a cable hundreds of feet above the East River. Not in real life. I would never do that in real life." A rocket whizzed by close enough to singe Molly's hair, and she speedily resumed her ascent. The higher they climbed, the stronger the wind grew, and the tighter they needed to hold on. Eventually Molly hauled herself onto the flat top of the stone tower and, after slapping out a small sleeve fire, helped the others up. She, Cassandra, and Emmett lay on their backs, catching their breaths, as enormous balls of red, white, and blue sparks blossomed overhead like electric dandelions.

"And I thought I was going to have to miss the fireworks!" Molly said, awestruck.

"Best seats in the city!" her mother yelled over the noise. "And we deserve it! Bell may not be happy with us, but we've foiled his plans! The robots are kaput and the city is safe!"

The blasts came rapidly now, the mushrooming sparks going higher and wider with each new boom. Balloons the size of hippopotami rose into the air around them, each carrying a basket from which rained fountains of gleaming sparks. And then, with one punctuating blast that seemed to shake the sky itself, the display was over.

"—eet again."

Molly, Cassandra, and Emmett bolted to their feet. Their masked enemy stood at the tower's edge.

"Sorry, did you say something?" Molly asked.

Bell huffed in frustration. "I said, 'So, we meet again.' I've said it three times! But you people are utterly oblivious! And now you've robbed the line of all its impact."

"How'd you get up here?" Molly asked.

"Ladder," he said, gesturing.

"Our way was more fun," Molly said. "Ladders? Pfft! Who hasn't climbed a ladder?"

"I've climbed hundreds," Cassandra said. Emmett tried to fake a laugh, but it came out more like sobbing.

"Silence!" the villain shouted with enough force that the Peppers actually fell quiet. "I bet you're all—" As the last spark faded, thunderous applause rose from below. Bell crossed his arms and waited for the noise to die down before continuing. "I bet you're all quite proud of yourselves. But if you think those automatons were the entirety of my plan, you are sorely mistaken."

Molly bit her lip.

"You know, when you first stumbled onto my plot, I was annoyed," Bell continued. "But after observing you for a time, my opinion of you evolved. What a motley and unexpected gaggle of antagonists! I began to think you three might pose a uniquely interesting challenge. What changed my mind, you ask?"

"No," said Molly. "Nobody asked that."

"I don't understand, Mr. Bell," Emmett said. There was so much pain in his voice. "Why are you doing this?"

"Oh, Emmett," Bell said in his softer, lilting voice. "You in particular deserve an answer to that question. And if you'd simply allowed me to capture you earlier, I would have happily given you a full explanation. Unfortunately, we are short on time now, so . . . you'll have to die unfulfilled."

Somewhere a beating drum was joined by French horns and trumpets. "Pomp and Circumstance." The second leg of the parade had begun its march from the Brooklyn side of the bridge. Bell reached into his coat and Cassandra pushed the children behind her. Molly gasped as something brushed across her back. One of the big balloons was floating by, its basket of sparklers burned out. She grabbed it and tapped Emmett on the shoulder. "Do you trust me?"

"I don't know," Emmett answered. She pushed him into the small basket and climbed in next to him.

"Mother, quick!" Molly yelled as the balloon immediately began to sink.

Bell withdrew a weapon that resembled a musket, but with a glowing orange coil where the barrel of the gun would be. Cassandra turned, but instead of joining the kids in the basket, she pushed the balloon away. "Three'll be too heavy," she said. "You two have fun!"

"Mother, no!" Molly shouted as she and Emmett began to drift out and downward.

"Mrs. Pepper, here!" With a grunt, Emmett reached out to another passing balloon and nudged it back toward the tower. But Bell was already aiming his strange weapon at Cassandra—no, past her, at the flapping American flag planted on the tower. The gun's orange coil glowed bright as the flagpole suddenly wrenched itself from its base and flew at Cassandra, knocking her off the tower's edge.

Molly felt her heart stop as her mother fell—and then start again at double speed as Cassandra caught herself on the basket of the other balloon.

"She's okay!" Emmett shouted. "She's okay!"

But Molly's relief turned to anger. "That was so . . . *stupid* of her! What was she thinking, pushing us away like that?"

"She was trying to save you," Emmett said. "It's what any good parent would've done."

"As if she could get by without me!" Molly snapped. She wasn't sure where this rage was coming from. "She needs me! She barely survives as it is!"

"Can we talk about this on the ground?" Emmett said, gripping the ropes tightly to keep himself in the cramped basket.

Below them, the band played the "1812 Overture," while above, Bell began to lower himself, spiderlike, on a long cord that extended from his belt. Halfway down, he pointed his bizarre, glowing weapon at a nearby steel beam. Two bolts ripped loose and zipped through the air like bullets. Molly and Emmett ducked.

"They missed," Emmett said shakily.

Then came the hissing sound.

"Or maybe not."

Their balloon had been punctured and they were descending fast. Very fast. Straight toward the parade.

Assassins!

MOLLY SPILLED FROM the basket, bowling over several important-looking men who hit the ground yelping, their neckties and mustaches in equal disarray. Some band members continued to play, while others stopped and screamed. Still more marched in circles, tooting out random notes as if the surprise had broken something in their brains. Police officers shouted. Bystanders shrieked. It was pandemonium. Molly couldn't find Emmett and had no idea whether her mother was down there with them or floating over Long Island by now. She stayed down and tried to crawl away, as people tripped over one another.

"Emmett?" someone said.

Molly stood to look and was knocked off-balance by a fleeing flautist. Stumbling deeper into the chaos, she crashed into a broad, fuzzy chest. A bear? No, a fur coat. She reached up to grab whatever handholds she could find.

"My word!" coughed a deep voice.

Molly gazed up at the horrified face of President Chester A. Arthur. She was clutching each of the man's ample sideburns.

"Assassin!" someone yelled. "Protect the president!" From all sides, men began fighting to reach their commander in chief.

"No," said Molly, releasing her whiskery handfuls. "I—"

Strong hands gripped her by the waist. She reacted quickly, spinning around and tripping the person who'd grabbed her—only to realize too late that it was her mother. Cassandra slammed the president to the ground, plopped on top of him, and was promptly tackled by three federal agents.

"Mother," Molly gasped. But before she could intervene, Emmett tugged the bottom of her dress.

"Down here." He was crouched between the voluminous skirts of two ladies fanning themselves melodramatically.

"But—"

Emmett tugged harder and began crawling away. Reluctantly, she crouched and followed him. While everyone's attention was on the president, they slipped under the railing and dropped down to a thin ledge along

146

the outside of the bridge. Balancing on tiptoe hundreds of feet above the fast-flowing river, Molly and Emmett peered through the guardrail and saw Cassandra, surrounded by police officers, her hands bound behind her back.

"I'm going to get Bell for this," Molly growled.

"It isn't Bell," Emmett said.

"What?"

"It wasn't Mr. Bell in the mask," Emmett explained. "I bumped into Bell. Up there, in the parade. He saw me too—called me by name."

It wasn't possible, thought Molly. Emmett still simply couldn't accept that his mentor was capable of the things they'd seen that night.

"Look, there he is now. Talking to Governor Cleveland." Emmett pointed to a tall, bearded man running his fingers through his thick, wavy hair as he surveyed the chaos around him. His was the same face Molly had drawn an eye patch over in that newspaper photo. It was definitely Alexander Graham Bell.

"He . . . he must've pulled off his mask to blend in," she said, refusing to believe that she could have been so wrong.

"And changed his clothes? Molly, it's *not* Bell." Emmett pointed up to the grid of girders overhead. Still lowering himself on a wire was the man in the crooked mask.

Accusations!

CASSANDRA PEPPER WAS being arrested.

Throughout the years, Molly had prepared herself for such an event, expected it even. But in the hundreds of times she'd played out the scenario in her mind, she never imagined she'd be watching it from afar. She always pictured herself in matching handcuffs, fighting by her mother's side. She also never dreamed the charges would rise to the level of high treason.

"Madam, you are under arrest for the attempted assassination of the president of the United States," said a federal officer in a long black coat.

"Assassination?" Cassandra scoffed as several aides brushed smooth the president's fur coat. "Poppycock! All I did was take a little tumble onto the man. How fragile do they think you are, Mr. President? Pleasure to meet you, by the way. I can't say I voted for you. But then again, I can't vote for anybody."

Around them, newspaper reporters jotted down notes.

"Even if our politics don't always align, Mr. President, I must add that my daughter and I are big fans of your sideburns," Cassandra continued. "They're like baby wolves suckling at your earlobes."

"Can somebody please tell me who this person is?" The president's eye began twitching.

"Cassandra Pepper," she proudly replied. "Inventor, pickle heiress, and lifesaving heroine."

"Um, Agent Clark?" the president nudged.

"Yes, Mr. President!" The officer shoved Cassandra into the hands of two local policemen. "Take her away!"

"But—" Cassandra was swallowed by the crowd.

Molly began to pull herself back up over the railing, but Emmett stopped her.

"Have you apprehended the rest of her gang?" Agent Clark asked of the remaining police. Any other day, Molly would have been flattered to have someone think she was part of a gang.

"We lost track of the girl and the Chinese one," an officer replied. "But a few of the guys think they saw one of those masked fellas down toward the Brooklyn end. They're after him now."

People gasped as Cassandra suddenly reappeared on the scene. "Those masked men are not part of my gang,"

Cassandra said. "*They* are the real criminals. We are trying to *stop* them."

"She's back," said President Arthur. "Cleveland, why is she back?"

Governor Grover Cleveland, nervously tugging at his push-broom mustache, simply shrugged.

"Are there two of her?" President Arthur asked.

Grover Cleveland shrugged.

"You mean to say that in running through barricades, climbing into restricted areas, and leaping on the president, you were trying to save his life?" asked Agent Clark.

Cassandra nodded. "Yes, but not today. We were trying to save his life next Friday."

The president rubbed his eyes. "Am I imagining this, Cleveland?" he said. "I knew I shouldn't have eaten so many of those fried dough puffs during the fireworks."

"Next Friday is the opening of the World's Fair," Cassandra continued. "And that masked man had a diabolical plot to unleash an army of killer robots there."

"Robots?" said Agent Clark.

"What in heaven's name is a robot?" asked the president.

Grover Cleveland shrugged.

"But the president and the World's Fair are safe once more, because *we* have destroyed the robots," Cassandra said with a curtsy. "You are all quite welcome."

"*What* is a robot?" the president asked again, his face reddening.

"And here is the *really* interesting part," Cassandra said. "The villain is someone you all know and respect! Someone no man in his right mind would suspect!"

Molly and Emmett cringed, knowing what was coming.

"You won't believe me when you hear it," Cassandra went on. "But I have proof! Go to the ruins of his secret lab! There you'll find the remnants of his robot death machines. And then you will know that the most vile villain in New York is none other than . . . *Alexander Graham Bell!*"

"Me?" A bearded man in a tweed suit and bow tie nudged his way to the front of the crowd. The look on Bell's face was one of both confusion and pity. "I'm sorry, madam, but I've been marching with my fellow inventors all night. And so . . . Wait, what was that about my lab?"

Cassandra's face went ashen; her lip trembled. It reminded Molly painfully of the way her mother looked when she first learned of her father's diagnosis.

"You can't be Bell," Cassandra said defiantly.

"But I am," said Bell. Hearing him speak, Molly had to admit that the masked villain, whoever he was, did a remarkable impression of the real inventor. "And, sorry, what was that about my lab again?" Bell continued.

"Don't listen to him!" Cassandra warned. "He must have taken off his mask to hide among the crowd!"

Molly shook her head silently. Cassandra was too flustered and disoriented; she wasn't paying attention to the details. The Bell before her wore a brown suit, not black like the masked man.

"Well, I can vouch for Alec." Thomas Edison sidled his way through the bystanders. "I mean, I can certainly understand how the old boy could get himself accused of sinister skulduggery—who *hasn't* caught Bell sneaking a looky-loo at their secret projects? Am I right? Kidding, Alec! Kidding! No need to be Mr. Scowly-Face. Wow, you should invent yourself a sense of humor. But anyway, yes, Bell's been marching with us the whole time."

"As if anyone would suspect otherwise," President Arthur said, patting Bell on the back. "Mr. Bell is our national treasure!"

"Well, *a* national treasure, perhaps," Edison said, stepping in front of Bell. "Certainly not *the* national treasure. I mean . . . I'm Thomas Edison."

Bell pushed past Edison and approached Cassandra. "Madam, please, my lab? What did you mean by the *ruins* of my lab?"

"The, uh . . . lab on Pike Street," she replied. "Squarish building, dull paint job? You really should take some decorating pointers from your fellow Guildsmen. Anyway, it . . . sort of blew up."

Bell looked stricken. "My automatons!"

"Aha! So you admit it!" Cassandra's eyes reignited. "You *did* build an army of killer robots to unleash upon the Fair!"

"That warehouse was filled with automatons!" Bell cried. "Clockwork figures! They were to be a surprise for the World's Fair! They were performing automatons!"

"Wait. What?"

"Those metal men! They're programmed to march and sing in unison. They were to sing 'Polly Wolly Doodle'!"

"Oh," Cassandra said sadly. "I would've enjoyed that. I love that song."

"They're . . . destroyed, you say? All of them?" Bell staggered. "They were to be the next great step in personal entertainment. More spectacular than a player piano. Miles above Edison's silly phonograph. At parties and celebrations, everybody was going to have their own clockwork quartet singing in perfect four-part harmony. But now . . ." The crowd parted respectfully as Bell shuffled off. He walked to the railing, dangerously near to Molly and Emmett, and gripped it as if the bridge were a great ship being tossed by violent waves.

"I think we've heard enough from this loony bird," Agent Clark said as the reporters scribbled frantically on their pads. "Mrs. Pepper, you have admitted to arson and destruction of property; you've cast baseless aspersions against the character of Alexander Graham Bell;

and you physically assaulted the president of the United States in full view of a hundred witnesses. You've given us ample reason to suspect you are criminally insane. You will be taken to the lunatic asylum on Blackwell's Island to await testing and trial."

"No, you can't! My daughter—" But Cassandra was already being jerked away. She cried out with rage, but her voice got smaller and smaller as she vanished from sight. "Don't trust him! He's lying! There's a lot you don't know about your national treasure! He sent a ship full of men to their deaths at the South Pole! Does he talk about that little incident? Does he?"

At the rail, Bell looked westward, watching the plume of thick smoke from his lab rising like a snake charmer's cobra. "Oh, Emmett," he muttered softly to himself, but loudly enough for Molly and Emmett to hear. "What have you gotten yourself into?"

Molly peered up toward the girders. The masked man was gone. She had no idea how long ago he'd slipped away. As the crowd dispersed, Agent Clark approached Bell. Molly and Emmett froze like gargoyles on the ledge.

"Mr. Bell," they heard the federal agent say. "I'm truly sorry you got caught up in this. Fire brigade is on its way to your lab now. Top priority, though, is locating the woman's accomplices. Including that Chinese boy. Now, I've just gotten word that you have a lab assistant at the Guild—"

"No," Bell said sharply. "I got a good look at the young man in question. It was not my assistant."

"Are you positive?" Clark did not sound convinced. "Maybe in the dark, you didn't—"

"It was not him," Bell repeated. "If you'll excuse me." He marched off.

After what felt like an eternity of inching slowly along the ledge, Molly finally dropped back onto solid Manhattan ground. There were still lots of people milling about, but it was unlikely anyone would recognize them in the chaos. She helped Emmett down, but he pulled away from her as soon as he was safe. "We ruined Mr. Bell's life," he said sourly. "I *knew* he was a good man. I should never have let you talk me into thinking otherwise."

"Hey!" Molly shoved him. "My *mother* is gone! Arrested! On her way to a lunatic asylum!" Her voice dropped. "I've never done anything without my mother." She started crying. It was the last thing she wanted to do. Especially in front of Emmett.

"Molly," he said softly. "Hey, Molly, I : . ." He reached for her, but now it was her turn to pull away.

"Stop." She didn't really know this boy, this stranger. They'd only just met. He obviously didn't really know her. Not if he thought she'd care a whit about some man she'd never met when her mother had just been taken from her. Her *mother*. Her friend. The person she laughed with and had adventures with and shared deep talks with . . .

She glanced at Emmett through teary eyes. In the forty-eight hours she'd known him, she'd done all those things with him already. She sniffled and, sort of, almost, smiled. The situation she was in terrified her. But she wasn't in it alone.

"Let's just go," she said. "Before someone sees us."

The children hurried off the street and slipped into a back alley, where, stretched on clotheslines above them, sheets flapped in the wind like the sails of the fantastic pirate ship Molly wished could carry her away.

PART II

22

Nowhere to Turn

"I KNOW WE'RE trying to stay out of sight," Emmett said after an hour of creeping through unlit alleys and forgotten side streets, "but this seems like a really long route to your shop."

"We can't go back there," Molly replied, climbing over a discarded sofa and startling a stray cat. "The police have my mother, so I assume they're looking for me and that's the first place they'll check. Besides, the Jägers have probably changed the locks on us by now anyway."

"So, where *are* we going?"

Molly stopped. "I don't know," she admitted. "I'm just trying to put distance between us and anyone who might be after us."

"That's a lot of people right now," Emmett said. His stomach growled audibly.

Molly sighed. Her mother would know where to go. "Don't you have some . . . you know, some Chinese people we could stay with?"

Emmett looked at her askance. "No, Molly, I do not *have* any *Chinese people*," he said. "I haven't even had a home for . . . Wait. I know where we can go. Follow me."

Hours later, they stepped over the fallen gate of a garbage dump. Mounds of soot and ash rose high against the night sky like netherworld versions of Saharan sand dunes. Here and there, men in rags gathered around small fires, drinking from old biscuit tins and roasting skewered who-knows-what. Emmett led Molly deep among the shadowy hills, behind the tallest ash pile of all, in the loneliest, most remote corner of the dump.

"Where are we?" she asked.

"Only place I could think of where no one will find us," Emmett replied. In the faint moonlight, Molly could see the silhouette of a small but fully enclosed wagon. It was not much bigger than the chicken cart they'd stowed away on the day before. She squinted to make out the words painted across the side:

MISS ADDIE'S BOOKMOBILE

"My home," said Emmett. "Until three months ago, anyway." He fished through his pockets and pulled out a small key. "Whew," he said. "So glad I didn't lose this. Without the key, this place is basically impenetrable."

"Tougher than the Bastille, I'm sure," Molly joked.

Emmett grinned slyly as he unlocked the cart's tiny door. "Duck," he warned. He crouched as he opened the door and Molly followed suit, narrowly avoiding a flour sack that whipped out of the doorway on a spring-loaded broomstick. That sack would have felt like a right hook from a boxer if it had hit. "The Bastille doesn't have one of those," Emmett said.

Molly followed him inside, feeling her way into the blackness. "So you haven't been here in months, right?" she said. "What are the chances this place isn't teeming with rats by now?"

"One hundred percent," Emmett replied. "I rigged tiny broomstick traps over all the mouseholes."

Molly laughed, even though she wasn't sure he was joking. Seeing this place reminded her that her friend was far more than just an inventor's assistant.

Emmett lit a candle on the wall and began turning a crank. The lighted taper began sliding along a wire, igniting the wicks of several other candles as it moved and glass covers—jam jars in a previous life—descended over the lit candles. Now Molly could see the books. There must have been fifty crammed onto those tightly packed shelves. Seventy, maybe! If she had to live alone in a garbage dump, she couldn't think of a nicer place to do it.

"And no, I haven't read them all yet," Emmett said, anticipating Molly's question. "A lot of them, though.

There wasn't much else to do in here." He sat on the edge of a homemade bed—the only furniture—and pulled a cord that sent a metal claw (crafted from forks and door hinges) along a second network of wires to pluck up a book and deliver it back to him. *The Tales of Edgar Allan Poe* dropped into his lap.

Molly grinned giddily. "You could read every single one of these books without lifting your head off the pillow! I'd call it lazy if I didn't know how much work it must have taken to make it."

"I mostly built it because I'm indecisive," Emmett said. "I could never choose a book, so I'd just close my eyes and let the claw pick for me."

"Emmett, you have *got* to be an inventor when you're older," Molly said, gaping at the complicated machinery around the room.

"I don't know." He shrugged again and it triggered a burst of frustration in Molly.

"Why do you say 'I don't know' whenever someone mentions you becoming an inventor?" she asked sternly.

"I don't know," Emmett replied. "Sorry. I mean . . . It's just . . . Could I?"

"The mechanical hand you built just grabbed a book for me!"

"So, you think . . . yes?"

"Aargh!" Molly cried. She threw open the Poe book, pursed her lips, and began reading.

"Sorry, I guess I've just always assumed I'd end up a sailor like my father. That's what he'd always wanted."

"Do you like boats?"

"No, I hate them. I get seasick. That's why my dad always left me reading on the docks while he worked."

"Then be what you wanna be!" Molly said. "Stop being so goosey about everything in your life! It's not like your father's here to stop you!" She looked back to her book, immediately regretting her choice of words. "Sorry," she muttered. "I didn't mean . . ."

"It's fine," Emmett said in a tone that told Molly it wasn't fine. "Maybe we should just stop talking for a bit. You'll probably like that book, by the way. Lots of dark, creepy stuff."

"Thanks, that's exactly what I need tonight." And yet, she was so overcome by exhaustion that, even as she flipped through the illustrations of devils and spirits, she drifted into a deep, peaceful slumber that lasted until morning—when she was jolted awake by a banging at the door.

23

An Unexpected Guest

"I THOUGHT YOU said no one would find us here!" Molly raised the Edgar Allan Poe book into bash-ready position.

On the floor, Emmett sat up groggily and put his eye to a peephole.

"It's Jasper," he said, sounding relieved. But Molly kept Poe ready to strike. She squinted as sunlight flooded through the open door.

"Emmett Lee! Where have you been? I thought you were never comin' back," said the stocky man in sooty gray coveralls who stood outside. "You know how long you been gone? Three and a half months! That's a *quarter* of the *year* that I been waiting to find out how Phileas Fogg and Passepartout are gonna get outta Hong Kong. You can't leave a man waiting *three and a half months* on somethin' like that! You know what that is? Cruel and unusual. That is cruel and unusual treatment, my friend. Forbidden by the Constitution. I half thought to bust my way in here and grab the rest of that book myself. You know what stopped me, Emmett? These eyes. I know you got the place all booby-trapped and I don't wanna lose one of these eyes. I got beautiful eyes, Emmett Lee. Or so I been told. I ain't so vain as to think of them that way myself. Still, I gotta take care of these beautiful eyes. And you know what these eyes are missing, Emmett? Chapter twenty-two of *Around the World in—*" A glimpse of Molly finally caused him to pause. "Excuse me, miss. I did not realize Emmett had company." He tipped his frayed cap and hustled away.

"Jasper, come back," Emmett called. "It's fine."

Jasper slowly made his way back to the cart and peered inside, cautiously, as if there might have been a tiger ready to swipe at him. He was probably in his early twenties, tall and thickly built. Molly lowered her book, but Jasper continued to eye her suspiciously.

"Jasper Bloom, this is Molly Pepper," Emmett said. "We're in some trouble. And we could use your help. You know I wouldn't joke about something like this."

"You don't joke about hardly anything, Emmett Lee," Jasper said, crouching to step inside. "A sense of humor is what you need. Keeps me alive, my sense of humor does. Remember what Miss Addie used to say about

165

jokes? Nothing. 'Cause she didn't make any. And where is she now? Dead. God rest her soul. Not me, though. I'm still walkin' this earth 'cause I can see the humor in anything. Except Balthazar Birdhouse. Nothing funny about that man."

"Who?" Molly asked, desperately trying to follow Jasper's rapid patter.

"It's not important," Emmett replied.

"You only say that 'cause you never met Balthazar Birdhouse." Jasper crossed his arms.

"Jasper works sanitation for a factory nearby. He hauls ash down here a few times a week," Emmett explained. "He was also an old customer of Miss Addie, so I made a deal with him. He helps me keep the bookmobile hidden by adding his ash to the piles around it, and in return, I give him books."

"*Parts* of books, you mean," Jasper said. "Which is why I'm still hangin' on a what's-gonna-happen-next from *three and a half months ago*. The boy only gives me portions of the books at a time 'cause he's afraid I won't come back. Ha. Who's the one of us who *shoulda* been harboring that particular concern? I'll give you a hint . . . it's me."

"I am sorry about that, Jasper," Emmett said.

"You should be," Jasper said. "It was supposed to be *Around the World in Eighty Days*, not *Halfway Around the World in Forty-Two Days*. Oh, and don't bother telling me

I can read the rest now, 'cause it's too late. I can't go back after three and a half months. That story is *over* for me. And because of you it had an unhappy ending. You may have ruined my love of literature forever, Emmett Lee."

"So you *don't* want the rest?" Emmett asked, reaching under the bed and pulling out a sheaf of loose pages held together by a clothespin.

"No, I'll take 'em!" Jasper grabbed the pages. "But only because it would be unfair to Jules Verne if I didn't see his artistic vision through to the end."

Molly let out an embarrassingly loud snort of laughter.

"This young lady understands the benefit of a good laugh," Jasper said.

Molly stood up and offered her hand. "Mr. Bloom," she said, "it is a pleasure to make your acquaintance."

"I can't argue with that," Jasper replied. "Now, Emmett, I believe there was a plea for help. . . ."

"Yeah, um, it's not good for Molly and me to be seen in public right now," Emmett said. "So can you possibly scrounge up some breakfast for us? And a newspaper?"

Jasper raised an eyebrow. "What in the name of Washington's wooden teeth have you gotten yourself into, Emmett Lee?"

Emmett pressed his lips together, obviously afraid to share too much.

"If you do these things for us, Mr. Bloom," she said, "we'll tell you everything."

He narrowed his eyes.

"And we'll give you a second book," Molly added. "A *whole* book."

"Which paper do you prefer?" Jasper asked. "The *Sun* or the *Herald*?"

Bad News

**PRESIDENT SAFE AFTER FAILED
ASSASSINATION ATTEMPT**

**BELL'S LABS ALSO TARGETED
—INVESTIGATION UNDER WAY**

MOLLY AND EMMETT bumped heads reading through the article together. Beyond a recap of the previous night's events, there was little new information, but it confirmed two points: one, police were indeed on the lookout for "a large-eared girl and dark-haired boy of Asian origin," and two, "deranged assassin Mrs. Nathaniel Pepper" had definitely been sent to Blackwell's Asylum.

Sitting in the East River halfway between Manhattan and Brooklyn, Blackwell's Island was New York's most notorious spot for punishment and incarceration. Molly slumped. There was now a mile of fast-moving water, hordes of guards, and who-knew-how-many walls and gates between her and her mother. Reuniting felt impossible. Not to mention figuring out who the masked man really was and why he was framing Mr. Bell.

"All done?" Jasper asked. He sat cross-legged on the floor, shelling nuts from a bag on his lap. "'Cause I think we can all agree I been very patient over here. Sit yourselves down and tell me everything while we share these peanuts. I traded Balthazar Birdhouse my bad hat for 'em. I didn't trade my good hat, mind you— no story's worth that. You'd understand if you saw my good hat. But that's neither here nor there—make with the tale-tellin'. I particularly can't wait to hear the part about how you two are *not* the fugitive children in that article. 'Cause if you was, I would seriously question the wisdom of me bein' here right now." He popped a peanut into his mouth.

Emmett looked to Molly, who responded with a shrug. They needed an ally. Jasper could have already turned them in if he wanted to.

"It started when that no-good Inventors' Guild stole my mother's spot at the World's Fair," she began.

Forty minutes later, Emmett finished with, "And that's when we came here."

Jasper stared at them with eyes that seemed to barely

fit in his head, until he finally broke his uncharacteristic silence with applause. "Wow. Just . . . wow. I take it back—that woulda been worth my good hat," he said. "Jules Verne got nothin' on you."

"Except our story is true," Emmett said.

"Who says Verne's stories ain't?" Jasper replied.

"I'm pretty sure Verne does," Emmett said. "He writes fiction."

Jasper scoffed. "*Pfft!* You really think that if the man had underwater ships and slingshots to the moon and such, he wouldn't pretend it was all fake? Course he'd *say* it was fiction! If the public truly believed there was giant, man-eating dinosaurs in caves below our feet, you know what we'd have? Chaos. Complete and total chaos." He popped the last peanut into his mouth. "Now tell me again about these man-eating robot thingies."

"Well, it turned out they were just singing robot thingies," Molly said with a twinge of guilt.

"*If* Bell's tellin' the truth," Jasper said.

"He is," Molly said. "Not even Sergio Vittorini could've faked that kind of confused reaction."

"Ooh, Sergio Vittorini," Jasper said. "Man of a Thousand and Twelve Faces. I can only make seventy-six faces, myself. And two-thirds of those ain't useful in the slightest. The other twenty-five, though—"

"Jasper, aren't you technically at work right now?" Molly asked.

The ashman jumped to his feet. "That reminds me, I'm technically at work right now." He brushed bits of shell from his coveralls. "I gotta get back before Baltha-zar Birdhouse starts slandering my good name with the foreman. Can't trust that Balthazar Birdhouse. He'd stab you in the back while looking you in the eye. Don't worry, though—he don't know about you two. When I traded him my bad hat, I told him I needed the peanuts to feed some baby ducklings." He grabbed the remaining pages of *Around the World in Eighty Days*, plus a copy of *Oliver Twist*, before opening the door and peeking around for possible spies. "You stay put," he added in a serious tone. "Everybody and his uncle's gonna be huntin' for you— the police, the Jägermen, the masked villains, maybe even Balthazar Birdhouse. . . . Safest place for you is right here. I'll be back when I can."

"Jasper, wait!" Emmett said. He grabbed a pencil, ripped a blank page from a book, and jotted a quick note.

"What are you doing?" Molly asked.

"We need to get a message to the one person who might be able to help us," Emmett said. "The one person who *knows* we're innocent."

"My mother?" Molly tried.

Emmett shook his head. "Mr. Bell."

"Do you see a wizard cap on my head?" Jasper asked. "How is it you imagine me getting a secret message to Alexander Graham Bell?"

"There's a service entrance in the alley between the Guild Hall and Madison Square Theatre," Emmett said. "In your ashman's uniform, no one will question you going in that way. Then just slip the note under Bell's door or something."

He handed the note to Jasper, who held it as if it were a bomb with a lit fuse. "Have I somehow given you the impression I enjoy danger?" the ashman said.

"Five books," Molly said.

"Whoa, hold on," said Emmett. "These are *my* books."

"Seven and you've got yourselves a delivery spy," said Jasper.

"Seven whole books," Molly agreed, and sealed the deal with a handshake.

The Letter

"WHY DON'T YOU speak Chinese?" For the past several hours, Molly had been slowly working through a cinder-block-sized copy of *The Count of Monte Cristo*, but she found it difficult to concentrate in the small, stuffy wagon. Plus, the protagonist's long, miserable imprisonment was filling her head with unwanted images. She shut the book.

Emmett looked up from the pages of *Black Beauty* and sighed. "I wish I did," he said. "But my father only spoke English to me."

"What about anybody else? You're not the only Chinese person in New York."

Emmett leaned back against a shelf. "I think I told you my mother died in childbirth back in Qingdao, so my father was alone with me," he said. "There'd been a lot of talk at the time about work opportunities in America, so he packed me up and took a steamer to California. But it takes a while for news to cross an ocean. We showed up just as American workers started to get really resentful of the Chinese immigrants in San Francisco. There were riots. It wasn't safe. My father felt like he'd brought his baby son into a nightmare.

"We left the West Coast to see if New York was any better. There were no riots here, at least, but it still wasn't exactly a welcoming environment. So my father gave me an American name, spoke English to me, fed me American food, sang American songs. He wanted me to fit in. But I still couldn't get into American schools. I still couldn't make American friends."

"Until now," Molly said.

One corner of Emmett's mouth crooked up like he was trying to hide a smile. "I just . . . I don't know who I'm supposed to be. The culture I was born into is a mystery to me, and the only country I've ever known doesn't want me. I mean, I've always been curious about my heritage. I used to ask my father about it all the time. But eventually I stopped because he was just so . . . It was the one thing he was strict about. I didn't like there being any problems between us, so I stopped asking."

"What about since he died? Have you tried to connect with other immigrants? Ones who came here before the Exclusion Act?"

"I've been too busy finding food and shelter and stuff. And anyway, I am the way I am because my father turned his back on his heritage. Other Chinese people might not take kindly to that." He paused and thought for a moment. "There was only one time I ever realized how proud my father was to be Chinese. . . ." From a drawer under the bed, he retrieved a yellowing sheet of paper. "Unfortunately, they were the last words he ever said to me."

Molly took the letter gently in her hands and read.

Emmett,

I will miss you terribly these next nine months, but I have taken with me a picture you drew when you were six, the one of you and me, very big, standing on a tiny ship that is barely bigger than our feet. Do you remember it? I know you are a more skilled artist now, but there is something about this drawing I have always loved. Perhaps I like thinking of us as giants.

I know you did not want me to go, but I also know you understand why I could not pass up this opportunity. I have never seen a vessel like the Frost Cleaver. *I truly believe this ship will get us through the Antarctic ice. The first ship to reach the South Pole is going to be captained by a Chinese man, a Lee, your father! And when a Chinese man becomes an American hero, that will change everything for us! So I hope that when I return, you will be less angry about me leaving and* more proud about what we have accomplished.

My only regret is that you will not be by my side when we set foot on that new continent. I would have brought you if Mr. Bell had let me, but he is right that you are too young. Even so, I am certain you would have made a better cabin boy than Silas Cotton, a sour-faced young man who does not seem pleased about taking orders from a "foreigner." None of the crewmen do, frankly. It is going to be a long enough voyage without needing to deal with a navigator like Ezra Hopper, who will only speak to our first mate, whether I am present or not. ~~I pray it doesn't come to this, but if Hopper~~

Pay no mind to that. We've not even left the dock yet. I will earn this crew's respect by the time we reach the Caribbean. And I'm not completely without friends here. Ambrose Rector seems an amiable fellow. Hard to believe someone so young designed this wondrous ship. We are on a perilous journey, but I feel completely safe in his hands.

Behave yourself for Miss Adelaide. And pace yourself on those books of hers. Something tells me you'll have read every page in that wagon by the time I get back. I look forward to hearing about all the adventures you are sure to have while I am away.

With love, respect, and pride,
Your father

Molly had been so focused on her separation from her mother that she'd never stopped to consider how much Emmett had already lost. She vowed at that moment that she would see Emmett through this. It was what her mother would do. She wiped a tear from her cheek and launched into the long story of the Pepper family and her own father's passing. They talked well into the night, occasionally wondering aloud why Jasper hadn't returned yet.

They continued to talk the next day, although their concerns about Jasper now made up a much larger portion of the conversation—especially after they finished off the last of the apples Jasper had smuggled to them the day before. Emmett peered through his peephole as the sun set on the dump for the second time since Jasper's departure. Between an empty stomach and a fretting mind, sleep was impossible. And then, sometime after ten p.m. on the second night, a knock finally sounded at the door.

"Which do you want first, the good news or the bad news?" Jasper asked as he ducked his head and stepped inside. "The good news is that I won the recipe contest at work. So much for Balthazar Birdhouse's famous pound cake!"

"What's the bad news, Jasper?" Emmett said, unamused.

Jasper handed him a note.

"This is *my* note!" Emmett cried.

"Now, listen here, Emmett Lee," Jasper said. "Do you know how many times in the last two days I tried to sneak in through that alley door of yours? No, you don't. And I'm not gonna tell you because . . . you might think it was not enough times. But suffice it to say that approximately two hours ago I finally finagled my way up to that fancy-fancy second floor of the Guild Hall only to learn that I had just missed Mr. Bell."

"He went home for the day," Molly said. "It's late."

"Not so, Molly Pepper," said Jasper. "Because a colleague of Bell's told me where he'd gone. He went lookin' for one Emmett Lee."

Emmett cringed. "He's out searching the city for me? As if I didn't feel guilty enough already . . ."

"Oh, he's not walkin' the streets, callin' out your name," Jasper said. "He thinks he knows exactly where to find you. And therein lies the dilemma."

"What are you talking about, Jasper?" Emmett asked, frustrated.

"They said Bell was heading to your home."

"Home? What home?"

"The address you gave him three months ago," Jasper said. "The place you *told him* you lived."

Emmett jumped up, tangling his head in the mesh of cords above. "Mr. Bell is going to Bandit's Roost?"

"The hangout of Oogie MacDougal and the Green Onion Boys?" Molly cried.

Emmett nodded. "If Alexander Graham Bell shows up there alone . . . at night . . . and starts throwing *my name* around . . . ?"

"He's not gonna make it out alive." Jasper nodded. "Shame too. His telephone thingie seems pretty great."

"Jasper, did you tell the police?" Molly asked urgently.

"The police and I are not on the best of terms," Jasper said. "You can thank a certain Balthazar Birdhouse for that. It would be a pointless errand anyhow. By the time I got to the police station and convinced them to believe me, Graham Bell would be kissin' the inside of a casket lid."

"You should have gone to the police first!" Emmett yelled, his face flushed. "We're kids, Jasper! What are we supposed to do?"

"We find Bell ourselves," Molly said, her voice cutting through Emmett's loud, anxious breaths. "We go to Bandit's Roost and stop Bell before he does anything he regrets. We're the only ones who know the danger he's in—we're the only ones who can act in time to do anything about it."

Jasper narrowed his eyes at her. "You do realize they call it Bandit's Roost because there's bandits there, right? And possibly a rooster?"

"You can't be serious, Molly," Emmett said. "The Green Onions probably have orders to murder me on sight. Haven't we put ourselves in enough danger already? The whole reason we wanted to contact Mr. Bell was because we need an adult to help us."

"A-*hem!*" Jasper raised an eyebrow.

"We're not just kids, Emmett," Molly said. "I've been running a business. You survived for years on your own—in a home *you* built, for crying out loud! We can do this."

"That's right, Emmett Lee," Jasper said. "You can do it."

"We all can," said Molly.

"*We* meaning *me*?" The ashman gulped. "I'm not sure how I feel about that part."

"Come on, guys!" Molly cried. "I know you're not Peppers, but I am. And Peppers don't quit." Molly's eyes scanned the bookshelves. "Did . . . Did Robin Hood call it quits when the Sheriff of Nottingham captured his friends?"

"No," Jasper said with enthusiasm. "He did not!"

"Did Tom Sawyer give up on Becky when she was stolen away to that cave?" Molly asked.

"Absolutely not!" cried Jasper.

"Did Jim Hawkins abandon his stranded crewmates on Treasure Island?"

"I have not read that yet!" Jasper shouted.

"This isn't a storybook, Molly!" Emmett yelled. "This is real life."

"All the more reason for us to act fast," Molly said.

"You feel bad about what we did to Bell? You wanna make up for it? Then let's go. Now."

Emmett nodded quietly. Molly knew he was scared. She couldn't blame him; she was too. She put her finger under his chin and raised his head so she could look into his eyes. "You're not alone," she said.

"That's right," Jasper said brightly. "You got Jasper Bloom with you. And if there's one thing I'm good at, it's saving famous people. I assume. I have yet to do such a thing. Unless you count the time I—"

"Jasper," Molly interrupted. "Take us to your ashcart."

Den of Thieves

"*OOF!* WATCH THE bumps!" Emmett whispered from beneath the tarp in the back of Jasper's ashcart.

"These eyes of mine might be beauteous pools of autumn twilight, Emmett Lee, but they cannot see in the dark," Jasper replied. "Speaking of which, we have arrived. Whoa, Prancey-Pie!"

The clip-clopping of pony hooves stopped and all was quiet. Molly squinted as Jasper whipped the tarp off, expecting a surge of light, but none came. She and Emmett climbed out, stretching their stiff limbs and brushing the ash from their clothes. There was one dim gas lamp on the corner where they stood, but across the intersection, the street appeared to vanish into nothingness, a black hole between two decaying buildings with boarded-up windows and doors riddled with bullet holes.

"It's over there?" Molly asked.

"That's right, Molly Pepper," Jasper replied. "Just across the street in that terrifying void of shadow and nightmare."

"Wishing your mother was here?" Emmett asked.

"Yes," said Jasper.

Molly was wishing it too, but rather than admit that—to herself or anyone else—she thrust her shoulders back and marched across the street. Emmett and Jasper hurried to follow. Some of the empty tenements they passed looked rickety enough to be brought down by the vibrations of a stray cough, but a light shone from within one.

"Well, looks like you found it," Jasper said. "So, I'll be back at the—" He turned to point back at his cart and saw a small man—maybe even a boy—untying his pony.

"Prancey-Pie!" Jasper yelped. "Hey! Stop!" He took off.

"Jasper, no!"

"Don't worry, Miss Molly, he's just a little one. I'll scare him off," the ashman said as he ran. "I swear, if Balthazar Birdhouse has anything to do with this . . ."

Molly and Emmett looked to each other, both unsure of whether to follow. But soon a second figure stepped into the lamplight and clubbed Jasper over the head with an unseen object. Their friend slumped over the side of his cart. Before the children could even react, the thieves were gone—along with Jasper, Prancey-Pie, and their ride back to the bookmobile.

"Oh, no," Emmett breathed.

"We can't chase those guys down on foot," Molly said, trying to think clearly through the sudden fog of panic.

"But Jasper—"

"We need Bell's help more than ever now," Molly said, motioning toward the one lit building. "Let's just find him and get out of here."

She hopped a fence and peeked inside a smudged window. Behind a bottle-lined bar and handful of stained tables, she saw walls adorned with dartboards, portraits of dancing girls, and a smattering of wanted posters, the faces on which most likely belonged to the very people in that room—a rowdy band of hooligans in ragged coats and patched bowler hats.

Molly checked around the corner. A rope ladder dangled from a second-floor window.

"It's probably for making sneaky exits during police raids," Molly whispered. "It'll work just as well for sneaky entrances."

She climbed up with Emmett close behind. "It's amazing," Emmett whispered, "what climbing the Brooklyn Bridge will do for a fear of heights."

Inside, they found themselves on a balcony, overlooking the barroom. They peered over the railing.

"That's not good," Emmett muttered.

The riled-up ruffians below had formed a circle

around one man, who stood fiddling with the brim of the hat in his hands.

"Fellows, fellows, we can all be civilized here," Alexander Graham Bell said as hooligans lobbed foul words at him. The men to his left were decked out in various shades of green—emerald-colored derbies, lime-tinted ties, pine-toned trousers. Those to the right all had pink carnations pinned to their lapels. While it was clear to Molly that these were two opposing gangs, Bell did not seem to pick up on that detail.

"For those of you who may not have heard me over all the buzz and huffle," the inventor went on, sounding more annoyed than intimidated, "I have already apologized—thrice, if I've not miscounted—for interrupting your . . . business transactions. Now, if you'll allow me one brief question, I'll be on my way."

This is it, Molly thought. *We're about to witness the transformation of Alexander Graham Bell into a human pancake.*

Emmett peeked through his fingers as a tall man in a kelly-green vest approached Bell, a wry grin beneath his waxed mustache. "Never has it been said that the Green Onion Boys are inhospitable hosts," he declared. He paced a slow orbit around Bell, whose sudden rapid blinking gave tell that he was beginning to understand the gravity of his situation. "So, let's hear it, Fancy Dan," the tall man said. "What's your inquestigation?"

"I, um, I'm trying to locate a boy. He . . . he gave this address."

"Please don't tell them anything else," Emmett prayed quietly. "Please don't tell them anything else."

"A Chinese boy, not quite twelve years old," said Bell. "His name is Emmett."

Several of the green-clad men whooped. "Little Emmett Lee," said the tall one.

"You . . . know him?"

"Oh, yeah," the tall man said drily. "Emmett's an old 'quaintance of ours. How do *you* know Emmett?"

"He works for me."

"Well, isn't that something!" The tall man cheerfully slapped Bell on the back. "Because we thought Emmett worked for us. And he owes us quite a bit of money. Seeing as you're his new employager, though, I think it's perfeckly fine if his debt gets repaid by you. Now."

Molly was afraid Emmett might melt through the floorboards.

"But . . . but Emmett's a decent boy," Bell said. "I have a hard time believing he was employed by such . . . such . . ."

Several men with shoulders like cinder blocks cracked their knuckles.

"How much is it the boy owes?" Bell asked, taking out his wallet.

"Two thousand," said the tall man. "Plus another four

hundred for the guns. And at least another five g's that we coulda earned *with* those guns. Plus interest. Plus a two-dollar inconvenience fee. Let's just round it off to ten thousand."

Bell goggled at him. "Dollars? I . . . I don't carry that kind of money on me. I daresay no one does."

The tall man turned to his brothers in green. "Notice he didn't say he doesn't *have* that kind of money." He tapped his head to show how smart he was.

"Is that Oogie MacDougal?" Molly whispered.

"No, his name's Pembroke," Emmett said. "And if we stand any chance of talking our way out of this, we need to do it before MacDougal shows up. For one thing, you can understand Pembroke. Mostly."

Below, Pembroke waved a switchblade in Bell's face. "Friends and fellow enterpenoors, I think we can temporarily put aside the deals we was working on," Pembroke said. "'Cause Fancy Dan here is going to lead us into more dough than any of that business."

"Stop!" Emmett shouted. "You don't realize who you have there!"

All heads turned up to the balcony.

"Emmett?" Bell gasped, seeming all the more puzzled.

Though his legs were shaking, Emmett placed his hands on the rail and held his head high. Molly had no idea what he was about to try, but she felt oddly proud of this dangerously bold move.

"Hey, if it isn't my old buddy Emmett," Pembroke called up with a smile.

"That man is Alexander Graham Bell, the famous inventor," Emmett said. "The Inventors' Guild will pay a king's ransom for him. But not if he's hurt."

"Oh, really?" Pembroke said sarcastically.

"That's what Oogie MacDougal told me," Emmett continued. "Yeah, that's right, I've been working with Oogie all along."

Molly beamed. Her friend had come so far.

As gang members on both sides began muttering, a man with an enormous carnation on his hatband gave Pembroke a fat-fingered poke. "You been holding out on us?" the man sneered. "You told us Oogie had a big job in the works, but you didn't say it was VIP-ransom big."

"Don't jump to delusions, Chaswick," Pembroke retorted, poking the portly man back. "That kid ain't trustable."

Molly recognized the lost look in Emmett's eyes. He was freezing up, doubting his own plan. She needed to jump in.

"Do you think anyone could really be that stupid," she said, rising to Emmett's side, "to steal from the Green Onion Boys?" She nudged Emmett with her foot.

"Certainly not me," Emmett said. "I am not that stupid. No, um, look, Oogie thought I'd be the right person to . . . infiltrate Bell's organization, pretend to work for him until I could lure him down here. The money and guns were my . . . payment."

When Emmett saw his mentor's face fall, his own did too. Molly nudged him again.

"Pardon my skepticasm," Pembroke said, squinting at them. "But why then did Oogie tell us you *stoled* it?"

"The plan was secret," Molly interjected. "No one could know the truth except Oogie and Emmett. And me. Penelope von Venturesworth, professional saboteur."

Chaswick elbowed Pembroke and whispered, "I think I've heard of her."

"Hey, don't believe me," Emmett said. "But I wouldn't want to be you when Oogie shows up and finds out what you did to his prize captive. Look, why don't—"

"Penelope," Molly whispered.

"—*Penelope* and I take Mr. Bell out back and babysit him while you finish up with the Carnation Boys—"

"Ugly Flowerpots!" Chaswick barked.

"Sorry!" Emmett sputtered. "You can finish up with the . . . Flowerpots and we can iron out this Bell business when Oogie returns."

Suddenly, behind the bar, a door that had been disguised as a shelf of liquor bottles swung open, and a reedy man in a long green coat strode into the room on spiderlike legs. Curly red sideburns framed his face and several gold teeth flashed when he smiled. He tipped his emerald top hat to Emmett and "Penelope."

"Nae need tae hauld yer wheesht," the man said in the world's thickest Scottish brogue. "Oogie's 'ere."

The Bandit King

"Oogie," Pembroke cried. "Is it true what the kid says?"

"Nae a word, Pembroke." Oogie MacDougal gave his lieutenant a crooked grin. He pointed to the balcony and ordered, "Fetch they bairns!"

Several of the gangsters looked to one another for a hint of what to do.

"The bairns, the wee weans!" Oogie barked. One gangster tentatively reached for a bowl of pretzels. "The children!" Oogie shouted.

Several thugs bounded upstairs to the mezzanine. There was probably time to duck out the window, but Molly saw Emmett's eyes locked with Bell's and stood fast by his side. The goons lugged them downstairs and dropped them next to Bell.

"Ah cannae hawp ye fell fur sic stories," Oogie said,

waving a long, thin finger in Pembroke's face. There was a clear cruelty in MacDougal's grin, but beyond that, nothing about the fragile-looking, rail-thin man seemed overly threatening.

"Stories?" Pembroke said. "Oh, the kid's stories. You think I believered them? Is that what . . . ? I *think* that's what you said. Well, no! I never doubted ya for a second." But the tremor in his voice betrayed him.

"Ah kin see it in yer een, gowk," Oogie sneered. "Gang tak' a nap." Molly had no idea what MacDougal had said, but she knew a threat when she heard one. The gang leader grabbed a fistful of Pembroke's shirt, hoisted the man over his head—one-handed—and threw him across the bar into a shelf of glass mugs.

"How the heck is a guy built like a drinking straw so strong?" Molly muttered to Emmett.

"I had no idea he was," Emmett replied.

"Shh. Hear that?" Bell whispered.

Hear what? But then Molly noticed it: With every step Oogie took, there was a metallic creak. MacDougal had some kind of machinery under his coat.

As two Green Onions hauled away the moaning Pembroke, Oogie strode over to his captives. "Emmett, mae wee mukker. Yer a pernicketie jimmy tae fin'."

"Emmett," Molly whispered out of the corner of her mouth, "I officially apologize for doubting your 'I couldn't understand him' story."

"He said you're a hard man to find," explained Bell. "I grew up in Scotland."

"I know," said Molly.

"I've git three questions fur ye, Emmett," MacDougal said.

"That's far fewer than I have," Bell muttered.

Oogie raised one finger. "Whaur's mah dosh?"

"Where's his money?" Bell translated.

Emmett looked down and bit his lip. *Just lie*, Molly thought. *Say it's stuffed in a tree, buried on an island, booby-trapped in a pit full of deadly vipers—anything.*

"In the river," Emmett said.

MacDougal's face grew a full shade redder. "Whaur ur mah guns?"

"Where are his . . . guns?"

"It was a mistake. I didn't know who he was," Emmett said to Bell. Then to Oogie, "The guns are with the money."

The gang leader sucked his teeth and took a step back. When the crimson in his cheeks faded, he raised a third finger. "How come shouldn't ah murdurr ye this minute?"

Bell winced. "He wants to know why he shouldn't—"

"I got that one," Emmett said. Wobbly and bleary-eyed, the boy looked as if he might have passed out had a burly gangster not been holding him up.

"Please, Mr. MacDougal," Bell said. "From one Scotsman to another—"

Oogie's laughter cut him off. "Quit yer havering, ye doolally auld gallus! Ye'v bin makin' hoose in the States fur sae lang noo, ye cannae tell a braw haggis frae a drookit pipe poke!"

Emmett and Molly looked to Bell for a translation, but the inventor shrugged. "Sorry, even I couldn't follow that one."

MacDougal gripped Bell by the collar. "Awright, muckle brain . . ."

"Wait!" Molly cried out. "I can answer your question. You're not going to kill us because . . ." She hoped to come up with a reason by the time she finished the sentence. She looked at Emmett, his face drawn with despair, and Bell, who stared upon Emmett with equal dismay. She looked at the Green Onion Boys thirsting for violence, and the Ugly Flowerpots with imaginary dollar signs before their eyes. She looked at Oogie MacDougal, a man with the apparent physical strength to hurl an elephant across the East River. And she knew what to do. "You're not going to kill us," she said, "because when you hear what we have to say, you're going to want to join us."

"Is that so?" MacDougal mocked.

"Absolutely," Molly said without a quiver in her voice. "Because however much you think the Inventors' Guild is going to pay you for Bell, I bet they'll reward you twice as much for saving the World's Fair from a madman."

The silence was painful. Finally, though, MacDougal

gave the smallest hint of a smirk and leaned closer. "Ye've git me interest, dearie. Let's blether it ower in back."

The gang leader guided Molly, Emmett, and Bell into the hidden room behind the bar. Their entrance interrupted the billiards game of two men who, based on their bruised, scar-adorned faces, had seen their fair share of violence.

"What was the hullabaloo out there?" the taller of the two called out as the door opened. But Emmett was the first one to walk in.

"You!" spat the shorter of the gangsters—who was still roughly the size of an orangutan. Wielding his cue stick like a club, he rushed at Emmett, but MacDougal thrust an arm out and the man fell as if he'd hit a brick wall.

"Settle doon, Crikes," Oogie said.

"But I thought we was supposed to kill this kid if we ever saw him again," groaned the man on the floor.

"Wee Emmett's under mah protection fur th' moment; least till ah hear the barry business deal th' lassie haes tae offer. Hulp him up, Tusk." Molly assumed the taller of the henchmen was called Tusk because of the one large tooth jutting up past his lower lip (either that or the man's parents had been awful at baby names).

She stepped confidently up to the pool table. After a series of catastrophic misfires, she was finally going to set things right. She and Emmett needed help if they were going to defeat the masked man—and the Green Onions certainly knew how to take down an enemy.

"Here's the deal," Molly said, taking a moment to look each gangster in the eye. "Emmett and I uncovered a plot to murder everyone at the World's Fair. At first, we thought Mr. Bell was behind it, but we were wrong. Sorry about that, Mr. B."

The inventor looked as if someone had poured a bucket of ice chips down his back. "But, but, but . . . What in heaven's name made you think I could be involved in such horror?"

"We found it in your office," Molly answered.

"My—?" Bell's indignation melted into disappointment. "The break-in. That was you, Emmett."

"No, just me," Molly said. "Emmett was only there because he was secretly living in your workshop and didn't want you to know he was homeless."

"Molly!" Emmett said.

"Might as well get everything out in the open now, right?" Molly replied. "Keeping secrets is what got us into this mess."

Oogie MacDougal scowled with impatience.

"We'll discuss this later," Bell said quickly. "Right now, I want to know what you found in my office that set your imagination running off."

Molly whipped the incriminating scrap of paper from her boot and slapped it down on the billiards felt. She pointed to the various notations. "Targets, victims, death machines . . ."

"I've never seen this in my life," Bell said, and the confusion in his voice was such that Molly believed him. "But there is something familiar . . ."

"You believe us?" Emmett asked.

"Well, whoever made this obviously had nasty intentions," he replied, scratching his thick beard. "I doubt, however, that this is anything more than an angry man's fantasy. There's no way one man could actually endanger tens of thousands of people like that."

"He's got a *death machine*," Molly said.

"*That*, my dear, is strictly conjecture," said Bell. He was talking to her as if she were a child and she did not like it. "D-E-A, M-A-C. Those letters could belong to any number of phrases."

Molly crossed her arms. "Name one."

Bell scratched his beard again. "Dead mackerels."

Molly rolled her eyes.

"Deaf Macedonians," Bell tried. "Deactivate Macy's?"

"The store?" Emmett said. "Mr. Bell, at first I thought Molly was overreaching too. But so much has happened in the past week. And it's clearly got some connection to the Guild. Since we found these plans in your workshop, we've been spied on, threatened, chased all over the city by masked men—men who confronted us at *your* lab. Their leader has a gun that makes flagpoles fly at you.

Whoever these people are, it wouldn't surprise me if they had death machines."

"Fur cryin' oot loud! It dinnae say deeth machines!'" MacDougal's outburst startled everyone.

Molly coaxed her heart back down her throat. "How would you know it doesn't say 'deeth machines'? I mean, 'death machines'?" she asked.

The gang leader reached into the pocket of his emerald coat and produced a rough-edged piece of paper. "'Cause Ah've git th' ither hauf." He set down his torn parchment, fitting it like a puzzle piece into Molly's. The whole thing was a letter. And the words that had been cut off were now clearly readable:

DEAR
MACDOUGAL.

"It was you," she said, stepping back. She glanced at Crikes and Tusk. Comedy and Tragedy. Why hadn't she noticed until now? "It was you three in the masks."

"These two, aye," Oogie said, gesturing to his henchmen. "But no me. Ah'm tae important tae play sidekick tae—"

He was cut short by a sudden commotion out in the tavern. Hushing his captives, he cracked the door.

"I don't like it, I tell ya!" growled Chaswick, the leader of the Ugly Flowerpots. "Now get outta my way! We're going back there to see if Oogie's holdin' out on us!"

MacDougal huffed. "Come wi' me, Tusk," he ordered. "Crikes, ye play nanny till Ah git back." He marched into the tavern, with Tusk at his heels. "Staun doon, ye clarty oxters!" The door slammed behind him.

"Now what?" Emmett asked.

Crikes opened a drawer and pulled out a long chain.

Chained!

MOLLY, EMMETT, AND Bell were chained to a rolltop desk in the corner, their gadget-filled carpetbags now on the pool table, frustratingly out of reach. While Crikes pressed his ear to the door in an attempt to eavesdrop on the muffled voices buzzing from the other side, Emmett fiddled with a pen and paper clip. *Nerves*, Molly thought. Her own insides roiled as well. Not even atop the precarious tower of the Brooklyn Bridge had she felt such desperation. How had things gone so wrong?

"I'm sorry, Mr. Bell," Molly said. Apologizing felt like the only good thing she had left. "For getting you involved in this. For Emmett lying to you. For blowing up your lab. It's no excuse, but we only did it because we thought your robots were the death machines."

"There's that ridiculous word again!" Bell grumbled.

"Can somebody please explain to me why you keep calling my automatons *ro-bots*?"

"*You're* the one who called them that," Molly shot back. "You etched it onto their name tags!"

"Name tags? I did no such . . ." Bell put his hand to his face and let out a mirthless laugh. "Robert . . . You must have seen a 'Robert' model. Each automaton sings a different part of the four-part harmony—Charles is the baritone, William the bass, James the tenor, and the lead is Robert. Perhaps you could use a pair of spectacles."

"It was dark!" Tears began to flow. Misreading a word was far from the worst mistake Molly had made that week, but it was the one that tipped her over the edge of despair. "I would have liked to see them sing!" she sobbed. "'Polly Wolly Doodle' is my mother's favorite song!" She couldn't believe she was crying in front of a Green Onion Boy. But Emmett started weeping too.

"Quit blubbering," Crikes barked. "I can't hear as it is!"

"Perhaps you can see my automatons sing yet, lass," Bell said, his eyes growing puddly as well. "I still have the four originals back at my Guild office."

"You do?" Emmett asked, chains clinking as he wiped his face. "But . . . *where?* Wait, are they behind that door that says 'Top Secret'?"

"Hold on." Molly was stunned. "You've been living for three months in a place with a door marked 'Top Secret' and you never once peeked?"

Her friend shrugged. Bell laughed deeply this time.

Molly wiped her face on her sleeve. "*I* would've looked."

"Oh, no question there," Emmett said, grinning. And for the first time, Molly noticed that he wasn't just nervously fussing with desk supplies—he was building something.

"Button it!" Crikes yelled as the angry voices from the tavern got louder. He spun his key ring on his finger. "Don't know what I'm doing here. I ain't a blinkin' babysitter. Not anymore. Not since that one kid went up the chimney. But he had it comin'. He— Hey, boy, what're you—"

Molly quickly leaned forward to block Crikes's view of Emmett. "So, Crikesy, why do you call yourselves the Green Onions, anyway?" she asked.

Crikes crossed his arms and glared. "'Cause if you cut us, we'll make you cry."

Molly snorted. "So in that analogy, *you're* the one getting hurt."

Crikes grinned smugly. "But *you're* the one crying."

"Yeah, *after* I've cut you."

Crikes raised his hand for a slap. "Don't tempt me, smart aleck."

"That's it!" Bell shouted, startling everyone. "The handwriting! I know the handwriting on those plans! Because the braggy blatherskite has been leaving notes

203

on my door for weeks. Notes like, 'Hey, Smart Alec, you're just like your telephone—all talk.' Or 'Hey, Smart Alec, just because your name is Bell doesn't mean all your inventions have to have bells.' And they don't, by the way—I've invented plenty of things without bells."

"Who writes notes like that?" Emmett asked.

"Edison," Bell growled.

"*Thomas* Edison?" Molly asked. "But you two are pals!"

"Far from it," Bell said bitterly. "Don't mistake a public handshake for friendship behind closed doors."

There was obviously more to that story, but it would have to wait. "Still . . . Edison can't be the man in the mask," Molly reasoned. "He was at the parade with you."

"I hadn't seen him all evening until he stepped up to defend me," Bell said, getting riled up. "Which I'm now certain was some kind of trick."

"You know, the masked man did disappear right before we saw Edison," Emmett said. "And at the Guild Hall, we were in *both* offices. Mr. Bell's *and* Mr. Edison's! Everything got mixed up."

Molly leaned out as far as the chains would let her and snatched the paper from the pool table. She flipped it over to show the autograph Thomas Edison had scratched on it when she saw him. The handwriting was a perfect match.

"Hey!" Crikes marched over to snatch the paper back

and noticed Emmett's little project. "Hold on, what've you got there—"

Emmett brought the shaft of a pen to his mouth, and, using it like a blowgun, he puffed a spurt of black ink into Crikes's eyes. As the gangster stumbled backward, Emmett scattered a handful of pencils under his feet. The gangster tripped and fell, his head smashing into the corner of the billiards table on his way down. He was out cold.

Emmett immediately began spitting. "Ucch! I got ink in my mouth. It tastes terrible! Like a sardine that's been in the sun all day. And then fell into a coal bin. And then got poisoned."

"I knew you could do it," Molly said, patting her friend on the back. "I had no idea what you were doing, but I knew you could do it."

Emmett smiled back at her with black teeth.

Suddenly, a crash sounded from out in the tavern. Followed by some murderous shrieks. And then some grunts, thuds, and howls. It soon sounded like a small earthquake was demolishing Bandit's Roost.

"It's a brawl," Molly said.

"And it's going to mean bad news for us, whoever wins," Bell said.

Emmett quickly swung a chain of paper clips to snag the key from Crikes's finger. In seconds, their shackles were off and the carpetbags strapped back on.

"Are you . . . barring the door?" Bell asked as Molly shoved a pool cue through the door handle.

"You want to go out into *that*?" she replied as a pained scream rang out from the tavern.

"Not particularly," said Bell. "But it's the only way out."

"This is a secret room with a secret entrance," Molly said. "So we just need to find the secret exit."

Emmett began running his hands along the wall.

"I'm sorry, children," Bell said, amused. "But that's not the way logic works."

"Only because you're thinking like a scientist and not like a criminal mastermind," Molly replied, without pausing in her opening of drawers and lifting of carpets. "Imagine an unexpected gang war erupts in the middle of your hideout. You need to beat a hasty retreat, so you slip away through the hidden door that you've built behind your bar. Do you want that handy escape hatch to lead you into a dead-end room where your enemies can trap you and then skewer you with billiard cues? Or do you want it to be the first step on a route *out* of the building?"

Bell stood silent for a second, then started peeking behind picture frames and feeling under cabinets. He pulled forward one whiskey bottle to find it was attached to a lever. A panel on the wall slid open to reveal a dark passage.

"Ooh! I found it!" the inventor said with excitement.

But the newly revealed tunnel was not empty. A man was standing there.

The man in the crooked mask.

"Gee," the villain droned sarcastically. "Thanks for ruining my surprise entrance."

Meet the Wizard

"I TRULY REGRET not throwing you off that bridge when I had the chance," the masked man said in his deep, sinister voice.

"You can quit play-acting, Edison," Bell said defiantly. "We know it's you."

"Bravo, you've deciphered all the incredibly obvious clues," the villain said, his voice changing to the familiar New York accent that Molly had heard at the Guild Hall. He removed his twisted mask to reveal the aquiline nose and tufted brow of Thomas Alva Edison. "Someone should write a series of detective novels about you."

"It's all true," Emmett said, gaping. "You really are working with the Green Onion Boys."

Edison stuck out his tongue. "Ugh, give me some credit, kid. Those buffoons are working *for* me. It's a very important distinction. The King of All Inventors doesn't work *with* anybody."

The noise out in the tavern was dying down, which meant that the victors of the brawl—whoever they were—would be forcing their way in shortly. The passageway Edison was blocking was the only escape route.

"Good point, Edison," Molly said. "You're the world's greatest inventor, so why—"

"Hey, I'm no slouch," said Bell.

Edison snickered. "Yeah, and which of us is the centerpiece of the World's Fair?"

"At least I'm getting by on honest work," Bell snapped. "Not chasing children around in a ridiculous Hephaestus mask."

"Hephaestus! Greek god of craftsmen!" Molly slapped her forehead. "That's who that is!"

"Of course!" Emmett chimed in. "I feel like we should've figured that out sooner."

"True," said Molly. "But Hephaestus isn't traditionally a villain, so . . ."

"Oh, you may think of me as a villain now," Edison said. "But that's just because I'm going to hold a hundred thousand people hostage. And what do I want in exchange for those hostages, you ask?"

"We didn't," Bell said. "But go ahead."

"I want the government!" Edison said. "This country needs a true visionary in charge. Enough with Jolly

Mister Muttonchops—it's my turn at the presidency. And with all those hostages—including bigwigs like Grover Cleveland and Ulysses S. Grant and silly Chester A. Arthur himself—the spineless weasels in Congress will happily pass a resolution to make me commander in chief. Don't you think? No, don't answer. I don't care what you think."

The door rattled. Molly needed Edison out of the way. Should she tackle him? But what if he had another hidden weapon in his coat? No, she had to attack the one weakness she knew this villain had. "So, you're planning to take a hundred thousand hostages?" she said, overplaying her skepticism. "How? By having the Green Onions block some exits for you?"

"Of course not!" Edison said, rolling his eyes. "I mean, that's *part* of the plan. Hence the letter you so inconveniently stumbled upon." He chuckled. "Do you realize how adorable it is that you thought it said 'death machine'? I loved that. No, it will be my greatest invention of all that takes care of those fairgoers."

"What's this invention?" Bell asked.

"It's basically a death machine," Edison said. "But I don't want to ruin the surprise. Now that I've caught the high and mighty Alec Bell, I'm gonna make you watch me use it. I want you to witness my ultimate victory firsthand. You kids, too. Consider it a thank-you."

"Thank-you? For what?" Emmett asked, as the door rattled again.

"Everything was going smoothly until you broke into my office," Edison said. "I showed up there shortly after you tripped my alarm and quickly discovered the missing shred of evidence. By taking that little strip of paper, you basically signed your death warrant. I mean, I couldn't have you running around, warning people to stay *away* from the World's Fair."

Outside, it sounded like Oogie MacDougal was yelling, *Bah! Get out the way!* Or possibly, *Beluga's a whale!* But probably the first one.

"After spying on you, however," Edison continued, "I was relieved—and frankly, quite tickled—to find that you thought the plan was Alec's. And when you discovered Alec's warehouse full of robots for me, I knew just what to do: frame him! So, thanks for that idea, kiddies. Credit where credit is due. I rigged the warehouse to explode—kinda hoping you'd be inside it when it did— and planted evidence to make it look like those robots really were the dangerous weapons you thought they were. Once the evil Alexander Graham Bell is arrested, everyone will believe the Fair to be safe again, wholesome fun for the entire family."

"You're despicable," Bell hissed.

CRUNCH! Everyone flinched as the pool cue snapped and the door exploded from its hinges. Oogie MacDougal, his emerald coat torn and top hat dented, stood seething with bruised and bloodied thugs at his sides.

Edison waved to him. "Oogie, old man! Nice to see you

making use of that exoskeleton I built."

"Children, run!" Bell yelled, and leapt onto Edison, knocking him away from the passage. For once, Molly and Emmett did not question an order from an adult. They ran.

"Ach! Th' wee neds are gaun!"

Molly and Emmett heard the unmistakable brogue of Oogie MacDougal reverberating through the darkness as they felt their way along the walls of what they *really* hoped was an escape tunnel.

"Still with me, Emmett?" Molly asked breathlessly as she stumbled on.

"Yes! Keep moving!"

The suggestion was unnecessary—stopping was the last thing on Molly's mind. Not even when her fingers brushed past something damp and furry did she consider pausing. Not even when she heard MacDougal's chilling calls echo down the passageway: "Oh, *Em*-mett! Ah'm *com*-in' fur ye!"

Molly gasped as a bobbing lantern light appeared behind them. The gang leader was gaining fast. Finally, her hand hit a metallic lever. She yanked it down and, with a raspy grinding, another wall panel slid open. They were now in one of the abandoned tenement buildings across the street from Bandit's Roost, and compared to the utter blackness of the tunnel, the dim moonlight seeping through broken windows was as welcome as the sun.

"Made it!" Molly cheered. They pushed open the paint-chipped front door, and were stopped in their tracks.

"Think we don't know where our own secret tunnels end up?" The tall, stoop-shouldered Tusk stood on the steps with a squad of Onion goons.

The children spun back inside to see MacDougal step out of the secret passage. They were trapped. Emmett spotted a craggy hole in the wall and began kicking moldy boards out of the way until they could squeeze through. He and Molly emerged into the kitchen of the next building over. Any crumb that had once graced its cupboards had been long since carried off by rats, and the rusty sink was drier than the mildew-coated floorboards. Oogie peered through the crevice at them; it was too small for his tall frame, but he grinned wickedly.

"Rin aroond tae th' next duir!" he called to his minions as he began ripping away chunks of wall by hand.

"Rin?" Tusk asked.

"Aye, rin," Oogie said. "Wi' yer legs. Move 'em." He wiggled two fingers back and forth like a pair of running legs.

"Oh, *run*! Yeah, right. Going!"

As MacDougal continued his one-man demolition job, Molly and Emmett tried the kitchen door, but it wouldn't budge. Something must have been blocking it from the other side.

"Ouch," Emmett yelped as a piece of plaster fell onto him. Suddenly, debris was raining all over, coming down in larger and larger chunks.

"Oogie, stop! You're gonna bring the whole place down!" Molly yelled. But the red-faced gang lord wasn't interested. He had almost torn a hole big enough for himself to fit through; he didn't seem to care about the long, snaking cracks that had sprouted from that hole, running across the walls and up to the crumbling ceiling. With nowhere else to go, Molly and Emmett huddled against the door.

"Say g'nicht, weans!" Oogie sneered as he stepped into the rumbling kitchen. Then a clawfoot bathtub crashed through the ceiling, and even the fury-fueled MacDougal had no choice but to leap back through the hole in the wall.

"It's caving in!" Emmett screamed. Molly tried to join him in his cries, but choked on the dust-thick air.

Suddenly, the kitchen door opened.

"Come with me if you want to live," said a young woman in the doorway. Her own arms were raised overhead to protect herself from the hunks of ceiling that were falling even in that next room.

"We'll never make it out," Emmett cried.

But the stranger grabbed each of their hands. "Believe in yourselves," she said. And that was the last thing Molly heard before a slab of door frame crashed onto her and she slipped into unconsciousness.

30

Mothers' Little Helpers

I DON'T KNOW if this is heaven, Molly thought as she blinked her eyes open, *but at least it's not the other place. Too cold.* She reached up to the frigid spot on her head and found a dripping ice bag, which she promptly removed. That small motion caused a wave of pain to ricochet through her skull. On the bright side, that probably meant she was still alive. But where was she? There was a surprisingly comfortable cot beneath her, bare brick walls around her, and not much else. As her vision came back into focus, a door opened, and a strangely familiar face appeared—mahogany complexion, tightly pinned hair parted down the center, and a bright, beaming smile. It was the woman who'd taken her hand in the collapsing tenement, a woman she'd assumed to be a dream.

"You're awake," the woman said.

"You're real," Molly muttered in return.

"I sure hope so," she said. "My name's Sarah, Sarah Goode." She turned and called, "Emmett, Molly's up."

Emmett! She sat up and swung her legs down, wincing from the pounding in her head, and Sarah steadied her.

"Molly!" Emmett shouted as he burst into the room.

"I'm happy to see you too," she said, wincing again. "Can we be happy a little more quietly, though?"

"Yeah, sorry," he said, much more softly. "How do you feel? Do you feel okay? I was worried. But you look okay. Are you okay?"

Molly nodded. She'd never heard Emmett speak this much, this fast.

"Oh, good, because I was worried. Molly, so much has happened. Did you meet Sarah? This is Sarah, Sarah Goode. She helped me drag you from that building. She's one of Hertha's people. There are more of them. Five, actually. This is their workshop—not just this, there's a bigger room out there. I know your mother didn't trust Hertha, and you trust your mother, but these are good people. And I don't just mean Sarah, Sarah Goode. Did you meet Sarah?"

Sarah, standing behind him, tried to hide her amusement.

"Emmett, are you okay?" Molly asked.

"Hertha made me some tea," he replied. "I'd never had tea before. It's good! I've drunk a lot of it. Maybe too much. Now I feel a little—*vrrrr!*—like the motor in your mom's crazy mop."

"Ha! Welcome to caffeine," Molly said. Laughing made her head hurt, but she couldn't help it. "You should've tried the coffee when I offered it."

Then Emmett surprised her with a hug. She could tell he was trying to be as gentle as possible. "Oh, but Molly, there's so much to tell you," he said, pulling away. "That whole building came down, you know, the entire thing. Nothing but rubble now. We were so lucky to get out alive. Thank you again, Sarah! Did you meet Sarah, Sarah Goode?"

"Yeah. Was MacDougal still in the building?"

Emmett shook his head. "He got out, told his men to search the debris for bodies. Sarah and I hid with you while that Tusk guy poked around, but stuff kept crumbling and he gave up pretty quickly."

"So the good news is that the Green Onions won't be looking for you anymore," Sarah said. "They think you two are rubbing shoulders with Saint Peter."

If Thomas Edison and the Onions really thought they were dead, that *was* one less thing to worry about, but it was far from the end of their problems. Molly looked Sarah over. She was young and friendly, not stuffy and proper. And her simple yellow dress was a far cry from

Hertha's feather-and-ruffle nightmare. Had her mother's snap judgment about Hertha's group been too hasty? Or had Emmett once again been too trusting? It was too soon to rule out the possibility that these women worked for Edison. Or that they had their own nefarious motives.

"We were awfully lucky that you showed up in that random tenement when you did," Molly said, making no attempt to hide her skepticism.

"You were indeed. But it almost became incredibly *un*lucky for me," Sarah replied. "When my friend Mary and I followed you from the dump on Rivington, we had no idea you were heading into a foofaraw with the Green Onions. I'd ducked into that building across the street, hoping to find a good spot to keep an eye on you. Little did I know that you would suddenly appear in that very building—or that you would bring the whole thing tumbling down!"

"Well, that wasn't us," Molly said defensively. "That was Oogie with his— Wait, how did you find us at the dump?"

"Oh, well, that came out of Mary observing your friend Jasper at the Inventors' Guild," Sarah said.

"Jasper!" Molly blurted with sudden concern. "We have to—"

"Oh, don't worry, Molly Pepper, I'm here too," Jasper said, poking his head into the doorway. "Sorry I did not make my presence known sooner, but I didn't want to intrude upon your heartfelt reunion with Emmett. I fig-ured it best I keep myself secreted outside the room here. Also, I know what part of the story's comin' up next and I did not want to see the critical expression on your face when you heard it."

Sarah grinned and continued her tale. "After hearing about what happened to your mother, we'd been on the lookout for you and Emmett for days. Then Mary over-heard Mr. Bloom shouting to a Guild Hall clerk about how there were going to be two very angry children waiting for him if he did not report back to the Rivington Street landfill with information on the whereabouts of one Alexander Graham Bell. So Mary grabbed me and we followed him back to your bookmobile."

"Jasper!" Molly said. "Really?"

"That's the look I'm talkin' about! That's the look I did not want to see," the ashman said, folding his arms defiantly. "But that side door Emmett wanted me to use was scary. And I thought I'd have a better shot at sweet-talkin' my way in to see Bell. I mean, you have seen these dreamlike eyelashes of mine, right?"

In truth, Molly was incredibly grateful to see Jasper safe. He was yet one more innocent person embroiled in this World's Fair fiasco on her account. She didn't know if her conscience could bear any more. "I'm just glad you're okay."

"Likewise, Molly Pepper." Jasper dabbed his eyes.

"And I'm doubly thankful to Mrs. Mary Walton, who swooped in like Robin Hood to rescue me and my Prancey-Pie from the brutish Green Onion gangsters who'd absconded with us."

"Oh, I'm pretty sure those boys weren't with the Onions," a woman's voice called from the next room. "Just a couple of random thieves, couldn't have been more than ten years old or so."

"Yeah, but they were some of those *extra-large* ten-year-olds," Jasper said melodramatically.

"Come," Sarah said, helping Molly to her feet. "If you're up to it, I can introduce you to the rest of the MOI." When Molly was on her feet, Sarah pulled a lever and the bed folded in upon itself, transforming into a fashionable cedar desk, complete with cozy chair and footrest. Whatever else these women were, Molly thought, they were inventors to be reckoned with.

Molly exited the bedroom—or office, or closet, or whatever it was—into a large warehouse space roughly the size of the pickle shop. And like the pickle shop, it had benches and worktables, a vast array of tools and materials, and dozens of intriguing prototype gadgets sitting about. Unlike the pickle shop, however, it was astonishingly tidy. The tables were clear, not cluttered. Instead of being piled willy-nilly into crates, the hammers, pliers, wrenches, and such were hung on hooks in orderly lines. Rather than shoved into random corners, the gizmos these women had created were proudly displayed on shelves. It gave Molly the shivers.

In the center of the big room was a large wheeled machine, obviously a work in progress. It looked like an open-top wagon, constructed almost entirely of metal and with three rows of plush seats. But there was no place to hook up a horse. And no reins—only something that resembled the captain's wheel of a ship. Molly was about to ask what it was when something caught her eye overhead: electric lights. Six big onion-shaped bulbs gave off a warm yellow glow.

"You've got electricity," Molly said, her mind filling with the many bad things that could mean. "Are you wired into Edison's grid? Because he—"

"Emmett has told us all about your encounter with Mr. Edison," Hertha said, her crisp English diction cutting off the question. "Have no fear. We are neither in league with nor reliant upon the man. We have our own electrical generator." She gestured to a humming, vibrating machine in the corner.

"Oh, yeah," Molly said, recalling her previous conversation with Hertha. "Electrics are kinda your thing, right?"

Hertha raised her eyebrows in an expression that Molly took for a smile, even though the woman's mouth didn't move. "Good to see you up and about, Miss Pepper." Hertha walked to Molly, her brocaded skirt swishing as she moved, and shook her hand. "Can I interest you in some tea?"

The mix of confusion, suspicion, and curiosity muddling Molly's brain made it difficult to play it cool. Plus, she was really thirsty. "Got any coffee?" she asked.

"Coffee?" Hertha scoffed, turning away melodramatically. "I'm not a heathen."

Another woman, with tufts of graying hair poking from beneath a flower-patterned knit cap, rolled her eyes. "Ignore her, dear. I'll make some."

"Hey, I know you," Molly said, recognizing the older woman's wry wink. "You're the lady from the Guild Hall—the one with the parasol who tripped those guards."

"Mary Walton," the woman said. She paused her coffee bean grinding to shake Molly's hand with a grip that was surprisingly firm for someone so grandmotherly. "Perhaps you know my work too, since you've grown up here in Manhattan. Do you have any recollection as to how New York's elevated trains sounded a year or so ago?"

"Yeah . . . ," Molly said with dawning enlightenment. "I used to cover my ears. They made me feel like my insides were gonna shake right out of my body. But the trains haven't been that way in a while."

"That would be my sound-dampening system," Mary said. "I firmly believe that technology need not spoil the world in which we use it. That's sort of *my thing.*"

"Oh, yes, where are my manners?" said another woman, seated by herself across the room. She closed the book she'd been reading—with a tasseled bookmark carefully placed between the pages—and stood to offer her hand in a way that struck Molly as very royal-ish. "Josephine Cochrane," the woman said. This was the fancy lady who'd been spying on them by the train tracks before the parade. She was dressed just as elegantly now: satiny dress with ruched skirt and lacy cuffs, pearl necklace, white gloves, and silver-framed reading glasses on the tip of her nose. "My *specialty*—I have too much respect for the English language to refer to it as a *thing*—is internal dynamics, moving parts. I've put this to use mainly in the creation of a few small mechanical devices for the home, but my pièce de résistance will be a fully automated dishwashing machine. It's certain to chip fewer wine goblets than the servants do, am I right?"

None of this helped change Molly's initial impression of the woman.

"Um, Sarah, you didn't tell Molly your thing—your specialty," Emmett said loudly, perhaps to distract from the odd look Molly was giving Josephine Cochrane.

"Oh, well, um . . . I design ways to fit big objects into small spaces," Sarah said. "Like that fold-up bed. I'm from Chicago, and apartments up there aren't very

223

generous in elbow room. So, as they say, necessity is . . ."

"The mother of invention," Molly finished.

"That would be us." Mary Walton handed Molly a cup of coffee.

Molly took a sip as she looked around at the various contraptions lining the shelves. "I thought there were five of you," she said.

At that, a fifth woman slid out from underneath the steel wagon in the center of the room. She wore crumpled, grease-smeared coveralls, multiple tool belts, and thick goggles that made her hair stick out like wings on the sides of her head. She looked like Josephine Cochrane's worst nightmare. "Margaret Knight. Boston," the woman said. "I make a lot of stuff. Started with the paper bag, just kept going." And she slid back out of sight.

"You invented those brown paper bags? With the flat bottoms?" Molly crouched to yell under the vehicle. She felt as awed as she had in the presence of Bell and Edison. "We use those in the pickle shop!"

"Margaret is probably the most accomplished of the five of us," Hertha said. "She already has eighty-seven patents to her name."

"That's crazy," Molly said. "Why have I never heard of her?"

"The answer, Molly," said Hertha, "circles right back to the conversation we had in your shop last week."

"So, you're all successful?" Molly was gobsmacked by the idea. "You all have *patented* inventions?"

"Not all. Not yet," said Sarah. "But someday. Someday I will be the first black woman to get a US patent. I believe it."

Molly's head was in a swirl, and not just because she'd been clobbered by a chunk of ceiling. Meeting these women—simply learning of their existence—seemed to change everything. Though Molly wasn't sure if it gave her more hope for the world, or less. On the one hand, her mother wasn't alone—she could be part of a community of female inventors, all of whom faced the same struggles and could support one another through it all. But on the other hand, none of these determined, accomplished, intelligent women had gotten recognition in their careers. Even the ones who'd actually managed to earn patents for their work were completely unknown. None had come anywhere close to the fame of Edison or Bell. None of them could even be members of the Inventors' Guild.

For so long, Molly had held on to the belief that, if her mother could just get her work seen, she would undoubtedly become a tremendous success, that Cassandra Pepper would change the world, that she would be part of history. Now Molly realized there were no guarantees. Not with the world being the way it was.

Still, she wasn't alone. That counted for something.

Perhaps if all these women worked together . . . "So, what's this wagon thingie you're building?" she asked.

"Ooh, ooh! Can I tell her?" Jasper jumped up and raised his hand like a schoolboy. "I ain't said anything in a long time and, you may not understand this, but that *hurts* me. It physically hurts me to be silent for more than a few minutes. Plus I'd like to show you ladies how well I paid attention when you was explainin' it earlier."

"Have at it, Mr. Bloom," Hertha said.

"Okay, well, this here is the Marvelous Moto-Mover," Jasper began.

"Mr. Bloom," Hertha scolded. "Not one sentence in and you're already embellishing. It is simply called a motor coach."

"I know that's what *you* called it," Jasper said. "But you gotta admit Marvelous Moto-Mover is a much catchier name."

"I'm with Jasper on this one," Molly said. Emmett nodded in agreement.

"It's tacky, if you ask me," said Mrs. Cochrane, who then went back to reading her book.

"Anyways, the Marvelous Moto-Mover is a horseless carriage," Jasper went on. "You understand what that means, right? No horses. So what pulls it? Nothing. Nothing pulls it. This thing moves by itself on account of they put an engine in there. And how does the engine work? I am not qualified to answer that question. Anyway, the

226

Mothers intended the Moto-Mover to be their joint entry into the World's Fair. But they ran into the same problem your mother had, Molly Pepper—the Guild made the Fair a no-go for lady inventors."

"Or as we like to call ourselves, *inventors*," said Mary.

"And we weren't going to let a little thing like the lack of an invitation stop us," said Hertha.

Sarah nodded. "Cinderella didn't have an invitation to the ball either."

"Yes, but we were going to be our own fairy godmothers, make our own magic," Hertha continued. "We reckoned we'd drive our motor coach all around the fairgrounds and let the people gawk."

"Tacky, if you ask me," said Mrs. Cochrane.

The others stared at her.

"I didn't say *no*, I said *tacky*." And she went back to her book.

"My mother and I thought about doing the same thing with her Icarus Chariot," Molly said. "Only flying, not driving." She was growing fonder of these women by the moment. (Except maybe Mrs. Cochrane.)

"Your mother made a flying coach?" Sarah asked.

"More like a flying boat," Molly said.

Emmett nodded. "She really did. I saw it. Well, I didn't see it fly, but I saw it in her shop."

Molly felt a warm surge of optimism she hadn't felt in days. It might take some convincing, Molly thought, but Cassandra Pepper belonged in the Mothers of Invention. These fun, exciting, brilliant ladies could be more than partners to her; they could be friends. Molly closed her eyes and envisioned her mother joshing around with Hertha and Sarah, trading tricks with Mary and Margaret, poking fun at stuffy Mrs. Cochrane. For the first time in a long time, Molly was able to imagine her mother happy about something beyond their little two-person family. And that thought elated Molly. Because, no matter how much she liked putting a smile on her mother's face, being entirely responsible for another person's happiness can be exhausting.

"Hertha, I know my mother didn't give you the warmest reception before, but if she got to know you all, I think she'd fit in great," she said. "She's an amazing inventor. I'm sure she'd have incredible ideas to add to your Marvelous Moto-Mover."

"The motor coach is not going to be finished for the Fair, Molly," Hertha said gently. "We have more important things to focus on now."

Molly was about to ask what could possibly be more important when it hit her. "Oh, Edison," she said. And her mood deflated once more.

Emmett put his hand on her shoulder. "But we have help now, Molly. This is a good thing."

"If what Emmett told us is even remotely true," Hertha said, "then everything must be put aside until we know Edison's plot is foiled and the fairgoers will be safe."

"Well, what are we sitting around talking for, then?" said Molly. She downed the rest of her coffee in one slug. "Let's stop Edison!"

"Please, Molly, give us some credit," said Hertha. "We've been working on it. We only stopped our planning session because you woke up." She motioned toward a table where empty teacups surrounded open notebooks, newspapers, maps, and pencils.

"I think better with a wrench in my hand," Margaret Knight said from beneath the motor coach.

But Molly was perplexed. "What's to figure out?" she asked. "Go to the police! Emmett and I couldn't risk it, but surely you—"

"We did," said Mary. "It's not so easy to convince a grumpy desk sergeant that one of the most beloved men in America is a dangerous criminal. Not without evidence."

"Or a mustache," Mrs. Cochrane said without looking up from her book.

"But what about Alexander Graham Bell?" Molly asked, exasperated. "Did you tell them that the Green Onions have him? We don't even know if he's still alive. Don't they at least want to find out if he's okay?"

"Oh, your constables were definitely interested in Mr. Bell," Hertha said. "But not to rescue him—to arrest him."

"What?" Molly was flabbergasted.

"Edison wasn't kidding, Molly," Emmett said, shuffling through news articles. "He's put a load of work into framing Mr. Bell. Not only did the police find traces of dynamite among the wreckage of Bell's lab, but also a set of instructions—signed with Mr. Bell's personal stamp—outlining a plan to have his robots attack the Fair. And yes, the papers are calling them *robots*."

"Those are new papers?" Molly said. "How long was I out?"

"Nearly a full day," Sarah said. "It was almost this time last night when you were knocked out. If you'd stayed asleep any longer, we were about to bring you to a hospital, arrest warrant or not." She handed Molly a copy of the *Sun* with the headline ALEXANDER GRAHAM BELL: FUGITIVE! "That's from this morning," Sarah added as she rushed to the workshop door and opened it, giving Molly a glimpse of the twilight outside. "We should check the evening edition for developments."

While Hertha nodded to Sarah, Molly scanned the *Sun*'s front page in confusion. "But—but—if they believe Bell's guilty," Molly stammered, "does that mean they're releasing my mother?"

"Sadly, no," said Hertha. "They still believe Cass was an accomplice who betrayed her boss in an attempt to save herself. They're looking for you and Emmett too."

"Just us?" Molly asked. "But what about the three men in masks?"

"The police think they've already got them," Emmett said through gritted teeth. Molly had never seen him look so bitter. "An 'anonymous report' led police to discover masks in the apartment of three Chinese immigrants. Those poor men barely speak English. They couldn't defend themselves. They might not have even understood what they were being accused of!"

Edison was flat-out evil. He had to be stopped. And if the authorities weren't going to do it, Molly would. "So, it's on us," she said. "Same situation as yesterday. Except now there are more of us. We need evidence, so let's go get some evidence! The Fair is only a few days away. Stop fussing around in notebooks and finish that vehicle of yours so we can ride it to Menlo Park and raid Edison's main lab."

"The motor coach is days away from completion, Molly," Mary said.

"Emmett and I can help," Molly said.

"I got two hands too, Molly Pepper," Jasper chipped in. "And probably no more job at the factory, seeing as I been here all day and not there. I bet Balthazar Birdhouse has already claimed my coat hook."

"And my mother!" Molly added eagerly. "Let's go get her! We can—we can break her out of the asylum!"

She saw none of the enthusiasm she hoped to see on the women's faces, only pity.

"Come on, people," she said, clapping her hands. "We all know she's not supposed to be locked in there, so let's—"

The door opened and Sarah burst back in. "Sorry to interrupt, but things just got more complicated." She handed the evening paper to Hertha. "According to this, Alexander Graham Bell just kidnapped a bunch of other inventors: George Eastman, Nikola Tesla, Levi Strauss, and Thomas Edison. He left a note threatening to kill them if the police don't call off their manhunt."

Everyone in the room stopped to ponder this new development. Even Margaret slid out from under the motor coach.

"Well, we know Edison wasn't really kidnapped," Emmett finally said.

"Yes, but the others," Hertha said. "Are they victims? Or co-conspirators?"

"Levi Strauss? He makes pants!" Molly cried. "Look, this cinches it. We have to act now! If your motor buggy's not ready, we've got Jasper's ashcart."

"Oh, I don't know about that," Jasper said. "I think Prancey-Pie's still traumatized from her ordeal."

"And you, young lady, are not going anywhere, anyway," said Mrs. Cochrane from her throne across the room. "In fact, you should be back in bed until we're certain you're in good health."

"That's ridiculous! I feel fine!" Molly snapped. The last part was a lie—her head was pounding and her gut was churning. But the suggestion infuriated her. "It's my mother whose life is at stake!"

"There are many more lives at stake than just hers," Mary said, sounding almost apologetic. "Don't worry, Molly. We're more than capable of working out a plan. And once we've dealt with the most immediate crisis, we'll do what we can for your mother, I promise."

"I know more about what's going on here than any of you," Molly shouted. "You can't just send me to my room! I'm not your prisoner! Or am I?" A surge of dizziness swept over her and she stumbled. Jasper leapt forward to catch her.

Hertha stood up, took Molly's hand, and led her back to the small office room. "I understand you want to help, Molly, but I'm afraid I agree with Josephine. You suffered a severe blow in that building collapse. You may have a concussion. Rest here, get the sleep you need, and trust us. By the time you're up and ready to help, we'll be able to tell you exactly what to do." She pulled the lever that transformed the desk back into a bed, and sat Molly down on it.

Molly wanted to fight it, but her gut was clenching with spasms of nausea. She looked through the doorway to Emmett, her eyes pleading for him to help. He knelt beside the bed as Molly's head hit the pillow.

"I'm not going to argue against making sure you're healthy," he said.

"My mother—"

"You can't help your mother if you're unwell," Emmett said.

She stared at him silently, not wanting to admit he was right.

"You may not trust them," Emmett whispered. "But please trust me." Hertha led him back out and shut the door, leaving Molly alone in the dark to wonder whether or not she could do what her friend requested of her. She knew Emmett would never knowingly betray her. Knowingly.

Molly began to ponder where the Mothers of Invention hid *their* escape tunnel.

Hero's Tribute

WHEN THE DOOR cracked open the following morning, Molly assumed it was Emmett sneaking in to her, but she soon figured out it was Jasper.

"Are you decent, Molly Pepper?" the ashman whispered. He had his eyes closed and bumped his head into a bedpost.

"Yes." She'd been sleeping in her dress. "What's going on?"

Jasper quietly shut the door and fumbled for the pull-chain on the electric light overhead. "I know it's early and I don't like bein' the bearer of bad news," he said. "But I figured this ain't ancient Rome and you ain't gonna kill the messenger, especially when that messenger is sneaking information to a girl who's supposed to be recoverin' from a—"

"Jasper, what?"

He handed Molly a newspaper—a fresh one, still warm from the printing press.

BELL KILLED!
HERO EDISON SLAYS "MAD SCIENTIST," SAVES LIVES OF FELLOW INVENTORS

The article told of how one by one, four prominent Guildsmen had been rendered unconscious by an unknown gas, only to wake up prisoners of Alexander Graham Bell, bound and gagged on a boat in New York Harbor.

Who knows how many more of our revered inventors would have been stolen from us, had the brave Mr. Edison not managed to free himself and fight back.

"Edison was spectacular," said George Eastman. "He slipped out of his ropes and climbed up on deck to confront that hooligan Bell."

"Through the hatch, we see them struggle," confirmed Nikola Tesla. "I see not where the Edison get his knife from—he must grab it from the Bell. But soon the knife go in and, splash, the Bell go into the sea."

"Kidnapping is a rough and tumble ordeal," added Levi Strauss. "Thank heavens I was wearing a pair of my new Levi's dungarees, the pants that are ready for whatever life throws your way."

"This makes no sense," Molly said.

"I know," Jasper replied. "Why's he so excited about the pants? The pants didn't do anything."

"No, all of it," Molly said. She couldn't believe her actions had brought about the death of an innocent man—a man who'd sacrificed himself to save her. She put down the paper, so it wouldn't rustle in her trembling hands. "Why did Edison fake this kidnapping? If he was going to kill Bell, why didn't he just do it at Bandit's Roost and get it over with?"

"If the man's as full of himself as you and Emmett say, maybe he did it for the adoration." said Jasper. "That's the kind of thing Balthazar Birdhouse would do." He picked up the article and read the end of it to Molly. "'And thus, thanks to the courage of one man, any threat of danger at Friday's opening of the World's Fair is over. The State of New York and the World's Fair Committee will formally show their appreciation to the heroic Edison with a special medal of valor. Governor Grover Cleveland and former president Ulysses S. Grant will personally present the award to the daring inventor in a ceremony at noon today in Union Square.'"

"He wanted witnesses," Molly said with quiet horror. "Not just witnesses to Bell's death, but to his own heroism. With the public thinking Bell was still out there plotting, people would be scared to go to the Fair. Edison

237

not only solved that problem, but he's made it so that even *more* people will show up for his lighting ceremony. They'll all want to bask in the glorious glow of the *heroic Thomas Edison!*" It was hard for Molly to imagine how things could get any worse. "Has Emmett seen this yet?"

Jasper shook his head. "He's still sleeping. He was up real late with those inventors talking plans and such. They're all still out too, I think. Except maybe that one under the Marvelous Moto-Mover. I can't see if her eyes are closed or not."

"It's going to destroy Emmett to find out about Bell," Molly said, trying to quell her own sorrows.

"I'm just glad I didn't read this story before seein' with my own pretty eyes that you and Emmett were really safe and sound," Jasper said. "Or I'd be a blubbering mess right now."

Molly grabbed the paper again. "What do you mean, Jasper?"

"Oh, did you miss this part?" He pointed to a paragraph toward the end of the article and read, "'With tears in his eyes, Mr. Edison told police how Bell murdered the two poor children he'd had working for him.' See? So I'm talkin' to a ghost right now. With Bell dead and those Chinese fellas in jail, you and Emmett were the only two alleged fugitives left. Edison probably figures if you're dead in real life, why not write you out of his fake story too."

"The whole world will think we're dead," Molly muttered. She grabbed a bedpost to steady herself.

"On the bright side, the cops won't be bugging you anymore." He awkwardly patted her head.

"Jasper, you don't understand," Molly said. "The *whole world* will think we're dead. That includes my mother. She doesn't even know Bell's been framed. She'll think he actually murdered me! If she believes that, I don't know what she'll do. . . ." She slid out of bed and strapped her boots on. "I need you to sneak me out of here."

"Oh, Molly Pepper, I don't know about that."

She put her hands on the ashman's brawny shoulders and stared into his eyes. "Back in my pickle shop, I have a chest full of books that my father gave me before he died. They are my most prized possessions. If you help me now, they're yours." She sat back on the bed and pulled all four corners of the blanket up over herself. "Now lug me outta here like a bag of laundry and if anybody sees you, tell them I threw up on myself and you're dumping my dirty clothes."

In the darkness of her makeshift sack, she waited, hoping Emmett would understand, that he would forgive her, that they could still be friends when this was all over. But she didn't have the time to argue with him, to convince him they had to confront Edison directly, publicly. If she accused Edison right there in Union Square, in front of a crowd of fans and reporters, if she proved him a liar by revealing herself to be the very girl he claimed to have seen murdered, if she pulled out the "Dear MacDougal" letter and demanded a handwriting sample from Edison for comparison—for once, *he'd* be the one trapped. And even if it didn't work, the news would get out that she was still alive. And maybe that news would reach her mother.

Eventually, she heard Jasper sigh and felt herself lifted into the air.

32

A Face in the Crowd

As BOTH A former president and commanding general of the United States Army, Ulysses S. Grant had given many important speeches in his time, but Molly wondered if the man had any clue of the importance of his words that day—if he had any idea he was doing the dirty work of a homicidal madman.

"It is my great pleasure to officially announce that the 1883 World's Fair will open its gates to the public this Friday!" he declared into a megaphone, setting off a cascade of cheers from the hundreds packed around the wooden platform in Union Square. Molly watched from across the street, having climbed a tree in order to see over all the big, flamboyant hats in the crowd.

"And you have my assurance, as well as that of the noble and learned men beside me, that this will be the safest fair to have ever been held in this or any other nation, since the dawn of . . . fairs." There was another round of cheers, presumably for the former president's sentiment, and not his phrasing. Molly huffed with frustration, unable to spot Edison among the cluster of dark suits, pale skin, and facial hair crammed on the platform. She couldn't make her move until she was certain he was there.

"And while we on the planning committee would love to take credit," Grant said, "there's one man we need to thank more than anyone—the hero who saved this fair from the diabolical machinations of his own colleague. Ladies and gentlemen, the Wizard of Menlo Park and a true American treasure, Mr. Thomas Edison!"

Finally. Molly swung down from her tree as Edison hopped up from behind the platform, did a little tap dance, and got a gold medal placed around his neck by Governor Cleveland. Molly squeezed in among the hooting, clapping fools celebrating a man who wanted to kill them. But no one would be applauding Edison once she got to that stage and proved him a liar.

"Hello, New York!" Edison crowed through the big white cone. "Thanks for coming out today. You people are the best." Molly wanted to gag. "In fact, I love you all so much, I'm going to hit you with a little surprise. I was going to save this for the Fair, but then I said to myself, 'New York has had a rough week. These folks deserve a little magic *today.*'"

The crowd went wild as Edison tossed aside the big, clunky megaphone and rolled out a blocky machine with several knobs and dials on top. *His death machine!* Molly gasped. *He's going to use it now!* Molly covered her ears as a loud squealing sound filled the air. And then . . .

"HOW DO YOU LIKE ME NOW?"

Edison's voice boomed, loud enough to be clearly heard not only throughout the park, but probably for several blocks beyond.

Molly looked up. Edison was speaking into a small circular device that was wired to the machine he'd brought out. But his voice was far louder than it had been through the megaphone—an effect, presumably, of the machine.

"This little baby is my latest innovation," Edison said. "I call it the Vocal Empowernator, a sort of sonic amplifier, if you will."

Molly was relieved, until she saw a tall man with a prominent, jutting snaggletooth walk up behind Edison and whisper something in his ear. It was Tusk! Edison covered his speaking device with his hand, while the henchman pointed to Molly.

No! This was her only chance to confront Edison in public before the Fair. She had to make this happen. She couldn't have betrayed the MOI for nothing. She couldn't have betrayed Emmett on a gamble that didn't pan out. She *needed* to reach that stage before Tusk could reach her. She began pushing and shoving, moving as fast as she could through the tightly packed crowd.

"My apologies, folks," Edison said through the Empowernator. "My lab assistant just notified me of an emergency at the Guild Hall. Apparently one of my colleagues needs help screwing in a light bulb. Ha-ha! See you all on Wednesday!" He took his machine and dashed off, leaving a gaggle of bewildered politicians onstage.

"No! Wait!" Molly cried out. "Look down here! It's me, Molly Pepper! I'm alive! He lied!" But none of the men onstage stood a chance of hearing her over the angry grumblings of the frustrated crowd. The only person on that platform paying attention to Molly was Tusk. The henchman hopped down and started working through the crowd toward her.

"Rats," Molly hissed. She turned and saw Crikes heading up from the rear.

"Double rats," she said.

But the unhappy crowd was surging toward the stage too. "ED-I-SON! ED-I-SON!" they chanted.

"Where did he go? What do we do?" Ulysses S. Grant asked.

Grover Cleveland shrugged.

Molly felt like she was trying to swim against the current of a raging river. She started shoving harder, but to no avail. "Gotcha," Tusk said, grabbing her by the collar. "Now you're gonna—*erk!*" A thimble flew into the henchman's mouth. He dropped Molly and bent over, choking.

"Emmett!" Molly sputtered. "How?"

Emmett tossed aside Molly's Thimble Cannon, having used up its sole piece of ammunition. He grabbed her hand as Crikes ran past them to pound his blue-faced partner on the back.

Emmett headed toward the rear of the crowd, but Molly tugged him back toward the stage. "We have to get up there and tell everyone," she said.

"Edison's gone," Emmett yelled back over the roar of the crowd. "And those two aren't the only Onions here!"

Molly's head zipped back and forth. There were green-suited men heading toward them from every direction. "Triple rats."

Holding tight to each other, she and Emmett forged off into the least green section of the mob. "How did you find me?" Molly asked.

"You really think Jasper Bloom can keep a secret?" Emmett ducked past a screaming man with a WE LOVE T.A.E. sign. "And I would've figured it out anyway, as soon as I read the paper."

"So you know?"

"I can't believe Mr. Bell is gone." He looked like he might have teared up if he hadn't needed to jump over a shrieking Edison fan who tripped into his path. They stumbled out of the throng onto University Place.

"Listen, Emmett," Molly began.

"Save it," he shot back. "I know everything you're

gonna say. You're sorry. You feel terrible about abandoning me. You'll never do it again. You'll— Oh, drat! Here they come!"

Green Onion Boys were pouring from the crowd, first one, then three, then seven. The gangsters charged after the children as they tore down the street toward Washington Square Park. Already out of breath, Molly didn't see how they'd be able to outrun them. "I finally want to see a cop," she panted. "And not a smidge of blue in sight!"

"I don't see anybody, period," Emmett puffed.

"They're all back at Union Square." Molly's legs were getting wobbly. "You came alone?"

"The MOI are not happy with you," Emmett replied. "They're doing things their way. You're on your own."

"Not anymore." She would have liked to have flashed him a smile, but her sides were aching too much. And the Onions were gaining on them. She stumbled again.

"You're still injured," Emmett said, reaching out to steady her. "You're not gonna make it."

"No, look!" she said, pointing to the next corner. It wasn't police, but it was the next best thing: a Jägerman was harassing a young flower-seller.

"Hey, baby cop!" Molly yelled. "Leave that small fry alone; take us!"

The Jäger agent looked up, perplexed. The flower girl fled as Molly cried, "We're orphans! Take us in!"

"Um, yeah," Emmett said, with less gusto. "We're, uh, turning ourselves in. . . . Molly, is this the best—?"

Molly squinted to read the man's badge. "Don't stand there, Agent Humbert," she barked. "Cuff us!"

"Um, we don't carry handcuffs," the Jägerman said. "And the name's Hubbard."

Molly glanced over her shoulder. The Onions were still heading their way. "No time for this, Hubbard. Do your job!" She marched past the agent, yanked open the rear door of the Jäger Society wagon by the curb, and climbed inside. She motioned for Emmett to join her and, hesitantly, he did. She shut the door.

She and Emmett both held their breath—and not just because of the foul stench in the dark, dank wagon.

"I hope you know what you're doing," Emmett finally said.

"Whatever home the Jägers put us into will be far easier to bust out of than the dungeon Oogie MacDougal likely had waiting for us. If he'd even let us live."

Emmett said nothing.

"Thank you," Molly said. "For coming for me."

"You'd have done the same for me."

"Darn right, I would've," Molly said. And she meant it. Emmett had quickly become the second most important person in her life. And she did feel terrible about abandoning him earlier. "It almost worked, you know. My plan. Edison got scared. He ran."

"It wasn't a *bad* plan," Emmett said.

"I just shouldn't have tried it alone. Lesson learned. Give me your hand."

She spat into her palm and reached out into the dark space before her. She was grateful to find Emmett's hand waiting for hers. "We never separate again," she said. "That's my promise."

"Did you spit in your hand?"

"Yeah, to make it an official oath."

"That's a disgusting oath. I'd have believed you without the spit."

They could hear Agent Hubbard talking to someone outside and Molly bit her lip, praying that the Green Onion Boys wouldn't somehow talk this Jägerman into handing them over. She breathed a sigh of relief when the talking stopped and the wagon began rolling. She'd done it. She'd masterfully avoided capture by the Green Onion Boys and was feeling better than ever about her strategic prowess. Edison might think he had a plan for every eventuality, but he hadn't planned for Molly Pepper.

Sometime later, the wagon stopped and the back door opened.

"Out!" a uniformed police officer called. He pulled Emmett down and handed him over to two men in dark suits.

"Hey, this isn't the Jäger Society," Emmett sputtered

as one of the officers pulled his hands behind his back and slapped a pair of handcuffs on him. Molly leaned out and saw a bronze sign on a stark stone wall. IMMIGRA-TION ENFORCEMENT. The Jägerman shoved her back inside the wagon. "Not you."

"But—" Molly barely had a chance to register the look of terror on Emmett's face before the slamming door separated them.

The wagon rolled off once more. Molly pounded on the wall behind the driver. "What are you doing? What's happening to Emmett?" she yelled. "You can't send him away! He's got nobody! He'll be alone! I'll be alone!"

"Settle down," the Jägerman called from the other side. "By tomorrow, you'll be in a real home, with a real family. So sit back and enjoy the ride. Oh, and by the way, Mr. Edison sends his regards."

Molly didn't sit back; she screamed. She screamed and she pounded with all her might. She screamed and pounded and promised herself she would run as fast as she could the moment those doors opened. And that she would not let anyone stop her. She screamed and she pounded and she promised until no more noise could come out of her mouth and she no longer had the strength to raise a fist. Until hours had passed, and she could do no more than lay her head down on the dirty floor and let sleep overtake her.

PART III

Queen of the Orphans

MOLLY DREAMED OF an earthquake, of angry titans thrashing about, shaking her world, leaving no safe place to hide. Walls rattled and the floor rumbled beneath her feet. But worst of all was the loud, piercing whistle.

Whistle?

Molly opened her eyes and sat bolt upright. "Holy whipsnorters, I'm on a train!"

"Oh, gee, is that what this is?" snarked a pointy-nosed girl with mop-like hair who sat across the aisle. She was one of the two dozen young, grime-smudged girls who filled the train car. "I thought we'd been swallowed by a big iron snake."

"Put a pin in it," Molly snapped back. She'd always wanted to experience train travel. Books made it seem so luxurious—plush seats, porters doling out refreshments, lush scenery sweeping past the windows. But the thin padding on these seats wasn't quite worthy of the name "cushion," no one was serving anything, and the window shades were all closed. "No time for fribbledy-frapp!" Molly said. "I need answers! Where are we and how did I get here?"

Mop-Head shrank back. "Um, we're on the Orphan Train," she said meekly. "You were asleep when that guy brought you on."

Her terrifying experience with Edison's crooked Jägerman surged back into her mind. *The Orphan Train.* At least that explained why every passenger was under twelve and in dire need of a bath. Molly had read about the Orphan Train in the *Sun.* Rather than cram the city's overstuffed orphanages with more neglected kids, the Orphan Rescue Society was shipping them out of town. It sounded all well and good for those who genuinely needed new families, but Molly had a perfectly good mother, thank you very much.

"I'm not supposed to be here," Molly said. "I have a mother."

"So?" said Mop-Head. "Half these girls probably got mothers somewhere. But if your ma don't want you—"

Molly leapt into the aisle and Mop-Head practically jumped into the lap of the thumb-sucking redhead next to her. "My mother wants me," Molly said. "The only reason she's not here with me—"

"Is 'cause she's not an orphan?" shouted a tiny girl in the next row, who seemed very proud of herself despite having a finger halfway up her nose.

Molly rolled her eyes. "No, I . . . My mother's in an asylum for the criminally insane."

"Ooh, that's more interesting," cooed Tiny Girl.

"She's not really insane," Molly said, frustrated. "She's the victim of an evil conspiracy!"

The thumb-sucker plucked a shiny wet digit from her mouth. "Wow, this story gets better every time you say something."

"It's not a story—it's my life!"

"Then, please, tell us about your life," said Mop-Head, leaning in eagerly. "This trip has been *really* boring."

Molly glanced at the pleading eyes around her. *Why not?* She started with the breakdown of the Icarus Chariot and ended an hour later with, "So now I have to get off this train so I can rescue Emmett *and* my mother."

"You," said Tiny Girl, "are the most interesting person I've ever met."

"Do any of you know whenabouts we're supposed to stop next?" Molly asked. "I'm gonna hop off wherever and find my way back downtown." She lifted the window shade. Nothing but grass and shrubbery.

"Um, I'm pretty sure we're long past downtown," said Mop-Head.

A red barn came into view, and fields of grazing cattle.

"Western Pennsylvania, I reckon," said Thumb-Sucker. "The old ladies said we should reach Cincinnati by dinner."

Cincinnati? Molly stared out at the alien landscape. There were already two states and several rivers between her and her mother, and the World's Fair was in two days. She had to get off the train immediately.

"I'm jumping," she announced. "Who's with me?"

The other girls stared. "Um, I think most of us kinda wanna be here," Tiny Girl said apologetically.

Of course they did. They had new beginnings waiting for them at the end of this ride. For Molly, there would only be an ending. "Well, wish me luck," she said. Walking on a moving train turned out to be an adventure unto itself. Every rocky step threatened to send Molly for a tumble, and she had to grab seat backs for balance several times. But soon enough, she reached the rear door, through which she could see nothing but open sky. She opened it and stepped out onto a wrought-iron ledge.

"Young woman!" came a shout from behind her. A grandmotherly type had entered the car, pushing a small food cart. She wore spectacles—of course!—and a thick gray sweater. "Get back inside this second! No children outside the train car!"

Now or never, Molly thought, stepping to the edge. The tracks spooled out rapidly beneath her, much faster than she'd anticipated. That jump was going to hurt. Badly.

And although she suspected she could still walk back to New York with one broken leg, two might be pushing it.

She huffed and returned to her seat.

After handing out both apples and warnings against horseplay, the scowling old woman pulled all the window shades down "to avoid unwanted stimulation." The moment she vanished back through the car's front exit, Molly stood on her seat. "Okay, ladies, you need to help me get off this train."

"Hee-hee. *Ladies*," Tiny Girl giggled. Her finger was back up her nose.

"Look, everything I told you is true," Molly said. "Thousands of people are going to die if I don't make it back to New York to stop Edison."

"Why don't you just tell the Orphan Rescue ladies about it?" Thumb-Sucker asked.

"Right now, those old ladies assume I'm some random kid. Which is fortunate, because I'm technically still wanted for attempting to assassinate the—"

The door opened and Molly froze. In walked Agent Hubbard, the Jägerman who had arrested—no, *abducted*—her. He walked down the aisle to her, frowning and holding a small stool. "They told me to get you as far from New York as possible," he grumbled. "They didn't warn me you'd be a jumper." He continued on to the rear exit and stepped outside with his little stool.

"Don't make me come back in here," he warned coldly before shutting the door.

"That's the Jägerman who kidnapped you," Thumb-Sucker helpfully explained, before returning to the remarkable feat of biting an apple without gnawing off her thumb in the process.

"Yeah, I remember him," Molly said dully.

"We're on a train with . . . a *killer*?" asked Tiny Girl.

"I doubt he's killed anybody," Molly said. "The Onions probably just paid him off after Emmett and I climbed into his wagon like morons."

"I still think we should maybe tell the old ladies about the killers," Tiny Girl said.

"Nuh-uh," said Mop-Head. "The old ladies are probably working *with* the killers!"

"Everyone relax," Molly said, hoping to calm the concerned murmuring that was bubbling up. "I'm sure the Orphan Rescue Society had no idea what this Hubbard guy is up to. They're not trying to hurt anybody. I mean, they just fed us."

Several girls began spitting out half-chewed apple bits.

"Tell us the truth: Are we in danger?" Tiny Girl grabbed the front of Molly's dress. "Are we on some kind of perilous journey?"

"Yes!" Molly stood up. "Of course we are. Look at us. We're all orphans or half-orphans or unwanted kids.

We've been living in tiny rooms or filthy alleys or abandoned book carts. We've been dining on bread crusts and cheese rinds. We've all been hungry and tired and sick, and we've had to will ourselves to get better and move on, because it's not as if we had another choice. And on top of that, we're girls! What *hasn't* been hard for us? What *hasn't* felt dangerous? So, yeah, we're all on a perilous journey. And we should feel pretty darn good about ourselves for surviving this far. But: think how much easier it'll be if we look out for one another."

The girls stared.

"You're not just talking about this train ride, are you?" said Mop-Head.

THUMP!

"What was that?" asked Tiny Girl.

"Something hit my window," said a girl toward the front of the car. "From outside."

THUMP!

"It's by me now!" shouted another, a few rows farther back.

"Is it one of those robot things you told us about?" Tiny Girl sputtered.

"Oh, *please* let it be one of those robot things," said Mop-Head, holding her hands together in prayer.

THUMP!

Molly threw open the shade and saw Emmett's face staring in at her.

34

The Great Train Rescue

THE GIRLS SCREAMED so loudly that Emmett nearly lost his grip on whatever he was clinging to outside the train.

"Keep it down!" Molly warned. "It's Emmett!" She pushed her face to the glass for a better look. Emmett was balanced on a long plank, his fingers in a vise-like grip around its edges. The swaying plank extended from a vehicle that was rolling alongside the chugging steam train. "The Marvelous Moto-Mover!" Molly cried. Hertha was at the wheel, with leather goggles over her eyes and a jaunty scarf flapping at her neck. Mary Walton, ever in her knit cap, sat at her side. Behind them, Sarah Goode waved enthusiastically and Margaret Knight tinkered feverishly with some new invention in her lap. Josephine Cochrane sat in the last row, working hard to hold a large-brimmed, orchid-trimmed hat on her head.

"Where's the horses?" asked Tiny Girl, as every window shade in the car shot up and all the kids piled onto Molly's side to look. "How's it moving?"

"Are those the Science Mothers you told us about?" asked Mop-Head, pressing her nose to the glass. "Whoa. I didn't know inventors got to ride big magic bathtubs. I wanna be an inventor too!"

Molly nudged past the others into the aisle. "They're here to rescue me," she said. "I've got to get out to them before the Jägerman sees."

"Um, too late for that," said Thumb-Sucker.

The rear door burst open. "That craziness outside has something to do with you, don't it?" Agent Hubbard waggled an angry finger at Molly. "I shoulda asked for more money." He began shoving children out of his way.

Molly felt trapped until Mop-Head grinned at her and said, "Go. We got this." Molly nodded and started for the front of the car, as orphans clogged the aisle behind her.

"Move!" Hubbard bellowed.

"Yes, sir," Mop-Head replied. She and several others began wriggling in place. "We're moving, sir! As requested!"

"You know that's not what I meant," the man growled. Tiny Girl skittered onto his shoulders like a squirrel up a tree.

While the girls distracted the Jägerman, Molly stepped out into the loud, windy, open-air space between cars. Where was Emmett? Holding the rail of a metal ladder for balance, she tried to lean out past the edge of the car for a look when a particularly bumpy rail almost sent her flying to her doom. She ignored the lump in her throat, and tugged open the door to the next car. It was full of orphan boys, all of whom turned to look.

"You again!" shouted the old woman in glasses. "What are you doing? Where's that nice man?"

"He's not a nice man," Molly said. "Thomas Edison paid him to kidnap—ugh, never mind. I've got a Moto-Mover to catch." The woman shoved her cart aside and marched toward Molly, and whooping orphan boys quickly pounced upon the spilled apples.

Molly popped back outside and shut the door again just as Agent Hubbard struggled out of the girls' car, shaking Tiny Girl from his leg.

"Oh, no, you don't," he sneered at Molly. But she was already on her way up the ladder. The train rocked and the wind whipped against her face and she had to drop flat to avoid being blown away. As she crawled, gruelingly, across the roof, she wondered whether the idea of President Edison was really *that* bad. Then she heard Sarah shout, "She's on top!" Molly pulled herself to the edge and looked down to see the motor coach bring itself alongside the boys' car.

"Hiya, Goosey," she hollered.

"You. Owe. Me. So. Much," Emmett grunted, his arms

262

and legs wrapped tightly around the plank.

"You're going to need to help the young girl down, Mr. Lee," called Mrs. Cochrane.

The motor buggy bounced over a large rock and Emmett yelped. "Yikes!"

"*Tsk!* Language, young man," Mrs. Cochrane scolded.

"Keep her steady, Hertha," said Mary. "No sharp moves."

"Thanks for the advice, love," Hertha replied in her droll British accent. "I'd been thinking about a fun little zigzag just now, but since you suggest otherwise . . ."

Molly reached down to her friend.

"You can do it, Emmett," Sarah encouraged him. "Believe in yourself!"

"I do," Emmett shouted. "I believe in myself. I'm here, I exist. If I didn't, this wouldn't be so terrifying."

"Then believe in us too," Sarah returned. "We built this thing! And we know what we're doing!"

Emmett held his breath and reached up. Molly stretched as far as she could and wrapped her hand around Emmett's—just as Hubbard appeared behind her and grabbed her legs. Molly became the rope in a human tug-of-war.

"Who are those ladies?" the Jägerman sputtered. "And what the holy heck are they riding in?"

"Language," scolded Mrs. Cochrane.

"The children are in a bad spot, Margaret," Mary said. "Are you finished?"

"Fourteen seconds," came the reply.

"Make it twelve, darling," Hertha called out. "Some fool put a curve in the track up ahead."

"Done!" Margaret stood up, whipped off her goggles, and raised what looked like a combination musket-teakettle-garden hose. She squirted a stream of yellow goop that splattered across Agent Hubbard's chest, knocked him backward, and pinned him to the roof of the train.

"What in the—?"

"Language!" warned Mrs. Cochrane.

Free from Hubbard's grasp, Molly went flying to Emmett. But their momentum was about to send them both tumbling from the thin plank, until—*SPLORT!*—a glob of Margaret's adhesive stuck her and Emmett in place.

Emmett looked astonished to be alive. "I've never been happier to be covered in sticky goop," he said. "In fact, I've never been *happy* to be covered in sticky goop."

Sarah flipped a switch and the long plank began to retract into the side of the vehicle. As soon as they were close enough, she and Margaret pried the children free and helped them into the motor coach. Safe inside, Molly waved to the baffled Jägerman. The Moto-Mover continued across the field as the train veered south. Smoke puffs on the horizon were soon the only sign they'd ever been near a locomotive.

Molly couldn't believe she was free and safe, or that she was on her way back to New York, or that she was riding in a *horseless carriage*. On the outside, the vehicle was sleek and lustrous, a majestic purple with glints of chrome reflecting from the spinning wheels. The interior was as lush as a sultan's palace—velvet cushions and fine-grained wood paneling. A tantalizing array of buttons, switches, and meters flanked the steering wheel, and when Molly craned her neck, she could see a series of pedals at Hertha's feet. But how was the motor coach able to move so smoothly and quietly over such bumpy terrain? Where were the chugging noises and thick clouds of soot? For the first time, Molly wondered whether there was a smidgen of merit to Jasper's theory about Jules Verne.

"The Marvelous Moto-Mover is even more marvelous than I'd imagined!" Molly shouted. "And I have a good imagination!"

"You haven't even seen its best trick yet," said Sarah.

Molly grinned giddily. "I'm surrounded by fairy-tale wizards!"

"In a fairy tale, they'd call us witches," said Hertha.

"*Only* in a fairy tale?" Mrs. Cochrane chimed in. "Which reminds me . . ." She pulled a book from a compartment on the seat back in front of her and began reading. Molly raised an eyebrow.

"One need not forgo leisure simply due to the presence

of mortal peril," Mrs. Cochrane said. She opened a second compartment and retrieved a steaming cup of tea.

"I thought it was going to take you days to get the Moto-Mover ready," Molly said.

"*Somebody* left us no choice but to work faster," Hertha said in a clipped tone. "Because she sneaked off on her own and let some corrupt public servants throw her onto a train and—"

"You can stop. I know it's me," Molly said. "I'm sorry. And thank you."

"You should really thank your friend Jasper," Mary said. "If he hadn't seen you two carted off by the Jägermen, we would never have known what happened to you."

"I never thought I'd be so glad to have a friend who can't keep his nose out of my business," Molly laughed. "But how'd you get Emmett from the immigration guys? Emmett, are you safe from deportation now?"

"Until they realize the papers Hertha gave them were forgeries," he said. "I'm just glad we got you back. It's been a long day." He rested his head on Molly's shoulder and promptly dozed off.

Content for the first time in ages, Molly leaned back and marveled at the passing scenery—waving wheat fields flanked by dense woodland, shy farmhouses hiding behind crowds of lumbering cattle, and mountains, real mountains, rolling along the horizon as if on an enormous conveyor belt. There was so much to the world beyond New York. How much more of it would she get to see? And would her mother be by her side as she did? These questions were running through Molly's mind as the motor coach slowly rolled to a stop along an old dirt path in the middle of a desolate scrubland.

"Drat," said Hertha.

"Language."

"Are we here?" Emmett asked, sitting up.

"Far from it, I'm afraid," Hertha said, re-closing the hatch that allowed her access to the motor. "It seems our battery has belched forth its last spark."

"You mean this thing can't go any farther?" Molly asked, not caring to hide her frustration. "Your battery didn't have enough power to get us back to Manhattan?"

"I would've loved to have spent more time charging it," Hertha said curtly. "But *someone* got herself carted off by—"

"Okay, okay, I get it!" Molly lowered her eyes. "So, what now?"

Hertha peered down the long, empty trail. "Walking shoes, ladies." The women all changed shoes and began climbing out of the Moto-Mover.

Molly and Emmett exchanged glances. "But we're in Pennsylvania," Molly said. "That's a loooooong walk. We won't get to New York until—"

"One forty-eight p.m. on Wednesday," said Margaret.

"I told you one of us should have stayed behind in New York," said Mrs. Cochrane.

"You wanted to stay behind so you could make us all matching outfits for the Fair," chided Mary.

"We'd have been the height of fashion," said Mrs. Cochrane.

"Maybe we can hire a coach along the way," Sarah said, unrolling a map. "We can do this," she said. "Believe in yourselves, ladies! And Emmett."

"But—but can't we just fix the Moto-Mover?" Molly cried. "Can't we . . . recharge the battery?"

"Not unless you know of a place between here and Manhattan that has an electric generator," said Hertha.

Emmett dove for Sarah's map. "How far are we from Menlo Park, New Jersey?"

Lab Break-In №3 (or Is It №4?)

TREKKING DOWN LONG stretches of lonely road for miles on end would have been a grueling enough task on its own. Doing so while pushing a dead, thousand-pound motor coach did not improve the experience—especially after the sun went down. It was nearly morning—precisely 3:57 a.m. according to Margaret's goggle clock—on Wednesday, May 30, opening day of the World's Fair, when they spotted the soft electric glow of Menlo Park, home of Thomas Edison's flagship laboratory. As weary and on-edge as they were, they still couldn't help smiling as they walked along Christie Street, the first roadway in the nation to have electric streetlights.

Thankfully, the town's residents were asleep at this hour, and the travelers reached their destination unnoticed—a corner property obscured by a tall picket fence.

Margaret removed a lockpick from one of her many belts and the gate was quickly opened. They left the Moto-Mover by the curb (with Josephine Cochrane volunteering to remain with it as lookout) and filed into the yard with much trepidation.

Molly frowned. Edison's world-famous research lab was even more boring than Bell's secret workshop. It was a house. A pleasant country house with an overgrown lawn. Laboratories were supposed to be tall and bricky with lots of pipes and chimneys jutting from them. Or steel and glass with lightning rods and rocket tubes. They certainly didn't have porch swings and gabled roofs. Menlo Park looked more like a place for shucking corn than manufacturing death machines.

"Exercise caution," Hertha warned. "The Fair opens later today, so Edison himself should be in New York. But there could be any number of henchmen, traps, or alarms inside."

Margaret made short work of the front door locks, scouted the interior, and gave the all clear. The others stepped inside as Margaret flipped on the turnip-shaped lights hanging in brass fixtures overhead. Molly's eyes went straight to a wall of shelves that held a seemingly endless array of glass canisters. She scanned the labels: Magnesium, Ammonium Nitrate, Phosphorus, Amber, Rubber, Horse Hair, Rabbit Hair, Goat Hair, Minx Hair, Human Hair, Deer Hooves, Tortoiseshell, Shark Teeth,

Peacock Feathers . . . "I know they call Edison the Wizard of Menlo Park," she said, "but I didn't think he was mixing actual potions."

"Shh," Emmett warned, crouching in expectation of an ambush.

"It's okay, kid," Margaret said. "I'm pretty sure we're alone in here."

"Yes, but stay focused," said Hertha. "We need to find that generator fast."

A pipe organ at the far end of the room caught Molly's eye. "Does Edison play music?" she asked, sitting down at the keyboard. "Because I heard he's deaf."

"Beethoven was deaf," Mary said as she peered under a table. "And Edison's not totally deaf in both ears, anyway. Just the left from what I've read."

"Really?" Molly puzzled over this bit of trivia. Something about it struck her as important. She absent-mindedly tapped some random keys and the organ screeched out a string of loud, long, cacophonous notes. The others covered their ears.

"Believe it or not," Molly said, "I've never had a single lesson."

A hidden door slid open on the wall next to the organ and Thomas Edison stepped into the light. "It's about time," Edison said. "Thank you, little girl, for being such a dismal piano player and—*aagh!*"

Molly launched herself from the organ stool and

271

knocked the inventor to the floor, where she proceeded to pound on him mercilessly. "You made me lose my mother! You evil, wicked beast!"

"Wha—? Why are—? Help!" Edison cried. There was a clinking of metal as he shielded his head from Molly's blows. "Please! Get her off me!"

"Stop, Molly," Emmett said. "Look, he's in chains."

Her teeth still gritted in fury, she glanced down. The man's wrists and ankles were shackled, with clanking links snaking back into the hidden room from which he'd emerged. Molly climbed off him as the others gathered around.

"What's going on here?" Emmett asked. "What are you up to?"

Edison rose cautiously. "So you're not here to rescue me?"

"Rescue you?" Molly scoffed. "You *belong* in chains after everything you've done!"

Edison furrowed his thick brows. "I take it you've had a run-in with that charlatan. Well, I assure you I am the real Edison. So, if one of you could kindly free me from these—"

"*Real* Edison?" Hertha asked skeptically.

"Yes, if you've heard some maniac spouting off about a ruckus at the World's Fair, I assure you that was not me! I've been locked in here for . . . well, months. I've lost track. Has the Fair happened yet? Did that jelly-faced wretch perform *my* lighting ceremony?"

"That suit certainly smells like it hasn't been washed in months," said Mary.

"Even if there are two Edisons," said Sarah, "how do we know you're not the imposter?"

"Seriously?" Edison said with a sigh. "Fine. Could the false Edison do this?" He tapped out a jaunty soft-shoe dance routine.

"Actually, yes," said Molly. "Yes, he can."

Edison huffed. "Well, mine would've been better with my hands free."

"He definitely *sounds* like Edison . . . ," said Emmett.

"I'm the real me!" he cried, rattling his chains. "Months cooped up in my own secret closet while a madman runs around besmirching my good name, and when I finally think someone's been smart enough to figure it out and free me, I instead get mauled by some elephant-eared waif!"

"Oh, that's a cheap shot," Emmett said angrily. "If you—"

"Emmett, wait!" Molly said with sudden inspiration. "I know how to tell if he's lying. With one simple question."

"What? What? Please, ask it," Edison said. "I apologize for the crack about your ears."

Molly stood on the piano stool and whispered into Edison's left ear. The inventor immediately turned and offered her the right. "This ear, sweetheart," he said.

Molly hopped down. "He's telling the truth. Deaf in the left. You can free him."

"How do you know he's not faking?" Hertha asked.

"Back in Union Square, I saw Tusk whisper into Edison's left ear," Molly said. "That guy—whoever it was—had no problem hearing him. It wasn't really Edison. It didn't hit me until now."

"Yes, yes, see? *I'm* Thomas Edison!" He sounded hopeful. "The man you saw must have been Vittorini."

"Sergio Vittorini?" Molly gasped. "The actor?"

"Yes, he's the one who locked me in here and started ranting about his plans for global domination," said Edison. "'First the World's Fair, then the world!' Nonsense like that."

"No wonder he was able to fool so many people," Mary said. "I daresay he's earned his reputation as the Man of a Thousand and Twelve Faces."

"And he's been performing at the Madison Square Theatre," Emmett added excitedly. "He's been spying on the Guild Hall from right next door!"

"Flaming flapjacks," Molly blurted. "That day at the Guild Hall, when my mother and I saw Edison come in and sign autographs, and then ten minutes later we saw Vittorini coming out through the alley between buildings—it was the same guy! He'd just taken off his Edison costume. And he must have followed us, Emmett.

That's how he found his way to Bell's secret lab!"

"This is all very interesting," said Hertha. "But why is a stage actor doing all of this?"

"Exactly! You'd think Vittorini would be grateful to me after I let him star in so many of my kinetoscope films," said Edison. "The man in 'Man Sneezing'—that was him. And the man who jumps over the hat in 'Man Jumping Over a Hat.' He was even the horse in 'Man Kicked by Horse.'"

"Again, very interesting," said Hertha. "But still not an answer to my question."

"If it's questions you're interested in, here's a good one," said Edison. "Who the heck are you people?"

"We are the Mothers of Invention," declared Hertha as Margaret used a miniature blowtorch to cut through Edison's shackles. "And I'm afraid Vittorini aims to follow through on his threats about the Fair."

The women introduced themselves and recounted the imposter's plot while Edison checked himself out in a mirror and grumbled about the sorry state of his suit. "Well, I thank you ladies for liberating me," he finally said. "I'll have my secretary send you a casserole. At the moment, however, I must rush off to New York to stop a madman."

"That's what *we're* doing," said Molly. "We just need to borrow your generator so we can charge the battery on our Marvelous Moto-Mover."

"It's an electric-powered horseless carriage," Mary

Walton explained, noting the man's puzzled expression. "It'll get us to Manhattan in less than two hours."

Edison laughed. "You women should write romance novels. You've got quite extraordinary imaginations."

"Thank you, but we'll stick to being inventors," said Hertha.

"Inventors?" Edison echoed, apparently not having picked up on the group's name. "Like, with inventions?"

"What do you think I used to cut through your shackles just now?" Margaret asked.

"Something one of my men left on his desk, I assumed." Edison shrugged. "Look, if you ladies fancy yourself inventors, have at it. As repayment for aiding me, I offer you free use of this lab. And I hope you understand what a privilege that is. I'm letting you work in a place where men make history! This is, of course, where I invented the light bulb."

"You mean you improved upon the design of the bulb, right?" Molly said. This Edison was better than the one who repeatedly tried to kill them, but he still rubbed her the wrong way.

Edison cleared his throat. "As I said, use anything you want. Including the generator, which is in that back room. But, really now, I must be going."

"Why not just call the Guild from here and warn them about the imposter?" Hertha asked. "You must have a telephone."

"One of Bell's ringy-dingy talk boxes here in Menlo Park? Ha!" Edison said haughtily. "I'd never give that showy Scotsman the satisfaction. Which reminds me, you should probably free him too." Edison pointed back toward the secret prison.

Gasping with disbelief, Molly and Emmett ran in to find Alexander Graham Bell sound asleep in the corner.

Ghost Sightings

BELL GROGGILY OPENED his eyes. "Emmett? Oh, no, he got you too?"

"No, we're here to rescue you," Emmett said.

"Technically, we're here to steal a generator from Edison," said Molly. "But we're happy to rescue you too."

Emmett nodded. "Yeah, me and Molly and the Mothers of Invention."

As Margaret cut through Bell's shackles, Hertha turned to Edison. "Why didn't you tell us he was in here?"

"I just did," Edison replied defensively. "And you would've heard him eventually. The man snores like a drowning badger."

"I'm so glad you're okay, Mr. Bell," Emmett said, helping his mentor from the cell. "I can't believe Sergio

Vittorini is behind all this. He *really* looked like Edison."

"And to think I had tickets to the man's show!" Bell said. "Although I suppose it would have been good."

"Mr. Bell," said Hertha after all introductions had been made. "Do *you* have any idea why Vittorini might be doing all this?"

"Not the foggiest."

Everyone jumped as the front door was kicked open. "Excuse me, ladies," yelled Josephine Cochrane, "but would any of you be so kind as to help me with these two ogres?" She was dragging two unconscious Green Onion Boys by the collars.

"Josephine," Hertha said, helping to tie up the gangsters. "How did you manage—? No, better left to the imagination."

"I agree," said Mrs. Cochrane. "And as I am a proper lady, I will withhold any sarcastic comments about those among us who did not believe I should remain outside as lookout."

"Vittorini probably sent those goons for Bell and Edison," Mary said. "When they don't return, he'll be onto us. We have to get to Central Park fast."

Bell looked at a clock. "We'll never make it before the lighting ceremony."

"What takes five or six hours by horse can be done in two by motor coach," said Mary. "We just need to charge our battery."

"Oh, you were serious about that?" Edison said. "Well, okay then, let's get that battery. I wouldn't mind taking a gander at this Moto-Whatsit you say you've constructed."

Bell joined Margaret as they ran outside. Margaret returned lugging a hatbox-sized cube with wires sprouting from it, and Edison pointed her to the back room with the generator. Bell followed, rolling a wheeled cabinet with a small round lens on its front and a crank handle on its side. "Found this in the criminals' wagon," he said.

"It looks like one of my kinetoscopes," said Edison. "That thief better not be ripping off my ideas too."

"But Mr. Edison," Molly asked, "didn't you base your kinetoscope on that Frenchman's moving picture machine?"

"Why is this girl here again?" Edison asked.

"The device contains a message meant for us, Tom," Bell said. "The note here says, 'Play for prisoners before bringing them back to NY.'"

"Well, let's check this doohickey out," said Edison. He placed his eye to the lens and began turning the crank, but jumped back as a bright light blared forth from within. Unlike Edison's kinetoscope, there was no need to look into this machine.

Everyone gaped at the blue-tinted figure projected onto the wall. It moved like a portrait come to life—or a ghost trapped in a two-dimensional state. But what shocked Molly most was that she knew the man on the wall; she'd seen him before. As had almost everyone in the room.

"It is I," said the man in the film. "Sergio Vittorini!"

Everyone gasped. Edison stopped cranking and jumped away. "It's talking! How is it talking?" Then his shock turned to anger and he tried to pry the machine open with his fingers. "Did he put one of my phonographs in here too? How dare the villain try to improve upon my work!"

Hertha pushed him aside and took over the cranking.

Vittorini removed his curly hair and detached the long braids from his beard to reveal another familiar face.

"And now it is I," the actor said with a soft Scottish accent. "Alexander Graham Bell."

"Don't look at me like that," said the real Bell. "It's obviously not me!"

The villain slipped off yet another wig and ripped away his remaining facial hair, uncovering a visage that looked remarkably like Thomas Edison.

"And now, I'm Thomas Edison," the imposter crowed.

"You people really thought that was me?" the true Edison said. "Pathetic."

In the film, the ersatz Edison peeled off his thick, bushy eyebrows and threw them down like a pair of severed squirrel tails. He then peeled away a fake chin and plucked a stretchy rubber nose from his face. When all was done, Molly was left looking at a face she didn't recognize at all—a plain, generic face. The guy was blander than bland, utterly forgettable. Molly wondered if she'd even be able to recognize him again if she saw him at the Fair.

"And finally, the real me," said the boring-looking man. "Your superior, your captor, your future lord and master. Ambrose Rector! And you—"

"Stop the film!" Emmett cried, and Hertha ceased her cranking. "How can that be Ambrose Rector?" Emmett asked. "Ambrose Rector's dead. He went down with the *Frost Cleaver*. Years ago."

"That's what I thought too," muttered Bell. His eyes were glazed over. He looked terrified, as if the image on the screen really was a ghost.

"It does look like him, though," said Edison. "I think. He didn't have what you'd call a memorable face."

"So this Rector fellow is really the fake Edison?" Sarah asked. "*And* he's Sergio Vittorini?"

Emmett furrowed his brow. "But—but Rector died with my father," he said. Then his eyes lit up. "Is my father alive too?"

"Who's your father?" Edison asked.

"Your father could be alive, Emmett!" Molly shouted, grabbing her friend's hands.

"Who's his father?" Edison asked.

"But—but—oh, wow. To see my father again," Emmett said, shaking his head. "I've spent three years believing my father was gone forever. And now, suddenly ... What would I say to him?"

"Will somebody please tell me who the boy's father is!" Edison steamed.

"Captain Wendell Lee," Bell said. "He was at the helm of the *Frost Cleaver* when it went down en route to Antarctica. The same wreck in which we all thought Rector died. Now I'm beginning to wonder if Rector was responsible for that disaster."

"But how could Rector be the madman behind all this?" Emmett asked. "My father *liked* Rector. He said Rector was his only friend on that expedition. He couldn't believe someone so young had built that ship."

"Rector built—?" Now Bell looked both puzzled and angry. "The *Frost Cleaver* was constructed from *my* designs. With that ship and that expedition I'd hoped to launch a National Geographic Society. But after it went down, I threw away those dreams. I thought my creation—my ship—had killed all those men. But apparently there was at least one survivor."

"But why would Rector tell the crew *he'd* built the ship?" Molly asked.

"Because he was a loser," Edison chimed in. "Believe me, if Rector really had built that ship, it woulda sunk before it left New York Harbor. Guy was the worst lab assistant I ever had. I fired him after he almost burned my workshop down trying to bake a doughnut on a light bulb."

"So, wait—Rector is a *bad* inventor?" Emmett asked. "Not just evil-bad, but *bad*-bad? How did he manage to get hired by both of you?"

"*Johann* Rector, the Guild's founder, was Ambrose's dear old dad," Edison said. "Papa Rector forced his son on all of us. Every man in the Guild had to deal with that milksop at one time or another."

Bell lowered his eyes. "I feel horrible admitting this, but the only reason I sent Ambrose Rector on that polar expedition was to get him out of my lab before he broke anything else."

"None of this makes sense," said Molly. "If he was so useless, how has he built something as advanced as that metal-bending ray of his?"

"Perhaps we should watch the rest of the film," Hertha said. The others became silent as she resumed cranking.

"And *you* are my captive audience," continued the ghostly image. "Like the million-year-old flies who watched helplessly from their amber prisons as the dinosaurs exterminated one another, you will have to sit, paralyzed, and watch as New York meets its doom."

"I'm pretty sure that's not how dinosaurs went extinct," Molly said. Mrs. Cochrane shushed her.

"Which brings me to why we're here today," said Rector. "Today, in case you've lost track of the time in there, is opening day of the World's Fair, at which I—in the guise of the vaunted Thomas Edison—will flip the switch that powers New York City's new electrical grid. Only your streetlamps will also be broadcasting signals from my latest invention: the Mind-Melter. Amplified by the sonic devices I've installed in the lamps, the invisible waves from my Mind-Melter will find their way into every ear at the Fair. Everyone will be immobilized, including the two of you. And I'll have broken the record for the most hostages ever taken in a single kidnapping. I assume. I didn't look it up, but seriously, who could've done more?

"Anyway, I'm reasonably sure I've got the machine calibrated so it merely warps the brains of its victims, rather than liquefying them, but, hey, you can't be certain until you try it, right? So, in case you die later, I recorded this moving message for you. . . . Get it? *Moving* message? There's a double meaning there. Imbeciles."

"I got it," Edison said defensively.

"I also recorded this message to show you how much better I can use light and sound than you two supposed masters," Rector said bitterly. "That's really why I'm doing all of this—to show the world I'm better than you, better than my father even! And the irony of it all is that, originally, I didn't even want to be an inventor. I once believed my true calling lay on the stage, that I was meant to be a thespian! But dear old Johann Rector considered acting far too vulgar a profession for his child. No, in his eyes, there was only one path for little Ambrose: follow in Father's footsteps; become a tinkerer, a constructor, a contrapulator."

Rector paused and frowned before continuing, "Though I fought it at first, I came to realize he was right. Look at the two of you—honored and worshipped by all. Inventing *is* a far more dignified profession. No one knows more celebrity than my father's Guildsmen. And I . . . I could have been right there among you, basking in the adoration of millions. But no! Because you and your inventor pals were too jealous of me. You were afraid I'd inherited my father's genius and would show you all up, so you looked for one excuse after another to get rid of me."

"That's not true," Bell muttered. "The Rector boy was genuinely terrible."

"That's why Edison blamed *me* for the flammability of his workspace," Rector went on. "Why Levi Strauss said I didn't have the hips for his blue jeans, why Alexander Graham Bell sent me on a suicide voyage to the end of the Earth. But Bell and his co-conspirators failed to take one thing into account: Ambrose Rector doesn't die easily."

"Oh, come now," Edison griped. "How were we supposed to take that into account when we thought you were a moron?"

"When the engine gears iced up," Rector continued. "And Bell's booby-trapped ship conked out on the shores of the seventh continent, the crew blamed me! Simply because I'd been telling them I was the one who built it. They booted me from the vessel, tried to maroon me like a savage pirate. But the joke was on them.

"Oh, what a breathtaking landscape. And I mean that literally—it's basically too cold to breathe. But still pretty. Let me paint a quick portrait for you: Snow. Ice. Loads of adorable penguins. Seriously, you would not go hungry down there with all those penguins to eat. And the lights. Beautiful, swirling, colored lights. The aurora australis, which so many of you 'scientists' assume to be some sort of atmospheric phenomenon, but which I discovered to be the emanations of . . ."

Rector reached out of camera range and retrieved a bowling-ball-sized hunk of glowing rock. "Ambrosium," he said, his eyes transfixed on the stone. "But what is Ambrosium, you ask?" said Rector. "It is, for lack of a better term, a space rock."

"I can think of a better term," said Molly. "Meteorite."

"My best guess is that the Ambrosium fell to Earth millennia ago," Rector continued. "It landed on the frozen wastelands of our most forbidding continent, and has been waiting ever since for me to find it. And while I may not have discovered the South Pole on my trip, this is much, much better. Because you see, the more I held this space rock, squeezed it, caressed it, broke off little bits of it and swallowed them . . . the more I knew. The rock gave me . . . knowledge. I suddenly *knew* that it could do things. Miraculous things." A spooky grin crawled across his face. "Like distort human brain waves. Render a person unable to control his own body. Cause the brain tissue to pulse so rapidly it eventually disintegrates. Also, it's a magnet—look!" Giggling, he flipped the luminescent stone and a fork came flying from somewhere off camera. *Clang!* "Neat, right?" Rector cleared his throat. "So, to make a long story short, I went back to the ship and experimented on the crew members. Completely useless lot otherwise. By giving their lives to science, their existence on this planet was finally justified."

Emmett pulled his hands from Molly's and clenched them into fists.

"Then I popped my Ambrosium into the *Frost Cleaver*'s engine—turns out the stuff is a terrific power source as well—and piloted the ship back to America all by my lonesome. I couldn't wait to show my father that I had finally become the man he knew I could be! But what did I learn when I arrived back in New York? Johann Rector was dead—dead from the grief he felt over his missing son!"

"I thought old Johann choked on an olive," said Edison.

"He did," said Bell.

"My father would never know that his dream for me had been fulfilled," Rector continued. "That's when I vowed revenge. I adopted the persona of Sergio Vittorini and began spying on you from across the alley at the Madison Square Theatre. Father might not have approved of my methods, but the *New York Times* most certainly did. They gave me a rave review for my turn in *Fancies of a Ukrainian Barber*. Did you see it? The show, not the review. Actually, both were . . . Oh, fudge, I think I'm about to run out of—"

The film abruptly ended.

After several seconds of silence, Emmett turned to Bell and said, "Did you do it? Did you rig that ship to break down? Did you sacrifice my father and those others so you could get rid of Rector?"

Bell looked Emmett in the eye. "Son, I swear to you, that expedition was only meant to get him out of my hair for a few months. Its failure will always haunt me."

"We can't trust Rector's account anyway," said Mary. "The stone might have given him knowledge, but it also obviously warped his mind."

Emmett looked away. Molly got the distinct impression he was unconvinced.

"Frankly," said Edison, "I feel better knowing the man ate a bunch of magic pebbles to get his newfound smarts."

"The ironic thing is, Rector's actually a gifted actor,"

said Mary. "If his father had allowed him to pursue his passion, would we be in this situation?"

"A question for another time, ladies," Edison said. "Look at the clock; the Fair begins in two hours. Show us what your wondrous wagon can do." He retrieved the sizable battery and everyone followed him outside. But Molly noticed Emmett lagging behind.

"I know," she said gently. "That had to hurt."

"Three minutes," Emmett said. "I had three minutes of hope. Three minutes where I thought I might actually see my father again. And then it got yanked away. It's like I lost him all over again. Worse, really. Because now I know he didn't die in an accident—he was murdered. By a man who pretended to be his friend."

Molly was afraid to ask if he meant Rector or Bell. "I know how I'd feel if I really thought I'd never see my mother again," she said.

Emmett wiped his sleeve across his face. "I thought I might be able to apologize."

"For what?" Molly asked.

"When I first received the letter—the one I showed you—I was so angry. I hated my father for leaving me, just like I was so angry with him for keeping my heritage from me and for wanting me to be just like him. But the next thing I heard about him was that he was gone. And I was so sorry I'd ever had those feelings."

Molly thought about those last moments before Cassandra's arrest, how angry she'd been at her mother just then. She put her arm around Emmett and led him outside. Sarah, Mary, and Hertha were gathered around a newspaper with sickened looks on their faces.

"What now?" Molly asked. "Is that today's? Was it in the Onion Boys' wagon?" The women hesitated to answer, so Molly pulled the paper from Mary's hands.

"Molly," Sarah started. "You don't want to read—"

But she'd already seen the headline.

FAILED ASSASSIN CASSANDRA PEPPER
TO UNDERGO ELECTROSHOCK THERAPY TODAY
DOCTORS SAY NEW TREATMENT COULD BE
THE CURE FOR CRIMINALITY

"Electroshock? What are they going to do to her?" Molly asked numbly.

"Nothing good," Hertha replied. "I'm so sorry, Molly."

Molly frowned. Her mother needed action, not sympathy. "Well, we're getting her out of there," she said. "First. Before they fry her brain. We get my mother, then we go to the Fair."

"Molly, we can't," Hertha began. "Look at the time. It's after eight; the Fair opens its gates at ten."

"But the lighting ceremony's not till six! What if this thing they're going to do to my mother—what if it kills her?" Molly cried.

"It's horrible, and I loathe even having to make such a decision," said Hertha. "But we can't weigh one life against thousands."

"It's too important, dear," added Mary. "We really are sorry."

Molly struggled for words. Emmett found them for her. "Actually, Mrs. Pepper might be our best chance of stopping Rector's machine," he said.

"How's that?" Hertha asked. Molly wondered the same thing.

"From what Rector said on that recording, his device attacks with sound waves," Emmett said. "Mrs. Pepper's Sonic Nullifier could be just the thing to counteract it."

Molly was about to ask what the heck Emmett was talking about, but Bell spoke first. "Nullifier?" He and Edison stepped over to the group. "Your mother created a machine that cancels out sound? All sound?"

"She did," Emmett answered for Molly.

"Molly, you should have mentioned this sooner," said Hertha.

"It didn't occur to me," Molly finally said, hoping she didn't sound too surprised.

"Well, that goes far beyond the work I did quieting the train system," Mary said. "Definitely worth a detour. Molly, can you take us to your mother's invention?"

"I don't know where it is. Or how to use it." Neither was technically a lie.

The adults looked to one another, contemplating their options.

"Do any of us have ideas for thwarting Rector

otherwise?" Bell asked.

No response.

"Then it's decided," Hertha said. "Sarah, plot a course to Blackwell's Island." Molly couldn't be certain, but something in her voice made her think Hertha was secretly relieved by this change of plans.

She didn't want to think about how that might change when they discovered the Sonic Nullifier didn't exist.

"We'll get her back, Molly," Emmett whispered. "They took my father from me. We're not gonna let them take your mother from you."

37

Transformation!

WEIGHED DOWN BY two extra people, the Moto-Mover puttered along at a slower pace than before. Still, Bell and Edison seemed impressed. Bell ran his hand along the switches and panels on the seat back before him. "I must say, you've done a cracking good job with this contraption," Bell said.

"Language," tutted Mrs. Cochrane.

Edison leaned far over the side of the car to watch the wheels. "You girls have taken a fantastic first step here. When I think of the improvements I can make to this vehicle . . . Why, it would change the way the world travels!"

"Thank you, Mr. Edison," Hertha said with mock gratitude. "I hadn't realized our revolutionary, one-of-a-kind creation was so severely lacking. Would you care to honor us with one of your myriad ideas for improvement?"

Edison looked around. "Cup holders?"

"Seriously, ladies, an innovation like this should not be kept from the public," Bell said. "Why are you not displaying at the Fair?"

"You're kidding, right?" Molly snapped.

"Perhaps you were unaware," Mary explained, "but every inch of display space at the Fair was awarded to the Guild."

"True, the Guild does sorta run the show," said Edison. "You ladies should join . . . Oh, that's right."

"I suppose you can't, can you?" Bell said sheepishly. "It's . . . rather unfortunate."

"Unfair, you mean," said Mary.

"Hey, it's not our fault!" Edison tossed his hands up defensively. "It wasn't *my* decision to make the Guild men only."

"So we should assume you've spoken up against it?" said Hertha. "Explained to your colleagues how 'unfortunate' it is?"

The men were silent.

"As directors, can't you change the rules?" Emmett asked, wriggling uncomfortably between the two.

"Any change to the Guild charter would need the votes of a majority of members," Bell said. Molly narrowed her eyes at him. "But perhaps it's something we can work on," he added.

Molly kept her face stony as she nodded in reply, then turned her eyes back to the scenery and allowed herself the grin she didn't want Bell to see.

After two hours on the road—and ten minutes after the official opening of the World's Fair—Hertha pulled the hand brake and stopped the motor coach on the banks of the Hudson River. A mile of fast-moving water lay between them and Manhattan.

"*This* is the best part," Sarah said.

"Or worst," said Emmett with a grimace. "Depending on how seasick you get."

Buttons were pressed, levers were pulled, and slowly, the Moto-Mover began to transform. A glass bubble rose up to envelop the seating area. Metal plates shifted at the front of the car, forming a pointed nose like that of a sailing vessel. Steel fins extended from the sides and rear of the vehicle.

"The Moto-Mover," Molly shouted gleefully, "has become a Boat-o-Mover!"

For once, Edison was speechless.

"This vehicle is seaworthy?" Bell asked.

"Absolutely," said Hertha. "How do you think we got to the Jersey side to begin with? Although we are currently too heavy to go back. When we built the machine, we didn't calculate for this many passengers."

"I've an easy fix for that," Bell said, climbing out.

"It's best if we split up anyhow. There's a ferry terminal within walking distance of here. Tom and I will take one to Manhattan and alert the authorities about Rector. You go to Mrs. Pepper. She may not have much time."

"I'll stick with the Guild boys," said Mary. She patted Hertha on the shoulder and climbed out with Bell. "The rest of you rescue Cassandra."

"I wanted to ride the wizard boat," Edison whined as he climbed out. Then he fished around in the pockets of his suit jacket and came out with two small gadgets that looked like thumb pianos. "Do any of you know Morse code?"

Everybody in the car raised their hands.

"All right then." Edison handed one of the gizmos to Sarah. "We can use these to communicate. They're miniature telegraph machines that transmit messages across invisible waves. Don't ask me what kind of—"

"What kind of invisible waves?" Molly asked.

Edison narrowed his eyes. "That's classified."

"Ha," said Bell. "Yes, classified until he figures it out himself."

"As long as they work, we can use them," said Sarah. "Thanks, and good luck. Believe in yourself!"

Bell, Edison, and Mary waved farewell as the Marvelous Moto-Mover rolled into the swells of the Hudson and skimmed through the water. It sailed into the harbor, drawing slack-jawed stares from the fishermen and sailors they sprayed past. Emmett kept his eyes closed and his mouth covered until their vessel rounded the southern tip of Manhattan into the East River and finally burst onto the rocky shore of Blackwell's Island. Hertha switched the Moto-Mover back to land mode, drove across the flat scrubland, and parked it behind a patch of skeletal shrubs.

"It's even creepier than I'd imagined," said Emmett.

The architects of the Blackwell's Island Lunatic Asylum probably meant for its grand dome and ivy-covered white tower to look elegant and majestic. But in Molly, they inspired only melancholy and dread. The vines looked to be choking the life out of those stark walls, while the shadows of gnarled tree limbs crawled across dark windows like invading snakes. Water stains ran down from the dome, as if the building itself were weeping.

Molly shuddered. This was where they had her mother.

Mrs. Cochrane opted to once more wait with the car. And Margaret, whose tool belts and coveralls didn't fit the wardrobe for this undercover mission, stayed behind as well—but not before presenting goodies to the rest of the team.

"What are these?" Emmett asked as he examined the baseball-sized metal orb she'd handed him.

"Contingency plan," Margaret replied.

"Neat," Molly said, examining the small cube she'd been given.

As they ascended the marble steps to the main entrance, Molly kept her eyes on the windows, hoping to see a familiar face, but the ones that peered back gave her shivers. Inside, the entry chamber was far less spooky than Molly expected. No droopy cobwebs, broken mirrors, or bats hanging from the ceiling. Instead, gold-framed portraits of rich old men surrounded a carpeted staircase that spiraled up to the top of the dome. Not a mote of dust dirtied the glistening ceramic tiles, nor did a single loose paper clutter the ornately carved reception desk. The only person in sight was a guard napping on a stool by a big, black door.

Hertha cleared her throat and the guard jolted awake.

"Norris, wake up!" he called. And from behind the large desk appeared a small head. The man had beady eyes and a bladelike nose that made Molly wonder if all desk clerks were related.

"Can I help you?" the clerk asked, squinting like a man who'd forgotten his eyeglasses.

"We're here to visit a patient," Hertha said. "Mrs. Cassandra Pepper."

"I'm sorry, no visiting hours today," said the clerk.

"Oh, dear, we hadn't realized," Hertha play-acted. "But we're her only family and we came all this way."

"Yer *all* family?" the guard asked, raising his

eyebrows at their motley crew.

"Doesn't matter," the clerk snipped. "No vis . . ." He cocked his head. "How did you get here?"

There was a slight pause before Hertha said, "Ferry."

"But the city reassigned the Blackwell's ferry for the Fair," said the clerk.

"Then how'd *you* get here?" Molly shot back.

"By ferry. But our ferry's for staff only, and— Why am I explaining myself to you?" He looked to the guard. "Bernard, watch them while I make a call."

Bernard the guard stood while the clerk picked up a telephone.

"Contingency time," Hertha said. She whipped Margaret's glue cannon from the folds of her skirt and pumped it at the clerk. A thick wad of adhesive pinned him to the wall.

"Jumpin' jellyfish!" the guard shouted. Molly followed the instructions on her cube: POINT LID AT HEAD. PRESS BUTTON. The contraption sprang open like a jack-in-the-box, and Bernard suddenly had a burlap sack over his face. Startled and blinded, the guard tripped over his own stool.

"Our apologies for all this," said Sarah, who was nearly done using Margaret's mini-blowtorch to cut the bolt lock from the door. "It's a matter of life and death. I hope you understand."

"I understand nothing!" the trapped clerk cried as

Hertha ran behind his desk and flipped through a log-book.

"Women's wing, Ward H," she announced as Sarah kicked open the charred door.

"Bernard, help me," the struggling clerk groaned. "This goo is impossible!"

"I can't find you," the guard mumbled as he crawled across the floor and banged his sack-covered head into the desk.

"Don't give up, boys! Believe in yourselves!" Sarah yelled as she and the others raced into the depths of the asylum.

The quiet cleanliness of the lobby had been sorely misleading. The innards of the asylum held all the spiderwebs, stained floors, and cracked walls promised by the building's eerie exterior. As the quartet raced along foul-odored, barely lit corridors, following signs to Ward H, Molly tried to keep her eyes straight ahead of her. To glance to the side meant seeing the wretched, moaning, weeping women in the beds they passed. Some were strapped down, yelling things like "Get me out!" or "Please tell my family!" Others lay in puddles or sat staring into corners, ignoring the rats and roaches that skittered around their feet. Molly trembled with fear and rage.

A thick-necked orderly in a stained white apron

turned a corner, startling them. *SPLORCH!* Hertha glued him to the wall before he could utter a syllable. "There," she said, pointing to the door marked H.

"Hey, you can't be back here!" Another orderly ran at them.

Emmett hurled his metallic ball at the man, who caught it and laughed. "Was this supposed to hurt me or some—" Bluish gas hissed from the orb and the man collapsed.

"Cassandra!" Hertha called. "Cassandra Pepper!"

"Mrs. Pepper!" Emmett joined in.

"Mother!" Molly cried. They reached an area so overcrowded, the women's beds were lined up in the corridor. One woman lurched forward and grabbed Molly's arm.

"Let go!" Molly begged.

"Cassandra," the woman said. Her eyes were bloodshot. "They took her away."

"Where?" Molly asked.

"Downstairs," the woman replied. Her long hair was dirty, but still tied up in a fashionable bun. "About twenty minutes ago. They're starting the treatment on her—the shocks."

"Thank you," Molly said, but the woman didn't release her.

"They put me in here because I couldn't pay my rent," the prisoner said. "Please. Tell someone."

Hertha placed her hand on the woman's and gently

lifted it from Molly's arm. "I have a friend. Nellie Bly; she's a journalist," Hertha said. "I think she'd be very interested to know what goes on behind these walls. Have faith."

The woman retreated to her grimy cot as Molly and the others ran downstairs.

When they reached the lower level, they heard a man's voice behind a closed door: "I can't say it's not going to hurt, but on the bright side, when we're done, you probably won't remember how much it hurt."

"I still think I'd feel better if you tried it on yourself first," came Cassandra's reply.

The rescuers exploded into the cold, tiled room to find Cassandra Pepper in a white hospital gown, her formerly lustrous hair shaved down to peach fuzz. She lay on a table, bound by thick leather straps, while an orderly steadied a lamp overhead, and a white-cloaked doctor began to lower a wired metal cap onto Cassandra's skull.

"Mother!"

"Molls?"

"What's this?" spat the doctor. *SKLERP!* A perfectly launched glob of adhesive pinned the metal cap to his chest. He staggered and his elbow tripped the switch of the machine behind him. Sparks shot from the cap. The man yowled, crumpled, and fell still.

"Eh, he'll be fine," said Hertha.

Sarah rushed to the table and began carefully cutting through Cassandra's straps with her blowtorch. "Don't move, Mrs. Pepper," she said. "I wouldn't want to accidentally scorch you."

The orderly took a step toward the table, and Hertha trained her glue cannon on him. The man raised his hands. "Whoa," he sputtered. "I'm just gonna loosen these for you." He unlatched Cassandra's straps and stepped out of the way.

"You made a fortunate decision," Hertha said. "For us. Because this thing's all out of gloop." She tossed the empty gun aside.

"Hey, I'm not gonna stop you," the orderly said. "This place is awful."

Free of her constraints, Cassandra leapt up, and Molly enveloped her mother in a hug she never wanted to end. But they soon heard the sound of footsteps on the stairs.

"Run now, cuddle later," Hertha said.

"Um, there's no exit from down here," the orderly cautioned.

"That's okay," Sarah said, holding up her blowtorch. "I've got this!" She ran out into the hallway and the others followed.

"I don't think that's gonna cut through the stone," the man called out as they left.

"Doesn't have to." Sarah held up the canister, which had a label on it: IF ALL ELSE FAILS, PRESS BUTTON,

THROW, AND DUCK. She pressed the noted button, and tossed the canister to the bottom of the brick wall at the end of the corridor.

"Everybody down, please!"

The Pocket Welder exploded, taking out the asylum wall with it. Waving dust and smoke from their faces, Molly, Emmett, Cassandra, Sarah, and Hertha crawled through the gaping hole in the bricks. Before them lay several yards of dead turf, the East River, and Manhattan beyond.

"Anyone for a dip?" Hertha asked.

That was when the Marvelous Moto-Mover zoomed around the corner.

"That looks fun," said Cassandra.

"We heard the explosion," Margaret called out. "Get in!" She leaned over the side and helped everyone on board, while Josephine Cochrane, who sat rigidly at the wheel, slowed the vehicle.

"Is everyone in their proper seats?" Mrs. Cochrane asked.

"Just drive!" Hertha shouted.

Mrs. Cochrane spun the wheel, revved the engine, and tore toward the water's edge. The car bounced over rocks and branches and splashed into the water.

"*That* was not the move I expected," said Cassandra.

"Make it a boat first!" Margaret shouted. "It's still a car! Make it a boat!"

The car surged out into the fast-flowing East River, water rushing over the sides and flooding the seating well.

"This might be a good time to tell you I can't swim," said Molly.

"I would like to remind everyone," Josephine Cochrane said, in a manner far calmer than one would expect from a person in a sinking Moto-Mover, "I made it quite clear that operating a vehicle was not part of my skill set."

"Everyone hold on," Hertha said as she scrambled over seats to pull the correct lever. Soon, the glass bubble began rising, the nose reshaped itself, and the hidden fins appeared.

"Oh, look! It's turning into a boat." Cassandra beamed. "So that's what the lady in the goggles meant when she said, 'Make it a boat.'"

The passengers were up to their waists in brackish water. Emmett spit some from his mouth. "And I thought the nausea would be the worst part," he muttered.

Sparks shot from the control panel.

"What was that?" cried Molly.

"Electricity and water do not play nicely together," said Hertha. She began cranking levers and pumping foot pedals to no avail. "This coach is waterproof from the *outside*. The river was never meant to be a passenger. The motor is dead."

The boat was drifting south with the current. It wouldn't be long before they were swept into New York Harbor and the Atlantic Ocean beyond.

"We can't let ourselves be washed out to sea," said Emmett.

"Are you certain?" Cassandra asked. "Because I think we already are."

"We have to paddle," said Sarah. She lowered the glass shield and stuck her arms over the side. "Come on, everybody! Believe in yourselves!"

The seven of them paddled with all the strength they could muster. Even Mrs. Cochrane did her part (though not without complaining about the water making her fingers all pruney). Together, they fought the current, and twenty grueling minutes later, they were climbing onto a Manhattan pier, much to the bafflement of the local fishermen.

"Bon voyage, Marvelous Moto-Mover," Hertha said mournfully as the vehicle disappeared beneath the surface.

"First boat ride and first shipwreck in the same day," Molly said, wringing out her dress. "But at least we—"

Her mother lifted her off the ground and spun until her dizziness overpowered her affection.

Sunken Hopes

HERTHA LED THE sopping-wet group away from gawking seamen and paused in a small portside park to debrief Cassandra on the events of the past week.

"I must say, part of me wishes it was the real Edison who'd been the villain," Cassandra said. "I would've liked an excuse to slap him with my hat."

"He may still give you one," said Hertha. "Speaking of which . . . Sarah, have we gotten any word from Mary and the boys? Any luck they've already put an end to Rector's skulduggery?"

Sarah pulled the handheld telegraph from a hidden pocket in her skirt. "Rescue success," she narrated as she tapped out her message in the dots and dashes of Morse code. "What is your status?"

After an excruciatingly long pause, the answer came

in blips and bleeps: "Trapped. Locked in Bell Guild office. Need help."

"You know," said Molly. "They may be fancy inventors, but Bell and Edison are not great action heroes."

"What's the time?" Hertha asked.

"Four twenty-two." Margaret tapped her goggle clock. "Waterproof."

"Mary, Bell, and Edison will have to wait," Hertha said. "We've barely ninety minutes until Rector throws his switch, and it will take half that simply to get uptown. Cass, I hope your Sonic Nullifier is nearby."

"My sonic what now?" Cassandra asked.

Molly's gut sank.

"There, um, there is no Sonic Nullifier," Emmett said shakily. Then he turned hopefully to Cassandra. "Unless there is? By any chance?"

Cassandra stared blankly.

"I'm sorry," Emmett said to the MOI. "It's just . . . we had to get to Molly's mother. You saw how close she came to getting her brain fried!"

"There are thousands of lives at stake!" Hertha snapped, directly at Molly. The other members of the MOI looked on uncomfortably.

"I never said there was a Nullifier," Molly mumbled.

"You never said there wasn't!" Hertha sounded just as hurt as angry.

"Stop," Cassandra butted in. "I see that Molly lied to

get you to come after me, and that was definitely wrong, considering all that's going on. But please don't blame her. This is my fault."

"Molly's a big girl, Cass," Hertha said.

"But that's just it," Cassandra said. "She's a child. Even if I haven't always taken that fact into consideration myself." She gently lifted Molly's chin and looked into her eyes. "I had a lot of time to think in that asylum. And I came to realize: I have been a terrible parent. You're twelve years old, Molls. And look at the situations I've put you in. Climbing bridges, blowing up laboratories . . . And for what? My success? My fame? It was wrong. And it stops now." She turned to the other women. "I will go to the Guild to free the men and your friend Mary. I owe you at least that much. The rest of you go after Rector."

"What about Emmett and me?" Molly asked. "Do we go with you or the MOI?"

"We don't need your kind of assistance," Hertha said sharply.

"You go nowhere," Cassandra said to Molly. "You go back to the pickle shop. And Emmett with you. No more danger for you. I forbid it."

Molly pulled away. "No," she said. "You don't get to start playing the protective mother now. You don't know the half of what I've been through this past week without you—getting kidnapped by gangsters, jumping off moving trains, hiding out in garbage dumps. And, yeah, it all started out because I wanted to help you, but it became something I had to do for myself, and Emmett, and these amazing ladies who might never want to speak to me again now. And for the world. Not everything is about you, Mother! You don't understand that, though, do you? Not when you're acting like breaking into the Guild was the first bad situation you ever put me in. I quit school for you, I run the pickle shop for you, I act as your assistant day and night!"

Cassandra blinked back tears, but her face stayed stony. "I never *asked* you to do any of those things," she said.

"You didn't have to," Molly snapped. "You needed me to do them. That was pretty darn clear."

"That's not—" Cassandra cut herself off and took in a long breath through her nose. She turned to Hertha. "I trust you will see that my daughter and her friend stay safely away from Central Park."

"They can stay with me," said Mrs. Cochrane. "I will escort them back to your shop."

Cassandra nodded and turned to her daughter. "I'm sorry about the past, Molls. But how can I make up for it if you don't allow me to start doing the right thing?"

Molly watched her mother walk away—a bald woman in a wet hospital gown. She barely resembled the Cassandra Pepper Molly knew. That helped in a way. Because Molly didn't want to believe the Cassandra Pepper she knew would abandon her again so soon.

Enemies at the Gate

"THIS STINKS." MOLLY kicked a pebble as they walked back toward Thompson Street and Pepper's Pickles.

"I'm sorry," Emmett said.

"About what?" Molly grumbled. "That the Mothers think we're awful now, that Blackwell turned my mother into a jerk, or that we're stuck with Mrs. Grouchy Bloomers?"

"My ears work perfectly well, you know," Mrs. Cochrane said behind them.

"About everything," Emmett said. "I just—I hated lying to everyone, but since my father, nobody's made a bigger impact on my life than you, Molly. I wanted to help you. And what I thought you needed most was your mother. Guess I was wrong about that."

Molly sniffled. "I don't blame you for anything,

Emmett. I'm still kinda shocked that you lied for me like that, but . . . I know why you did. And I'll never forget it."

"Chin up, children," Josephine said, stepping between them. "Everybody's emotions are running hot right now. I'm sure Hertha will have forgiven you by tomorrow morning. Provided we're still alive."

"Um, thanks," said Emmett.

"As for Mrs. Pepper," Josephine continued, "I think you should both allow her a little leeway. Your father did most of the child-rearing when you were younger, didn't he, Molly?"

Molly stopped and turned, casting Mrs. Cochrane a curious glance.

"Your mother spent most of her life as an inventor. Then she suddenly had to raise a child all on her own. As a widow, at that. I can tell you from experience that when you've been part of a team for a long time, it's not easy to suddenly be by yourself."

"How do you know so much about my family?" Molly asked suspiciously.

"Hertha told you we did our research. Your mother's story struck a chord with me. My husband passed away not too long ago."

"I'm sorry," Emmett said. Molly just looked down.

"Thank you, dear," Josephine said. "As a way to move on, I threw myself into inventing. It turned out,

313

I'm quite good, but even so, it has been difficult to shed the identity of businessman's wife."

"Well, if you want to drop the prim and proper stuff, my mother can definitely help with that," Molly said.

"Perhaps that's why I recommended her for membership in our club."

Molly looked at her askance. "Are you trying to make me warm up to you?"

"I have no such plans," said Mrs. Cochrane.

"Plans!" Molly shouted with sudden urgency. "I still have Rector's plans in my boot! Without that evidence, how are the others going to get anybody to believe them? We have to catch up with them!"

Mrs. Cochrane pursed her lips. "It's not ideal, but we'll just have to hope that Hertha manages to convince the authorities without that paper. Or that your mother gets the real Edison to the Fair in time."

"But what if neither of those things happens?" Molly said. "You know this paper will make it much easier for them."

"I promised I would keep you safe!" Mrs. Cochrane thought for a second, then held out her hand. "*I'll* take the paper to Hertha. You two continue to the store."

"You think leaving us unsupervised is gonna keep us safe?" Molly scoffed. "As soon as you're out of sight, we'll just go to the Fair anyway. And think of all the reckless stuff we'll do without you *tsk*-ing at us."

314

"She's not bluffing," Emmett said with a shrug. "You have a much better chance of keeping your promise if you come with us."

Mrs. Cochrane sighed and began hustling after the children.

"Woo-hoo! I'm going to the World's Fair!" Molly hooted. "We're gonna stop Rector! And ride the Ferris Wheel! Ooh, and can we get candy corn?"

"Remember that we're going there to stop a madman," Mrs. Cochrane chided.

"Yeah, I remember," Molly replied. "So can we get candy corn?"

Twenty-two minutes later, the trio squeezed out of a packed train car and hurried up the block to Central Park. Molly could see enticing hints of the Fair's hidden wonders rising above the tall striped fence that surrounded its grounds: bejeweled spires, stained-glass domes, mosaic-tiled minarets. And towering above it all was George Ferris's Big Wheel. It looked like a gigantic mill wheel, only instead of paddles, it had steel gondolas filled with gleefully shrieking passengers.

Molly paused across the street from the main gate, where, in the shadow of a spinning, wrought-iron globe, ushers were herding throngs of people into the park. "Step right up! No tickets needed! Everybody in! Free admission today only!"

"I didn't read anything about free admission," Molly said.

"Green jackets," Emmett pointed out. "They're Mac-Dougal's men, trying to fill the park with as many victims as possible for Rector."

"Don't miss yer chance," yelled one fake usher.

"But I'm on the way to the doctor," said a passerby. The usher grabbed him by the lapels and tossed him in through the gate anyway. "There's doctors in the Fair!"

"Shall we?" Mrs. Cochrane headed for the gate.

"But those are Green Onion Boys," Emmett said. "They might be looking for us."

"Walk fast without any fuss and we'll be fine," Josephine encouraged them.

"C'mon," said Molly. "You think every random Green Onion can recognize us on sight?"

Emmett took a deep breath and headed for the entrance.

"This way, this way!" called the usher nearest them. "Don't miss this uniqueous bargain! Come—" The man thrust a wicker cane out to stop the children in their tracks. Pembroke, the Green Onion who'd first questioned them at Bandit's Roost, blinked at them through swollen, black eyes—a result of the brawl, Molly assumed. Did he recognize them?

Mrs. Cochrane pushed Molly and Emmett through from behind. "Move along, children! We adults would like to get inside too!"

"Heh." Pembroke grinned at her. "Juvenilians today, am I right?"

"A blight on society," Josephine muttered as she hurried past him.

As soon as they were inside, Mrs. Cochrane steered the children behind a snack vendor's wagon. "Did that man rec—"

"Candy corn!" Molly cooed. She tried to sneak her arm past the vendor to grab one of the little orange-yellow triangles. But Mrs. Cochrane smacked her hand down and pulled the children off the path, to a shady spot behind an elm tree.

"I was just lookin'," Molly said apologetically.

"Hush!" Mrs. Cochrane chided. "Now, did that gangster recognize you?"

"You can be most ascertained of that," Pembroke sneered as he strode up behind her, swinging his cane. "These are the brats that got me demotivated. And I'm gonna be most empleasured to—"

Mrs. Cochrane grabbed the cane from his hands and broke it over his head. Pembroke fell flat.

"Wow, Mrs. Cochrane," Molly gasped. "I didn't know you had it in you."

"I'm a woman who keeps my promises," she replied.

"What's that in his ears?" Emmett asked. He crouched and removed two tiny silver devices from Pembroke's ear canals. "They're meshed," he said. "Some kind of filter, maybe?"

"They must be special earplugs to protect Rector's men from his machine," Molly said. "He doesn't want to brain-melt his own minions, right?"

"Put them in," said Mrs. Cochrane.

Emmett looked at the plugs and cringed. "But . . . these were in Pembroke's ears. They're all . . . waxy."

"I'll take 'em." Molly popped the plugs into her own ears. "I can still hear. I hope they work. Next pair is yours, Emmett. We just need to steal a few more from some unsuspecting Onions."

"Come, children." Mrs. Cochrane dragged Pembroke's unconscious body behind the tree. "The world awaits."

The World Awaits!

THEY SPED BY a group of raucous men in lederhosen dancing with beer steins, then followed weaving paths past a replica of the Sphinx and a man selling kebabs. They turned past an Australian boomerang demonstration and cut through a parade of beret-wearing children singing "Alouette." Then they followed the trail around a Swiss chalet bedecked with cotton-fluff snow and past a group of raucous men in lederhosen dancing with beer steins—

They'd gone in a circle.

"Drat! We need a map," said Emmett.

"Wait, we have one!" Molly stopped and leaned against the fence of a Peruvian petting zoo, complete with llamas roaming fake Andes Mountains. Digging into her damp boot, she found Rector's plans and unfolded them. The ink had run, but the map was still mostly legible. "We're set!" she cheered. She waved the paper overhead to show Emmett, and a llama lurking behind her promptly ate it. "No!" Molly cried. "You are so—so—bah, you're actually cute. But why did you do that! Now we're—"

"No time for yelling at animals," Mrs. Cochrane said, nudging Molly back onto a side path, past the Warsaw Sausage Works. "The other Green Onions might have discovered our friend Pembroke by now. We need to warn Hertha and the others."

"What if the Onions already got them?" Molly asked with sudden horror. "What if we're the only ones left who can unmask Rector? What if—?"

"Molly!" Emmett blurted. Strolling out of the Sausage Works were two familiar faces: Crikes and Tusk.

Crikes spit out the kielbasa jutting from between his teeth. "Shove my uncle in a pumpkin!" he sputtered. "It's them!"

"Ooh." Tusk grinned. "I don't care if Oogie said to keep you two alive, I'm gonna—"

"Is *that* what he said?" asked Crikes. "To *keep* them alive?"

"I think so," said Tusk.

"'Cause I thought he said to burn them alive."

"Burn 'em? Wow, that's really different. Maybe you heard him say 'bairn.' He says that sometimes when he means 'kids.'"

"I thought that was 'weans.'"

"I think both, actu— Aw, crud! They're running away!" He tossed his tray of wieners onto a puzzled boy and charged after them.

Molly, Emmett, and Mrs. Cochrane ran as fast as they could, but Mrs. Cochrane quickly fell behind. The short, stilted steps her tight dress forced her to take would never allow her to catch up.

"Tear your dress!" Molly yelled to her. "Loosen the buttons!"

"What?" Mrs. Cochrane sounded appalled. "I can't—"

Molly dashed back and yanked hard at both sides of the woman's fancy skirt until several buttons popped onto the stone path. "Now run."

Mrs. Cochrane marveled at the long strides she was able to take. "Oh," she said. "Oh, this is ... Oh."

The three zigzagged around women in shimmering kimonos and men with colorful kaffiyehs on their heads, and ducked through the beaded entryway of the first building they saw, the Persia Pavilion. Inside, a man in puffy silk pants juggled curve-bladed scimitars amid walls draped with intricate hand-woven rugs. The children slipped into the crowd.

As the juggler caught his final sword and took a bow, Molly plucked one of the weapons from his hand. "Grraaaarrrr!" She charged at the villains.

The gangsters shrieked and dove in opposite

directions, crashing into clay urns and getting buried by falling carpets. Molly bowed for the applauding crowd until Mrs. Cochrane dragged her back outside.

"They're still coming," Emmett said.

Mrs. Cochrane and the children hurtled past the Siam Pavilion's dancers in demon masks and into the Holland Pavilion, where they ducked the spinning arms of windmills on their way to the exit. When they burst outside once more, they found themselves before the massive golden temple of the China Pavilion. Bright red pillars held up tiered, sloping rooftops, and serpentine dragon statues flanked a door with a sign that read CLOSED FOR PRIVATE FUNCTION. But by the corner of the building, a smaller door stood open, and a woman in a shimmering pink robe waved. "*Nǐ hǎo*," she said as Emmett ran by.

He stopped and turned to her. "We need help," he said, panting. "Can you hide us? There are two men—"

"*Duìbùqǐ. Wo bù dǒng*," the woman replied.

"I—I don't—" Emmett grew flustered. "Do you speak English? We need—please. Inside?" He tried to step past her into the pavilion, but the woman raised her hands to stop him. Or possibly calm him. Molly took hold of Emmett's arm to do the same.

"We need to keep moving," Molly said. "The lighting ceremony's gonna start any minute."

"*Qǐng shāo hòu*," the woman said, going inside and shutting the door.

"But . . . ," Emmett started. "Maybe she went for help?"

"Emmett, dear," Mrs. Cochrane warned, though not without sympathy.

"I know, I'm sorry." He shook his head. "I just—I should have been able to . . ."

A few yards down the path, Tusk and Crikes were marching in their direction.

"No time for sorries," Molly panted as they darted down another path. But all three paused as they reached a tall, silver archway in the form of two bearded wizards holding a sign between them. Sparks shot from the sorcerers' tin fingertips, splashing colored flashes across the sign: INVENTORS' ALLEY.

Molly peered down the long, bustling avenue of booths. Some were adorned with clockwork figures, while others featured flashing lights or curling glass pipes that puffed pastel clouds into the air. And in each, a man gesticulated wildly as he demonstrated some strange gadget.

"One of these guys must have something that can help us," Molly shouted. She leapt the partition into a booth manned by photography genius George Eastman.

"I believe there was a line," Mr. Eastman scolded as he cranked his latest handheld camera. "But you're here, so . . . Say 'cheese'!" The flashbulb popped right in front of Molly's eyes, and suddenly the Fair was gone. All she could see were swirling colored blotches. She staggered, disoriented, until Emmett and Josephine each grabbed an arm and dragged her out over the other side of the booth. She blinked rapidly, grateful to see that her vision was returning.

"Don't forget to stop by next week and pick up your photograph," Eastman called as he screwed on a new flashbulb. Crikes and Tusk bounded into the booth. "I guess we've given up on the line," Eastman sighed. He snapped his camera at the gangsters, and Crikes, dazed, fell into his partner's arms.

Struggling with her skirt, Mrs. Cochrane clumsily climbed into the next booth, startling a dapper fellow with a waxed mustache and jet-black hair that rolled in waves across his head. He was showing off a large glass sphere that appeared to be full of lightning.

"It's Nikola Tesla," Emmett said as he climbed in with still-blinking Molly.

"Yes, I am Tesla!" the inventor said cheerfully. He ran his fingers along the surface of the orb and the sparks followed his fingertips. "And you are volunteer?"

"Not I, sir," Mrs. Cochrane said as she hoisted the children over the other side. "But the two gents behind us are good for a go." She gracelessly tossed herself over the partition as Tusk and Crikes clambered into the booth.

The inventor stepped into their path. "Hello, I am Tesla! Please to touch my sparky ball!"

"Mrs. Cochrane, we could have used one of Tesla's

devices against them," Molly said as they ran.

Cochrane responded with a curt, "No."

"Look." Emmett pointed. "That man has an auto-mated mallet. Mallets make good weapons."

"Or over there!" Molly said. "That doodad's got hooks on it."

"I know what I'm doing," Mrs. Cochrane snapped. She headed straight for one specific booth.

"Levi Strauss?" Molly asked.

"We don't have time to figure out electric transference whatsits," she replied. "But pants? I know how pants work." Muttering an apology, she swiped a pair of denim dungarees from Strauss's booth.

"They're coming!" Emmett yelled.

Tusk, his hair standing on end, was still struggling to get past Tesla. But Crikes was charging like a mad bull.

"I'm gonna burn you," Crikes growled. "But not all the way. Just to be safe." He leapt for Molly, but Mrs. Cochrane stepped in. Holding one pant leg in each hand, she looped the blue jeans around the gangster's neck. The crotch of the pants hit Crikes's Adam's apple, and Mrs. Cochrane swung him in the opposite direction. He staggered away, sputtering and holding his throat.

"See, everybody," Levi Strauss called out to the mes-merized bystanders. "That's one tough pair of pants!"

Mrs. Cochrane and the children had a clear path to

the end of Inventors' Alley. But something caught Molly's eye as she ran.

"Hoity-Toity Boy," she growled.

She veered over to Thaddeus Edgerton's booth, where the teenaged Guildsman was waggling his eyebrows at a pair of young female fairgoers. ". . . Not that I'd ever need to use these glasses on a couple of Venuses like yourselves," he was saying.

Molly snatched the spectacles from his hands, snapped them in half, and threw the pieces into his face, before running back to rejoin Emmett and Mrs. Cochrane.

Even if Rector kills us all, she said to herself, *at least I will have done that.*

But suddenly, there was a veritable wall of people blocking her path, a seemingly endless line of fairgoers. She looked up. She'd been so distracted, she hadn't even noticed they were standing in the shadow of the Ferris Wheel.

41

On Top of the World

THERE APPEARED TO be no way around the gigantic wheel and its long queue of waiting riders.

"We'll go under it," Mrs. Cochrane said. "Up ahead, see where that man is letting people on and off?"

Molly nodded.

"The bad guys are still coming," Emmett said.

"Normally, cutting in line would be a tasteless breach of etiquette," Mrs. Cochrane said as she rammed her shoulders into waiting patrons. "These, however, are extraordinary circumstances."

The children followed her lead. But when they finally pushed through the grumbling crowd to the base of the wheel, Tusk was right behind them.

"Quick, get on!" Molly yelled. They dove past the startled ride operator into a moving gondola. Within seconds they were rising above the crowds.

"Um, they're *still* coming," said Emmett. "And I'm getting *really* tired of saying that."

Molly looked over the side to see Tusk and Crikes in the next car down. The goons glared upward, but couldn't reach them. Molly stuck her tongue out.

"You were pretty great down there, Mrs. Cochrane," she said. She smiled at the former fancy lady's disheveled hair, torn dress, and scuffed cheeks.

"Please, call me Josephine."

"I'm sorry about before, at the China Pavilion," Emmett said. "It's just . . . If I only knew Chinese, I might have been able . . ."

"It's okay," Molly said. "When this is over—"

"Children, look," Josephine said as they reached the wheel's highest point, a good ninety feet above the Fair. Thousands of people, looking for all the world like dollhouse toys come to life, roamed the labyrinthine pathways, swirling around exotic temples, palaces, and villas. Molly wished she could have focused on the fun bits, like the vendor chasing a runaway balloon or the llama eating a man's hat. But instead she took note of the exits, which had already been barricaded with overturned wagons. And just on the other side of the wheel, on a stage at the far end of a jam-packed central plaza, was the man they were looking for: Ambrose Rector in his Edison guise.

Rector was already speaking to the crowd. They could

hear his voice amplified through the speakers in the lampposts, but were too high up to make out his words.

"He's going to turn on his machine any second now," Emmett said. "I hope Hertha gets to him in time."

"She will," said Josephine.

"But we should try too," said Molly as their car began its descent.

"By all means," Josephine replied with gusto. "No reason to let Miss Marks hog all the glory."

"Psst!"

Molly turned to see Crikes's face upside down, mere inches from hers. Tusk held him by his feet, dangling him from their gondola, which was now above Molly's. She yelped as Crikes threw his arms around her chest and Tusk began hauling them both up.

Emmett grabbed Molly's legs. The cars swayed, and Molly and Crikes both squealed nervously.

"Let go of the girl, before they both die," Tusk called down.

"You let go," Emmett shouted back.

"I'm not gonna let go," said Tusk. "Then you'll have Crikes."

"Yeah, don't let go," Crikes said to Tusk.

"Then you let go," Molly said to Crikes.

"I'm not letting go," said Crikes. "If you get away, Oogie'll burn us alive. Hey, maybe *that's* what he said! He'd burn *us*!"

"Well, somebody has to let go!" shouted Emmett.

"And it will be you, sir," said Mrs. Cochrane. She stabbed the back of Crikes's hand with something long, thin, and silvery. "A proper lady never leaves home without a hairpin." Howling, the gangster did indeed let go. And before he could be hauled back up by his partner, Molly plucked the little metallic plugs from his ears.

"Hey, I need those," Crikes whined.

"We know," Molly retorted gleefully, tossing the plugs to Emmett.

As their gondola swooped to ground level, the three leapt off. Molly shoved the ride operator aside and pushed his control lever as far as it would go, speeding up the wheel and sending the Green Onions for another go-round.

"Put those earplugs in," Molly said to Emmett, ignoring the furious cries of the ride operator.

Emmett stared at the slimy nuggets. "These are worse than Pembroke's."

"Do it!"

Emmett closed his eyes and jammed the devices into his ears.

"Hurry, children," Josephine said. "To the plaza!"

They charged into the dense crowd, squeezing their way toward the stage. "Where is Hertha?" asked Emmett.

"It's okay," said Molly. "We can do this ourselves! We're not too late!"

But they were too late. The imposter Edison's voice echoed through the park. "And now for the moment you've been waiting for!" Molly knew it would be more than just the man's voice issuing from light poles all around the park if they let him pull the lever on the humming, silver machine before him.

Standing at Rector's side was President Chester A. Arthur, vying for attention with his floor-length fur coat, fluffed-out sideburns, and a jeweled ring on every finger. Beside Arthur, looking only slightly less spectacular in his medal-festooned Union Army uniform, was Ulysses S. Grant. And next to him, in a brown suit and derby, staring at his feet with eyes that said "I should have worn something more exciting," was Governor Grover Cleveland.

"Ladies and gentlemen, we are living in a new age," Rector said. "It is an age of automation, innovation, and electrification!" He paused as the massive crowd gave a deafening cheer. "But most importantly, this is the age of Ambrose Rector!" The politicians on the platform exchanged puzzled glances.

"He's gonna do it," Molly said as she shoved between two men in fezzes.

"Hurry, children!" Josephine urged. They were halfway across the plaza.

"And who is Ambrose Rector, you ask?" the villain continued. "Of course you ask that, because the petty members of the Inventors' Guild made sure no one ever got to hear the name of Ambrose Rector. Oh, I'm sure you've all heard of his esteemed father, Johann Rector, founder of the illustrious Guild. But did you even know Johann had a son? No, because Johann Rector never talked about his son. He was ashamed of his son. And so were his Guildsmen! They kept Ambrose Rector down because he was smarter, more imaginative, more ambitious than any of them could ever be!"

President Arthur leaned over and whispered something to the governor. Grover Cleveland shrugged.

"Mr. President, stop him!" Emmett cried. "Don't let him pull the switch!"

"He's a fake!" Molly screamed. "He'll kill us all!"

But no one onstage could hear them. Rector began speaking faster. "Now Ambrose Rector is about to burst free from his prison of obscurity! And no one will ever forget his name again!" He peeled back his fake eyebrows and twisted off his false nose.

"*I* am Ambrose Rector!" the madman howled. "Welcome to my world!"

And he pulled the lever.

The Main Event

NOBODY'S BRAIN EXPLODED. That was a good sign. Maybe Rector's machine hadn't worked?

But then, as electric lamps lit up throughout the park, people began to cover their ears. In moments, everyone Molly and Emmett could see dropped to the ground, Mrs. Cochrane included.

"Josephine!" Molly cried.

Onstage, Arthur, Grant, and Cleveland collapsed into a pile. And Molly knew that any police or emergency workers who might rush to the rescue would fall the moment they set foot in the park. She, Emmett, and Rector seemed to be the only people unaffected.

The earplugs worked.

"Get down!" Emmett hissed. "Pretend it's affecting us too."

Molly nodded and joined Emmett on the pavement. Josephine's eyes were open. Was she still awake? Could she hear and see what was happening, even if she couldn't move? Molly looked into her pleading eyes and whispered, "You kept us safe. Now we'll help you. That's *my* promise."

"What you are currently experiencing is the effect of my patented Mind-Melter Machine," Rector said to his incapacitated crowd. "Well, it's not technically patented, of course. It's not like the government would grant a patent to someone who is legally deceased. But that will change when I run the government. Which should be in, oh, ten minutes, give or take.

"What's that you say? Nothing. You say nothing, because your mouths don't function. But if you're thinking, 'How is he going to take over the US government in ten minutes?'—watch and enjoy. It's not like you can do anything else."

A telephone sat on a small table next to the pile of politicians. "United States Capitol, please," Rector said into the mouthpiece. "Ahoy! This is Ambrose Rector, your new president, king, and supreme overlord of all things. . . . Yes, I'm serious. . . . I've taken the World's Fair hostage. All of it, everyone. I can melt the brains of a hundred thousand people with a slight twist of the intensity knob on my doomsday device. And if losing a slew of random sidewalk slugs isn't high enough stakes for you, consider that I also have every member of the

Inventors' Guild, the governor of New York, and the man you called your leader up until thirty seconds ago, Chester A. Arthur. I also have Ulysses S. Grant, although, you know, what has he done lately?"

Rector crouched and poked a set of his special plugs into President Arthur's ears. Arthur sat up, gasping, relieved of the Mind-Melter's power. Rector held the telephone to him and the president shouted into the mouthpiece, "It's true! He's got us all! We're at his whim! But—"

Rector plucked the plugs out and Arthur flopped back to the floor.

"And there you have it," Rector said into the telephone. "You all work for me now. What's that? Oh, I see. Congress will have to vote on it. Well, sure. Rules are rules. I want this to be official. Go vote. I'll wait. Just keep in mind that if you vote no, I kill a hundred thousand people instantly."

Rector tapped his foot and whistled while he waited. Molly and Emmett began crawling away, inch by inch, trying not to attract attention. They were unsuccessful. A hand clamped over each of their skulls and, with a metallic creak, lifted them off the ground.

"How come haven't ye two meltit?" asked Oogie MacDougal.

"What's going on down there, MacDougal?" Rector asked from the stage, his voice still echoing through the loudspeakers.

"Th' bairns, they're no frozen," Oogie shouted, as

Molly and Emmett writhed fruitlessly. "Ach, Ah see. Looks lik' thay git thair hauns on some o' yer fancy wee lug plugs."

"Marvelous," Rector said with a sigh. "Must've stolen them straight out of the ears of your oh-so-capable goon squad. That was sarcasm, by the way."

"Whit dae ye want ah shuid dae wi' thaim? Crush thair skulls?"

"That *is* why I gave you a superpowered exoskeleton," said Rector.

The thin man in the emerald overcoat and shimmery top hat held his captives at arm's length. "Emmett," he said. "Miss von Venturesworth. Normally, ah dinnae care fur crushin' the noggins o' wee bairns, but fur ye pair, I'll mak' an exception."

Molly tried scratching at MacDougal's hands, but her fingernails clinked against the metal beneath his green gloves. Then she heard a voice from behind her.

"Blink, kids!"

Sarah! She must have gotten her hands on some earplugs! Had any of the others? Molly shut her eyes tight and heard the click-pop of George Eastman's camera. Oogie MacDougal dropped the children and staggered, blinded by the flash.

"Come on," Sarah said, tossing the camera.

They scrambled away from the masses of unmoving people toward the eerily still snack kiosks on the edge of the plaza. Oogie tromped after them, blindly swiping his fists through the air. One wild swing bent a steel lamp-post in half. Molly dove through the gangster's gangly legs, snatching the tail of his long coat and yanking it right off his back. Steel bands encircled Oogie's bony chest, shoulders, arms, and neck. Hinges squealed at every joint, and a shiny power pack hummed on his back.

"Mah favrit jaiket!" the gang lord howled, blinking as his sight cleared.

He raised an entire candy corn stand overhead, ready to drop it on Molly. *Oh, the irony,* she thought.

And then someone yanked her out of the way—quite painfully, by her braid—as the snack kiosk was smashed into splinters. "Hi, kid," said Margaret Knight, standing over her. "Sorry about the hair, but, you know, better than dying, right?"

Molly nodded.

"Get with Sarah," Margaret urged. "I'll take care of this tin-plated string bean." In her hand was one of Tesla's sparking glass spheres.

"I *knew* we should've taken one of those," Molly said.

"Go!" Margaret yelled as Oogie crashed through what was left of the candy stand and curled a mechanized arm around her.

"This day isnae endin' wi'oot me crushin' soombody," Oogie growled.

"You're gonna regret your choice of wardrobe," Margaret said as she shattered the globe against MacDougal's steel-encased chest, sending sparks up and down his body. Oogie collapsed. But the jolt also blew Margaret across the plaza. She landed among the other unmoving fairgoers.

"No!" Emmett screamed.

Sarah and Molly scrambled to Margaret's side. Sarah felt for a pulse. "She's alive. But we can't help her now."

Molly was about to protest when she noticed who Margaret was lying next to. "Jasper," she said sadly, gently patting the immobile ashman. "Why did you come here, you big fool? You knew what was going to happen. Were you trying to help us? Now how are you going to find out what happens to Phileas Fogg?"

Emmett tapped her shoulder and pointed to the stage. Rector was throwing a foot-stomping tantrum. He stopped only when he spotted Hertha skulking onto the platform from behind. Hertha froze. She was still a good twenty feet from the Mind-Melter. But Rector was even farther, at the opposite end of the platform.

"Ah, Miss Marks," the villain said coolly. "You'll never reach it, you know."

"Expecting some Green Onion Boys to come to your aid?" Hertha said. She fluffed her collar. "Your minions are on the ground with everybody else. My women and I saw to that. Thank you for the earplugs, by the way."

Rector waved his hand dismissively. "First rule of world domination: never pin your hopes for success on henchmen. No, I'm going to stop you myself. Because, you see, like the badger who has cleared the bees from a honeycomb only to have his paw stung by a deadly scorpion, you too have tragically failed to anticipate the *true* danger."

"Why is there a scorpion in a beehive?" Hertha said. "You know, the children were right about—"

"You, Miss Marks, have not met my Magneta-Ray!" He drew his glowing orange weapon and aimed it at a set of wrought-iron steps that led up to the stage. A humming filled the air and the steps levitated. Rector then flicked his wrist, and the iron stairs hurled themselves at Hertha, sending her tumbling off the back of the stage.

Molly gasped. Rector smiled as he hopped down and started walking toward her, making no attempt to avoid stepping on the immobile people in his path.

"Run!" Sarah yelled, and they raced back toward the Big Wheel.

They heard the hum, and a metal chair crashed to the ground right next to Molly. A bench whipped by. And then a trash can. Each projectile missed them by mere inches.

"If he doesn't kill *us* with that stuff, he's going to kill some poor person on the ground," Sarah said as they ran. "The things he throws keep dropping right before they can reach us. We need to stay out of range!"

"He'll just keep coming closer, though," Emmett said as they reached the silently spinning Ferris Wheel. "We need to keep him away somehow."

Molly cupped her hands by her mouth and yelled, "Now, Mother! We've lured him away from the machine! Turn it off now!"

Rector paused, but did not turn around. "You're bluffing," he scoffed. "If your mother weren't a lifeless lump on the floor like the rest of these meatbags, she would have already made her move."

"You sure about that?" Molly asked slyly. "Believe me, it's going to be a member of the Pepper family who dismantles your machine."

Rector snuck a quick peek over his shoulder. It was working.

"How many gangsters did you hire, Rector?" Emmett asked. "'Cause that's how many pairs of earplugs are floating around for the taking."

Rector pursed his lips and started backing toward the stage. But as he did, an ear-piercing shriek of rending metal rang out above their heads. Rector was using his Magneta-Ray to pull the Ferris Wheel off its frame.

"Move!" Sarah pushed the children ahead of her as the gigantic wheel broke free of its moorings and rolled after them. As Rector directed the wheel with his ray, Sarah and the kids ran along the far edge of the plaza, trying to keep the runaway amusement ride from flattening scores of people. But within seconds they hit a dead end.

Seeing no alternative, Molly started to climb into a Polynesian fruit stand. But Sarah pulled her back. "No, it'll be crushed!" she yelled. Sarah shoved both children aside as the Ferris Wheel toppled onto its side and demolished the tropical food stand. Dust choked the air. Minutes passed before Molly was able to see and breathe.

"Sarah!" she called between coughs.

"Molly! I'm trapped!" Sarah's voice came from beneath one of the wheel's gondolas. It was lying upside down atop the splintered ruins of the fish stand. Emmett tapped Molly's shoulder and pointed out the unmoving passengers who had flopped out of that very car: Crikes and Tusk. From the pained looks on their faces, Molly knew the fools had tried to share one pair of earplugs.

She turned back to see Rector, pacing onstage. Then, suddenly, a ringing. Rector picked up the phone. "Ahoy! Ah, yes . . . Wonderful! First order of business—round up everyone who didn't vote for me and throw them in the congressional dungeon. . . . What's that? Okay, first order of business—build a congressional dungeon."

The children began hauling splintered beams from the rubble. "We'll get you out, Sarah," Molly said.

"It'll take forever," Sarah replied from beneath the debris. "I'll dig out through the back. You two need to stop Rector. I believe in you!"

They glanced over to see Rector twisting a knob on his ray gun. He aimed it at a lamppost, which blew off its foundation and spun through the air, far out of the plaza, landing in the thatched roof of the Congo Pavilion.

"Hey, guess what I just figured out?" Rector said. "Magnets have two ends—one that attracts and one that repels. And when I reverse the polarity of my ray—voilà! More range! Gotta love science!"

He positioned himself behind a metallic urn with a large fern in it. *Hummm!* The planter hurtled toward the children at a terrifying speed. Molly and Emmett pushed each other to the ground as it zipped over their heads.

Molly didn't know what to do. She'd made one mistake after another, and now she was facing the end of her country. Possibly the entire world. Maybe if she hadn't fed their evidence to a llama. If she hadn't given herself over to the Jägerman. Or if she'd gotten a better look at those robots. Or trusted the MOI from the start, like Emmett wanted her to. Maybe if she'd never dragged Emmett into her ridiculous schemes. Or if she'd just told her mother she didn't want to be an inventor.

She threw her head back in despair, and visions of all

her mistakes appeared before her eyes, hovering in the air above her. Her mother. Bell. Edison. Even the robots. She blinked, but the visions remained.

Then she noticed that Emmett was looking up too.

Help from Above

"THE ICARUS CHARIOT!" Molly couldn't believe her eyes. And she was instantly jealous that Bell and Edison got to ride it before she did. As soon as this was all over, she told herself, she was taking a turn on that thing. And having some candy corn.

As the flying machine's motor purred, Cassandra, in the pilot's seat, pulled the steering levers to angle the canvas wings and begin their descent. The other three seats that circled the central mast held Alexander Graham Bell (gripping his safety straps for dear life), Thomas Edison (waving his hat in the air), and Mary Walton (who looked cozy enough to fall asleep).

As surprised as Molly was to see the chariot and its passengers, she was even more shocked by its cargo. In a large bin that dangled by chains from the bottom of the craft stood four of Bell's singing automatons—the original prototypes from his office, Molly assumed.

Cassandra flew low enough for the cargo bin to touch ground and flipped a switch to release the chains. She then brought the Icarus Chariot down next to it on the empty concrete base where the Ferris Wheel once stood. Molly's arms were around Cassandra before the woman could disembark. From the stage across the plaza, Rector simply crossed his arms and watched.

"That was one heck of a ride," Edison hooted, jumping from the Chariot. The smile fled his face the moment he saw the carpet of bodies covering the plaza. "Those are people . . ."

"Dear God, the devastation," Bell muttered.

"They're alive," Emmett said. "They just can't move, because of the waves from Rector's machine. Speaking of which, why can *you* move?"

"Oh," said Cassandra. "Turned out the bad guy had stationed a quartet of goons back at the Guild to guard these three. After I took them out, I found some gadgety bizwits in their ears, and we borrowed them."

"You took down four guys by yourself?" Molly gaped. "How?"

"Three words," said Cassandra. "Corn cob boomerang. Or is corncob one word?"

"We can fill each other in later," said Mary. "Right now, we need to help these people, which means cutting the power to that contraption. Where are Hertha and the others?"

Emmett shook his head.

"Oh, dear," Mary muttered. "We must waste no time, then. Cass, let's put your plan into action."

"Rector's got a magnet ray," Molly warned. "We can't get any closer without him hurling a big hunk of metal at us." *CRACK!* A cash register crashed through a nearby wall. "Like that."

"No fear, Molls," Cassandra said. "We needn't move one step closer to the man."

Bell and Edison were hoisting the automatons out of the bin. "Let's hope your adjustments work, Mrs. Pepper," Bell said as he handed small black boxes to Cassandra, Mary, and Edison.

"Rector's got a Mind-Melter, so I thought we could use some allies who didn't have any minds to melt," Cassandra explained. "I did some retooling on Mr. Bell's metal friends here. No reason they couldn't do more than just sing."

"You turned them into warrior robots?" Molly asked, agog with excitement.

"Well, I taught them to walk and grab things," her mother replied. "Which is basically all they need to do: Grab a lever and pull, right?"

"But the Magneta-Ray," said Emmett. "Rector will—"

"He will be annoyed to all heck when he finds out his

magnet doesn't work on these fellas," Edison said with a waggle of his eyebrows.

"In order to ship these fellows nationwide, I wanted them to be lightweight," said Bell. "So I constructed them entirely from aluminum—a metal which, as luck would have it, is not magnetic."

Cassandra clapped her hands together. "Let's get to work."

Each of the four inventors opened the chest plate of their assigned automaton and wound the key inside. Pectoral hatches closed once more, Cassandra stepped back, held her little black box to her mouth, and said, "Robot, walk." At her command, the automaton Bell had dubbed Robert began taking big, clunky steps into the plaza.

"You added the vocal recognition from the automated secretary," Molly said, swelling with pride. "I can't believe you did it that fast!"

"Charles, walk," Edison said into his controller.

"William, walk," said Bell.

"James, walk," said Mary.

The others joined their aluminum brother on the field.

"You didn't call yours Robert," Molly said to her mother.

"Robot is a better name," Cassandra said with a wink.

Across the plaza, Rector stood onstage and watched the four shining figures march toward him. "Looks like this finally got interesting," he said smugly.

For years, Molly had awaited the moment the Inventors' Guild would recognize her mother's genius. Now, here were its two most accomplished members standing by her side, using *her* technology. *To save the world.*

"Oh, I went down south, to see my pal Sal, singing polly wolly doodle all the day!" The voices of the marching automatons rang out in perfect four-part harmony.

"They still sing?" Edison asked incredulously.

"Of course!" Cassandra replied. "I love this song."

"Aaaaargh!" Rector howled. "I hate that song!" He aimed his ray at the approaching robots and pulled the trigger. Nothing. "Aluminum, I assume," Rector grumbled. "Well, like the Egyptian asp that thinks it's found a safe perch upon the brow of a mighty river horse—"

"No more metaphors!" Cassandra screamed.

"Fine!" Rector barked back. "My point was going to be that aluminum is a *very thin* metal!" He turned his ray on the telephone, which ripped from its cord, flew through the air, and caved in the shiny skull of one of the automatons. The robot collapsed onto its back and ceased moving.

"Not my William!" Bell cried out.

"You monster!" Cassandra cried. "The song sounds all wrong now without the bass!"

"Split them up," instructed Mary. "He can't attack all three at once. James, left!"

"Robot, right," Cassandra commanded.

"Charles, you keep doing what you're doing, you beautiful piece of manly machinery," said Edison.

The automatons avoided the signposts, frying pans, and storage cases that Rector hurled at them, and Mary guided James to the sole remaining set of steps that led to the stage.

"James, climb," Mary said.

Bell wrung his hands. "I can't watch."

A dozen metal skewers flew from a nearby kebab stand and impaled the poor robot like a pincushion. James toppled down the steps and fell still.

"Are there really only two more?" Rector called out. "'Cause this is fun!"

"Your fun is about to end, imposter!" Edison bellowed. "Prepare for the wrath of . . . Charles!"

And with that, Automaton Charles stopped and stood completely still.

"Move, Charles," Edison shouted into his controller. "Walk! Bell, what's wrong with your stupid, defective toy? Why did it stop?"

"Looks like the motor ran down," Bell said. "You didn't wind it enough."

"If I'd built the thing, that would've been enough winding for hours."

"Gentlemen," Cassandra interrupted. "I programmed them to re-wind themselves."

349

Edison looked skeptical, but lifted his controller. "Charles, wind yourself."

The automaton opened its chest plate, turned its motor key several times, and resumed marching on Rector. The inventors cheered. And then Rector used his ray to hoist the skewered body of James and hammer it down onto Charles. The two robots ended up one pierced, dented mass of metal. Rector did a victory dance.

"You stink, Bell. Everything you make stinks." Edison threw his controller to the ground. "If we survive this, I'm gonna make a much, much better version of these things."

"Mother, where's yours?" Molly asked.

"Shhh!"

Onstage, Robot was approaching the Mind-Melter behind the obliviously tap-dancing Rector.

"Robot, grab," Cassandra said.

The automaton reached out for the Mind-Melter's long, red lever.

"Robot, pull!"

Crunch! The robot tore the lever straight out of the machine. Across the plaza, six people slapped their foreheads.

Rector cackled. He plucked the broken lever from the robot's hand and held it aloft like a victorious knight thrusting his sword to the heavens. "No lever, no off!" he shouted with wicked glee. "And how about no annoying inventors either?" He aimed his ray at the mangle-tangle mess that once was James and Charles, and launched it across the plaza.

"Look out!" Cassandra cried as the mass of arms, legs, and pointy iron skewers flew at them. She pushed the children down seconds before the soaring automatons sent her sailing through the fake palm tree entryway of the Tahiti Pavilion. The broken robots cracked the fake trees in half and the building began to shudder.

"Mrs. Pepper!" Bell and Edison both rushed inside to aid her.

"Stay down," Mary warned the children before racing after them herself. She was just about to step across the threshold when the pavilion collapsed.

Molly tried to scream but couldn't find her voice. She and Emmett ran to the crumbled Tahitian palace and saw Mary Walton on the ground.

"Are you okay, Miss Walton?" Emmett asked, bending to help her up.

"I . . . think so," Mary said, starting to stand. "I just . . . I . . ." Her face looked suddenly pained. "I think . . . I may . . . have lost a . . ." She felt around her left ear and then suddenly flopped back to the ground.

"One of her earplugs fell out," Molly cried. "Find it!" She and Emmett scoured the nearby ground, but came up empty.

"No," Molly said, still on her hands and knees. "We're

right back where we were. My mother's gone, our friends are gone."

"They are," said Emmett. He sounded quiet, but determined.

"I'm terrified," Molly said.

"I know," said Emmett. He didn't sound scared.

"It's just you and me again."

Emmett nodded. "Yeah, just us."

"Yeah . . . so why aren't you panicking?" Molly cried.

"Because I'm with Molly Pepper."

Molly didn't know what to say, and Emmett continued. "I've spent the last week trying to be more like Molly Pepper. Molly Pepper is unflappable. She's not *too* scared of anything. And she never lets me give up. Remember her? Remember *that* Molly Pepper?"

Molly closed her eyes and waited for her breathing to slow. "We still can't get near Rector," she said. "And there isn't even a lever anymore for us to turn off the machine. What can we do?"

"What would Molly Pepper do?"

Molly thought. Then she nodded. She knew.

Showdown!

"Ahoy? Washington? This is your supreme leader speaking. Hello?" Rector had retrieved the telephone and was on his knees trying to reinstall it when Molly and Emmett snuck up behind the stage. They carefully crawled around Rector's paralyzed victims—until one of those victims moved. Hertha moaned and rubbed her head.

"Shhh. Rector's right up there," Molly warned. "Are you okay?"

"A bit groggy," she mumbled. "How are we faring?"

"Terribly," said Molly. "But don't worry. Emmett and I have got this. You rest. But not too long. If this stage blows up, you won't wanna be back here."

"Thank you, I feel utterly secure now," Hertha said weakly as she laid her head back down.

Molly gave Emmett a silent nod that said, *Thank you for trusting me with this.* To which Emmett responded with a nod that said, *Thank* you *for believing in me. We won't let each other down.* And Molly was happy to have a friend who could say so much with a nod.

"Ahoy? Ah, yes, there you are, Mr. Senator," Molly heard Rector nattering into the phone. "Actually, no, you're not a senator anymore. It was senators who killed Caesar. Your new title is . . . Boot-Polisher."

Molly pulled herself up on the stage. In order for her plan to work, she was going to have to trust in the abilities of two inventors: her mother and Emmett. She held her mother's little controller box to her lips. "Robot, walk," she whispered. The automaton started toward Rector. Her trust was well placed.

The villain dropped the phone, spun, and aimed his ray gun at her. "Make that tin can stop or I will."

"Robot, stop," Molly said quickly.

Rector grinned. "Good choice. I'd like to keep at least one of these clankers intact so I can take a look inside and see how your mother made them work like that."

"As if you could understand it," Molly scoffed.

The villain laughed. "Ah, Little Miss Pepper. I should've guessed it would come to this—me against an eleven-year-old girl. How impressive a final victory for me."

"Actually, I just turned twelve."

"Well, in that case, I surrender."

Molly kept her face stony, trying to act braver than she felt. She was careful to keep Robot between her and Rector.

The madman glanced around. "Where's your little friend? Did I flatten him along with your mother? Oh, I can see from the sneer on your face that I did. A shame, really. If I'm to speak truthfully, you two came ridiculously close to thwarting my plans. If only you'd been smart enough to realize how similar we are."

"Similar? Us?" Molly said, her disgust evident.

"You're willing to break a few rules when you believe your cause is just, are you not?" Rector said. "Do you recall what you were doing when you first stumbled onto my plans?"

Molly kept her lips shut tight.

"You and the boy certainly would've made better sidekicks than those Green Onion morons," Rector continued. "Hey, perhaps there's still a place for you in my government. Interested?"

Behind Rector, Molly saw Emmett climb onto the other end of the platform. She nodded to him.

"Was that a yes?" Rector asked with surprise. "Wow, that took less convincing than expected. Perhaps you're even more devious than I thought. Pardon me if I don't completely take you at your word, though. Before we continue this conversation, let's have you toss that little black box, eh?"

Grumbling, Molly crouched, set the robot controller on the stage floor, and slowly stood up.

"Good girl," Rector said smugly. "That was easy, wasn't it?" He loosened up and relaxed his arms, his ray gun finally pointing away from Molly. "You know, I like this whole 'you obeying what I say' change. Makes things go so much more smoothly. A man could get used to—"

Molly quickly tapped the button on the special bracelet Emmett had fashioned for her just five minutes earlier. The controller at her feet leapt back into her hand, reeled in by a near-invisible thread. Once again, trust well placed. "Robot, grab!" Molly yelled into the black box. Robot reached out and grabbed the barrel of Rector's weapon.

"Hey! Let go, teapot!" the villain growled, but the automaton's metal fist held tight. With a snap, the barrel of the ray gun cracked open to reveal the small chunk of glowing meteorite.

"Robot, pull!" Molly shouted again. And the robot plucked the luminous stone from the gun.

"That's mine!" Rector shouted. He began beating at the automaton's hand with his busted ray gun.

"Robot, wind yourself!" Molly said.

With one hand, Robot opened his chest plate, and with the other—the hand that still clutched the meteorite— he reached inside himself for a fresh cranking. Then

Robot resealed his chest compartment—with the space rock securely inside.

"Ha!" Molly crowed. Rector pounded his fists against the robot's torso, but backed away as the automaton suddenly began to tremble. A low hum sounded from deep within its chest, and soon the stone's orange glow began to seep through every seam and joint in Robot's aluminum exterior. Molly feared the metal man might explode. But instead, he began to levitate. At first, Robot hovered a few inches above the ground—and Molly swore the look in its ceramic eyes was one of confusion. Then it took off, zooming headfirst into the sky and out of sight.

"Well," Rector said. "That was unexpected."

"Robot, come back!" Molly shouted into the controller. But the automaton was gone.

"I suppose the space rock's magnetism caused it to repel itself right off the planet," Rector muttered. "That's how magnets work, right?"

Then he noticed the grin on Molly's face. He turned to see Emmett standing by the Mind-Melter. "Oh, you're *not* dead," he said, clearly disappointed.

"But your death machine is," Emmett replied.

"How are you planning to turn it off?" Rector asked smugly.

Emmett held up a bucket. "Electricity and water don't play nice together."

"Oh, bravo!" Hertha said from the ground. "You've been paying attention! The Marvelous Moto-Mover did not die in vain."

Rector screamed as Emmett poured three gallons into the open hole where the lever used to sit. Loud pops sounded from deep within the Mind-Melter's workings, and wisps of black smoke leaked from its seams.

Almost immediately, people began to stir. Throughout the park, fairgoers were standing. And some—like Jasper and Josephine, whom the children were very pleased to see among the living—rushed toward the stage, where President Arthur sat up and shook his fuzzy jowls. "Did that really happen?"

Grover Cleveland shrugged.

Rector grabbed Molly. "I'm going to wager none of you want to be responsible for the death of this brat." He held her in a headlock, the back of his hand against her throat. "Anybody gets in my way and I inject her with the deadly dose of Antarctic sea spider venom stored in my ring."

Rector forced his captive over to his broken Mind-Melter. Keeping one arm around Molly, he used the other to pry open the side of the smoking machine, reach inside, and pull out a small hunk of orange rock. "Nobody gets their hands on this," he said, jamming the Ambrosium into his pocket.

He and Molly then hopped down from the platform,

and the crowd parted for them. Molly was heartened to see Emmett follow as they warily crossed the square. Just as she was comforted to see Sarah helping Margaret to her feet. But none of them could do a thing to help her.

Once across the plaza, Rector prodded Molly into the Icarus Chariot. He strapped her in, then took the pilot's seat and immediately began pedaling. The generator hummed, the rotor spun, and the Icarus Chariot lifted off.

"I hope you don't think I'm beaten, Molly," Rector said as they ascended. "This shard in my pocket is just one tiny chip off the old space rock. There's plenty more where that came from."

"Antarctica?" Molly asked. Below, Emmett was reaching fruitlessly up to her. "That's where you're going?"

"Where *we're* going," Rector corrected her.

"I see," Molly said flatly. "And if I don't come with you, you'll stab me with your poison ring."

"Oh, there's no poison ring," Rector said. "Although it is a *great* idea—I gotta write that one down. No, you'll come with me because you want to. Being an Antarctic explorer is more your thing, anyway, right? Besides, what's your alternative? Go back to the mother who wastes your true talents by forcing you to be her assistant? She doesn't deserve you. Look at her, standing down there, all buddy-buddy with Bell and Edison, the very men who hold her back from—"

"My mother's okay?" Molly looked over the edge. Cassandra was standing right below her, arms outstretched. Molly unlatched her safety harness.

"What are you going to do, jump?" Rector asked, pedaling faster. "If she misses, you break every bone in your body."

Molly stepped to the edge of the flying rowboat.

"If you don't come with me, you'll never find out if Emmett's father is still alive," Rector said quickly, holding a hand out to her. "He was when I left him down there."

Molly's head whipped to her kidnapper.

"I couldn't bring myself to kill him. He was the only one who argued for me when the rest of the crew kicked me off the ship. I even left him with some supplies. Probably not enough to survive three years in Antarctica, but, hey, Captain Lee was a resourceful guy. Seemed to really love his kid, too; that might've been enough to keep him going."

Molly stared at him. Emmett's words echoed in her head: *What would Molly Pepper do?*

"Really, he could be alive," Rector said. "Strap yourself back in and we'll go find out."

Molly looked down. Her mother's arms were wide open, beckoning. She jumped.

History Is Written by the Victors

THE NEW YORK City police flooded into the fairgrounds soon after, followed by the US Army and squads of federal agents. They saw to the wounded, protected the president, recorded eyewitness testimony, and rounded up the remaining Green Onion Boys, all of whom claimed to have been duped by Rector. When they caught Oogie MacDougal, his heavily accented protests were taken for the ravings of a madman and he was shipped to Blackwell's Asylum.

Keeping a low profile, Hertha Marks and the Mothers of Invention congratulated Cassandra on a world-class job of daughter-catching. They reminded her that their offer of membership still stood, and then quietly slipped away. Though not before Josephine Cochrane presented Molly with a long-overdue bag of candy corn.

Molly waved goodbye and tossed one of the sugary kernels into her mouth. She grimaced. "Ugh. They're terrible." She popped in a second piece.

"Then why are you still eating them?" Emmett asked.

Molly shrugged. "They're candy."

Jasper found Emmett and the Peppers sitting on a fallen pillar outside the China Pavilion. "You children are hazardous to my health," the ashman said. "I don't know what kind of mystical, wizztical spell took hold of my mind to make me think I should come here and try to find you two. I mean, why in the name of Lincoln's mole would I—"

Molly threw her arms around him.

"I suppose that's why," he said. "I really should go now, though. Balthazar Birdhouse has been unsupervised for way too long."

Molly, Cassandra, and Emmett sat for a bit longer and watched soldiers clear people from the park. "So, will you join the MOI?" Molly asked her mother.

"Perhaps," Cassandra said, trying some candy corn and wincing. "Or perhaps I will get all of *them* into the Inventors' Guild with me."

"You really think Bell and Edison will convince the Guild to change its rules?" Emmett asked.

"After what we did today?" Cassandra said. "I should think so. We just saved the country! The Peppers have finally made the history books!"

"I congratulate you both," Emmett said.

"Don't discount your own part in this," Cassandra said.

"We might never have disarmed Rector without your Snap-Back Wrist Retrieval Cord Thingie," Molly said. "I'd like to see Edison build something that useful with only the odds and ends in Mary Walton's purse."

"And Emmett, our housing arrangement may be somewhat complicated at the moment, but I hope you know you will always have a home with us."

Emmett looked as if he might cry. "Thank you," he said. "America is my home. And I want more than anything to stay here. But I was reminded today that my Chinese heritage is also a part of me. A part I know nothing about."

"I understand," Molly said. She rolled a piece of candy corn between her fingers. Molly couldn't get Rector's words out of her head. Would Emmett be better off knowing about his father? Or would that knowledge only torture him further? "Emmett, there's . . . something I have to tell you."

"Can it wait, Molls?" Cassandra interrupted. "I see Bell and Edison over there. I haven't gotten to thank them for freeing me from that collapsed pavilion. Of course, I freed *them* from imprisonment before that. . . . But, still."

She strode off and Emmett, misty-eyed, followed. Reluctantly, Molly did as well. The news about Emmett's father would have to wait.

Bell and Edison stood in a huddle of dark-suited men that included Presidents Arthur and Grant, Governor Cleveland, and several Molly didn't recognize. Cassandra was about to tap Bell on the shoulder when they heard President Arthur say, "The world must never know of this."

"But there are literally thousands of witnesses," Bell said, incredulous.

"Mass hysteria," said a bespectacled man in a dark gray suit. "I'd wager more than half the people present legitimately don't understand what happened to them."

"Call it some kind of electrical disturbance," offered another unidentified man. "Or a gas leak, perhaps. Something that addled people's brains, made them hallucinate."

"A chemical explosion!" President Arthur said, nodding. "That would explain the structural damage as well."

"*Or* we could just tell everybody," Cassandra said with obviously forced congeniality.

"Who is this woman?" asked the man in the glasses.

Cassandra offered her hand to the man. "Cassandra Pepper. National hero, savior of the World's Fair, and inventor of the flying machine you saw today."

"The flying machine Rector used to make his escape?" the man asked pointedly.

"Cassandra and the others risked everything to help us today," Bell said with equal bite.

"Alec is right," added Edison. "Are we planning to

sweep those women under the rug?"

"If they are the heroes and patriots they say they are," said the gray-suited man, "they will understand the importance of keeping secrets for the sake of our nation."

"Secrets are what caused this whole problem!" Molly said, forcing herself into the circle of men. "Hiding what happened to the *Frost Cleaver*, hiding the real reason Rector was on that ship, hiding what goes on in the Guild—"

"Little girl," said the gray-suited man. "I'm going to pay your mother a compliment by assuming she's intelligent enough to understand what would happen if the American people became aware that a man as dangerous and powerful as Ambrose Rector was at large."

"Oh, yeah?" Molly rolled up her sleeve. "Well, I'm gonna pay you a—"

"Molly, stop." Cassandra put her hand on her daughter's shoulder.

"Fear not, Mrs. Pepper," said President Arthur. "We are aware of your contributions today and we will see to it that the charges against you are quietly dropped."

Cassandra muttered words that sounded like "thank you," but might also have been something less polite. And she led Molly away.

"So that's that," Ulysses S. Grant said with a sigh. "We'll dismantle the entire Fair immediately. As far as the history books will know, the 1883 World's Fair will never have happened."

"Mother, we can't let them get away with this!" Molly said.

"But they have a point," Cassandra said sadly. "If people knew what Rector could do with those space rocks, there'd be mass panic."

"So?" Molly said.

"So letting this go is the responsible thing to do."

"But what about us?" Molly asked, distraught. "It's like we're back where we started! What do *we* do now?"

"*You* can do whatever you'd like," said her mother. "Even if that means I need to look for a new assistant. You have many talents, Molly. I won't hold you back from exploring any of them."

Molly wiped away the tear that formed in the corner of her eye.

"As for me, however," Cassandra went on. "I'm an inventor. I'm going back to inventing. What should I make next?"

Molly sniffled. "Can you create something that could get us to Antarctica?"

"I can create anything," Cassandra said with utter confidence.

Molly smiled, then checked over her shoulder to make sure no one was listening. "Mother, there's something I need to tell you. It's about Emmett's— Wait! Where's Emmett?"

"Molly! Mrs. Pepper!" Emmett called from behind

the Polar Pavilion's igloo. The Peppers ran, kicking up paper-shred snow, and found the boy pointing skyward. They looked up to see a silver figure descending from the clouds. Robot made a graceful, controlled landing and settled his gaze on Molly.

"What would you have me do next, mistress?" asked the robot.

The query was met with a lot of blinking.

"Mistress?" repeated Robot.

Molly turned to her mother. "I didn't know you programmed him to speak on his own."

"I didn't," Cassandra whispered.

"If the space rock made him fly," said Emmett, "do you think it did . . . other stuff?"

"Other stuff?" echoed Robot. His chest flared with an orange glow.

"We need to tell Mr. Bell about—" Emmett began.

Molly shook her head. "Like the men in the suits said, we're very good at keeping secrets."

Cassandra grinned. "We might make the history books yet."

"Come, Robot," said Molly. "Come, family. Let's go."

And with that, a woman, a girl, a boy, and an aluminum robot left Central Park and headed home to their abandoned pickle shop.

Afterword: What's Real and What's Not in 'A Dastardly Plot'

This book is a work of fiction, but many of the people, places, and things that appear in these pages actually existed in American history. So, what's real and what's not?

Thomas Edison and Alexander Graham Bell: Obviously, these two men really existed. They're quite famous. But are all the details about them in this book factual? Many, but probably not all. Edison really was totally deaf in his left ear. And his lab in Menlo Park really had all those crazy things in jars that I mentioned. Bell actually was a founding member of the National Geographic Society. And he really did experiment with talking automatons. I have no hard evidence, however, that Edison was a good tap dancer.

The International Inventors' Guild: While no group with this name may have existed, it was not uncommon in the nineteenth century for professional organizations like it to have all-male membership. (There might even be a few places that still have rules like that today.)

The Mothers of Invention: While I can't say whether the MOI members teamed up in real life, all of these women were real inventors. Hertha Marks really made groundbreaking discoveries about the nature of electricity, Sarah Goode really built folding furniture, Josephine Cochrane really created the dishwasher, Mary Walton (known to some as the mother of green technology) really developed a noise-control system for railroads, and Margaret Knight really was one of the most prolific inventors of her day. Not-so-fun fact: Margaret Knight almost didn't get credit for inventing the paper bag! A male colleague tried to claim the idea as his own, but luckily, several witnesses stepped up to shoot down that scoundrel's lie and make sure the world didn't miss out on Ms. Knight's genius.

The Chinese Exclusion Act: Sadly, I did not make this up. Signed by Chester A. Arthur on May 6, 1882, this legislation marked the first time the United States ever banned an entire class of immigrants based on their country of origin. The law was intended to be in effect for only ten years, but didn't get repealed until 1943.

The Jäger Society: This group is loosely based on the New York Society for the Prevention of Cruelty to Children (aka the Gerry Society), founded in 1875 by lawyer Elbridge Gerry. Back then, some of its officers—known as Gerrymen at the time—got a reputation for being overzealous in their mission, but the Society eventually took care of its rogue agent problem and changed its focus to helping abused children—an important cause the NYSPCC still fights for today.

The New York City Lunatic Asylum on Blackwell's Island: Totally real and totally scary! Luckily for all of us, it was shut down a few years after this story takes place, thanks to the investigative reporting of a true American hero, Nellie Bly. Blackwell's Island is today known as Roosevelt Island and is much less terrifying.

Robots: I hate to break it to Molly, but in 1883, they really would have been called "automatons." The word "robot" was coined by Czech playwright Karel Čapek for his 1920 play, *R.U.R.—Rossum's Universal Robots*. (Or did Capek just overhear the word from a precocious twelve-year-old New Yorker?)

The Brooklyn Bridge: It was originally called the "New York and Brooklyn Bridge"—since New York and Brooklyn were separate cities at the time—but that name is simply too long to keep writing over and over in a book. The opening ceremony happened pretty much as described here. Except no one reported any assassins climbing the cables. (Then again, that's exactly the kind of detail they'd want to keep quiet, isn't it?)

The 1883 World's Fair in New York: If you do a little research (and I strongly suggest you do—research is awesome), you will most likely learn that there was no World's Fair in 1883. And that poor Mr. Ferris would have to wait a whole decade to debut his wheel at the 1893 World's Fair in Chicago. But if you dig a little deeper, you will learn that a World's Fair really *was* scheduled to be held in New York in 1883. And Ulysses S. Grant really *was* on the planning committee. And yet, there are no reports of that Fair ever taking place. So what happened? The official story is that New Yorkers rejected the Fair because they thought it would ruin Central Park. And that's most likely the truth. (Or is it . . . ?)

—Christopher Healy, 2018

Acknowledgments

I'm not nearly as amazing and awesome as the women of the MOI, but one thing we have in common is that we all recognize the benefits of collaboration. Which is why I have so many people to thank in helping me put this book together. Thanks, as always, to my first line of defense, my home team, Noelle, Bryn, and Dash—without you all, some of the best parts of this story might never have made it onto the page, and some of the worst parts might not have been deleted. Thanks, of course, to my editor, Jordan Brown, and to Debbie Kovacs at Walden Media, for believing in this book from the start and skillfully ushering it to fruition (looking forward to Book 2!). Thanks to Cheryl Pientka and everyone at Jill Grinberg Literary for all your support, both literary and emotional. Thanks to Kevin Chu at the Museum of Chinese in America for so graciously answering my many emails. Thanks to Martha Brockenbrough, Jennifer Chu, Geoff Rodkey, Shenwei Chang, Tiffany Dayemo, Barry Wolverton, and Christine Howey for all your invaluable input. Every opinion I got on this book helped shape what it has become. And lastly, thanks to the fans of my Hero's Guide books who said they'd stick with me for a trip to a very different world. Your promises meant more than you know. (And, obviously, I believed them, otherwise why would I be assuming you're reading this now?)

Turn the page for a sneak peek at

A Perilous Journey of
Danger and Mayhem, Book 2:
The Treacherous Seas

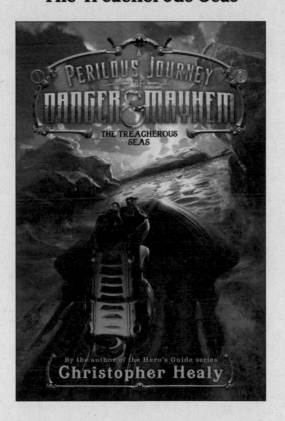

Pick a Peck of Pepper's Pickles . . .
Please
New York City, September 12, 1883

"Boop! Boop! Boop!"

Emmett Lee screamed and fell off his bed, accidentally tearing down the sheet that hung between his cot and Molly Pepper's.

"Emmmmmmmett," Molly moaned, wrapping her pillow around her head. "What are you doing?"

"What am *I* doing?" Emmett sputtered. "Robot's the one making the noise." Beside his bed stood a tall metallic man with a scuffed oil-barrel chest, clunky aluminum-tube arms, and a rather dapper straw hat. The automaton's handlebar mustache spun like a pinwheel as he continued to *boop*. "Robot, please stop," Emmett moaned. "Why are you doing this?"

"I was trying to anticipate your needs," Robot said. His trap-hinged jaw sometimes clicked as he spoke, but,

1

as he'd been originally created to sing at parties, he had a delightful tenor voice.

"And you thought we *needed* to be startled out of a deep sleep?" Emmett asked.

"I thought you needed to be awakened," said Robot.

Molly squinted at the clock on the wall and, giving up, slipped on her eyeglasses. "Oh, bother beans! It's seven twenty!"

"That is what I was going to say," said Robot. "Except for the 'bother beans' part. Should I start saying 'bother beans'?"

Emmett double-checked the clock. "The shop's supposed to be open already! And we're going to be late for school! Okay. Okay. Don't panic. We can figure this out. The walk to school takes, what, a half hour?"

Molly leapt from her bed. "Robot, lights!"

Robot began igniting the gas lamps that sat atop teetering piles of books, while Molly shook her mother, who lay snoring on yet another cot only two feet away. "Mother!"

"Was somebody booping?" Cassandra mumbled.

"The booper was I, Mrs. Pepper," said Robot.

Molly ripped the blanket from her mother and shouted, "We were supposed to be up an hour and twenty minutes ago! We're late for everything!"

"Oh, yes, I almost forgot! We're late!" Cassandra bounced from bed onto her tool-strewn workbench (for the bedroom was also the Peppers' workshop) and ran across the tabletop to a counter stacked with pots, mugs, and cans (for the workshop was also the Peppers' kitchen). Cassandra often took this route to avoid tripping over the half-built inventions littering the floor of the cramped little room. There were plenty of benefits to living with a brilliant inventor like Cassandra Pepper, but uncluttered living space was not one of them.

Cassandra hopped down and flipped the toggle on her Brew-Master 1900, which instantly began spouting steam.

"I'm still doing the math, but I don't think we have time for coffee," Emmett said from behind the sheet that Robot helpfully held up for him while he changed into school clothes.

"There's always time for coffee," said Cassandra.

"Well, let's see," said Emmett, misbuttoning his shirt. "If we leave right now and take Bleecker Street to— no, at this hour, we should probably go up West Third, unless—"

"Robot, can we make it to school on time?" Molly asked, squeezing into her ankle-length black dress.

"Your average walk to school takes eighteen minutes," said Robot. "You should arrive for the morning bell if you leave within the next eleven minutes, thirty seconds."

"See, plenty of time for a hearty breakfast," Cassandra

said cheerily as she dropped a full loaf of rye into the Mega-Slicifier. With a grinding noise, the device began shooting thin squares of bread onto the table like a riverboat gambler dealing cards.

"There's one thing I don't understand, though, Mother." Molly climbed over an open crate of nails while weaving her dark hair into a long braid. "What happened to the clock you built? The alarm didn't go off."

"That's because I didn't set it," Cassandra said, passing a hot mug of coffee to her daughter.

"You, um, you did this on purpose?" Emmett said. He fell over in a frantic attempt to pull his pants up. "Can I ask why?"

"Molly said mornings were boring, always the same old routine," Cassandra explained. "So I decided to spice things up!"

"Congratulations, you've succeeded," Molly replied as she fed bread slices through the Toastinator with one hand and buttoned her dress with the other. While she didn't want to say so in front of Emmett, she was genuinely enjoying the frenzy. It wasn't that she wanted to return to the terror and chaos of last May, when Ambrose Rector and his henchmen, the Green Onion Boys, were constantly trying to kill them, but she had been longing for a little chaos to be thrown back into their lives. Emmett, however . . . Well, Molly was pretty sure that, after years of living on the streets, hiding from

4

Jäger Society goons who wanted to deport him back to his birth country of China, Emmett was fond of finally having a "same old routine." Moments like these, Molly hoped her friend wasn't regretting his decision to stay with the Peppers.

"Get over here and eat, Emmett!" Molly called, sliding aside some loose screws to make space at the worktable (which was also the dining table).

"I really just want to get to school." Emmett, fastening his brown tweed vest, stumbled over a partially constructed Multi-Broom PowerSweeper. "It took an escort from government agents to get me into that school in the first place. I'd rather not risk it."

"I understand, Emmett, but you'll be fine as long as we abide by the contract," Cassandra said as she launched dollops of butter onto the toast with her Pat-a-Pult. "In the meantime, you children are twelve years old—I can't send you out without a proper morning meal." She cracked three eggs into the coffee maker and held a bowl by its spout to catch the coffee-speckled yellow mush that spewed forth.

Molly wasted no time digging into her bowl of slop. "This is surprisingly un-awful," she said. She flipped open a folded copy of yesterday's *New York Sun*. Emmett gave her a sideways look. "Just because we're late doesn't mean I can't be informed," she said. "Don't worry, I'm only scanning."

She took off her glasses, slid them surreptitiously under a napkin, and began reading.

PRESIDENT CALLS OFF SEARCH FOR SOUTH POLE

In the sixty years since a Russian vessel first spotted the mysterious "Seventh Continent of Antarctica," many intrepid souls have set out in search of the fabled South Pole—which scientists believe to lie deep at the heart of Antarctica's forbidding, snowcapped landscape. But most are thwarted by the miles-thick ice shelf that surrounds the continent and turn back before even reaching shore. Those who manage to make landfall fare worse. Many expeditions do not return at all.

Tragically, this appears to be the fate of the research vessel *Slush Puppy*, America's most recent attempt at victory in the race to the Pole. The wreckage of the ship washed onto an Argentine beach last week. All crew members are presumed dead.

The fate of the *Slush Puppy* signals the end of our Age of Antarctic Exploration, as President Chester A. Arthur today signed an executive order forbidding further attempts to locate the fabled Pole. "Too many fine American lives have been lost," Arthur said. "It's not going to happen. We might as well try reaching the moon!" The president then turned his attention to the new set of bronze mustache combs presented to him by the king of (continued on p. 5)

"Hey, Molly," Emmett said, wiping his mouth. "I know you like to recap the news for me on the walk to school, but we're probably going to be running today, so—"

"That's okay! Nothing interesting, anyway." Molly quickly refolded the paper. There was no need to share what she'd just read with a boy whose father *died* on a failed mission to Antarctica. It was Ambrose Rector who was responsible for Captain Wendell Lee's death too—though not in the way that Emmett or Cassandra thought he was. They believed that Rector had outright murdered Captain Lee along with the rest of the crew of the *Frost Cleaver*, but Molly alone knew otherwise. Rector had revealed to her that he'd actually marooned Emmett's father in Antarctica, leaving the poor man to slowly die of starvation and frostbite. It was, honestly, a much more gruesome death, which was why she'd never told Emmett about it. She struggled over that choice daily, but always came to the same conclusion: Why fill Emmett's head with images of his father suffering a lonely, painful demise? Emmett's feelings about his long-gone father were complicated enough as it was. It was better to spare him. She hated Rector for burdening her with this secret—among a million other reasons.

Molly shivered. She was thinking about him again. There hadn't been a day since the attack on the World's Fair that Ambrose Rector hadn't wormed his way into her head. It didn't matter that the villain had been spotted fleeing New York Harbor in the *Frost Cleaver* months ago; she knew he'd return eventually. And with more of his deadly "Ambrosium."

Bam! Bam!

Molly jumped. "Robot, is that you?"

Robot tilted his head. "That is not me. I am me."

"No, the knocking," Molly said.

Somebody was pounding on the front door, beyond the tall folding screen that separated the Peppers' living/working quarters from the actual pickle shop.

"We have a customer!" Cassandra announced.

"I'll get it!" Molly said.

"But—*school!*" Emmett sputtered.

Molly ducked under the table and squeezed around the screen.

Unlike the messy rear half of the Peppers' pickle store, the front half, where customers entered, had not a mote of dust on the floor, nor crumb on the countertop. Not a single drop of brine meandered down the side of a jar. Keeping the shop neat, however, wasn't difficult when there were generally no pickle purchasers to wait on.

Molly threw up the sashes and squinted as sunlight burst in, revealing the morning buzz of Thompson Street outside. Jasper Bloom, a stocky, stubble-cheeked young man in gray coveralls, waved at Molly as she unlocked the door. Jasper was a friend—and the Peppers' only regular customer, which was why she felt bad about the unenthusiastic nod she greeted him with that morning.

"And a howdy-do to you too, Molly Pepper," Jasper said, tipping his cap. "I must say I was not expecting to see your charming self here at this hour. Not that I'm displeased, mind you. Although you do have what appears to be muddy eggs on your face. Anyhows, I'm surprised because I was under the impression that you and Emmett left for your daily jaunt to school at seven. Then again, I was also under the impression that this store *opened* at seven, and yet there I was at 7:27, standing pickle-less in the sun. And doing far too much door knocking. Do you know what all that knocking does to a man's knuckles, Molly Pepper? It chafes them. I got chafed knuckles now. That sorta thing never used to happen to me when I was an ashman. I've gone soft, Molly Pepper. Soft like a puppy's floppy ear. Do you know what Balthazar Birdhouse would say about these soft, chafed knuckles of mine? No, you don't—'cause you still never met the man. And that's a good thing. So, why is it you're not at school? You're not sick, are you? 'Cause if you're sick, I'm not sure you should be handling my pickle."

"We're running late!" Molly blurted, grateful to get a word in before Jasper rattled on for another twenty minutes. "So take your daily pickle and go. No offense." She plucked a fat garlic dill from a jar and handed it to him in a piece of wax paper.

"Hmmph, 'no offense,'" Jasper echoed. "Do you know

9

what I think whenever Balthazar Birdhouse says 'no offense'? That was a trick question—Balthazar Birdhouse never says 'no offense.' He just offends you and takes full credit for it. Emmett Lee! You're here too?"

"Yes, Jasper." Emmett had come running from behind the screen with his and Molly's schoolbags. "And if we don't leave in the next four minutes, we're going to miss the bell."

"I made them late on purpose," Cassandra said, poking her head out while she got dressed behind the screen. "To make morning more fun."

"Okay, Jasper, pay up so we can get going." Molly held out her hand.

"Well, you see, Molly Pepper, that brings up another question," Jasper said, dropping a nickel into her palm. Molly braced herself. He was going to ask for a job. Every day, he would come in, buy a pickle, and ask for a job. "As you know, I used to be an ashman—probably the best in New York City, if I'm being honest. You might hear differently from Balthazar Birdhouse, but seriously, which of us are you gonna trust? Anyhows, I was relieved of that job after I missed several days of work helping some certain children deal with a certain diabolical madman, and I am now among the unemployed. Although I did keep the uniform—please don't tell anyone."

"Jasper, we've told you we can't afford to pay another worker," Molly said.

"Come back tomorrow, Mr. Bloom," Cassandra said, stepping into the front shop area. Her button-down black dress was askew, but her hair had been pinned up into an almost-neat bun. "Here, Molly, you almost left without your spectacles again."

Jasper perked up. "Tomorrow it is!"

"Nothing's going to be different tomorrow," Molly grumbled as her mother slipped the round wireframes onto her face. "Except maybe I'll do a better job of misplacing these glasses."

"What makes you so certain nothing will change, Molls?" Cassandra grinned coyly.

Molly narrowed her eyes. "Is there something you're trying to tell us, Mother?"

"To hurry off to school?" Emmett said, nodding hopefully. "That's what you're telling us, right? To go to school now?"

"Oh, I can't hold it back any longer: *Everything* is going to change!" Cassandra gleefully exclaimed. "Today is the day the Guild votes!"

That brought Emmett back from the door. "Wait—the Inventors' Guild? They're voting *today*?"

"To finally change their membership policy?" Molly asked.

"Yes!" Cassandra bounced with excitement.

"How do you know?" Molly asked, flabbergasted.

"Yes, how do you know?" asked Jasper. "I have no idea

11

what you're talking about, but if a conversation takes place in my presence, I *will* be part of that conversation."

"The Inventors' Guild—you know, the fancy club where all the most powerful inventors work and never have to worry about money because the Guild seems to have endless resources?" Molly said. "Well, they have a strict 'No Girls Allowed' policy."

"And they've never seemed keen on changing it," said Cassandra. "Until the World's Fair, that is, when their stodgy old hides got saved by a bunch of brilliant scientists who happened to be ladies. Alexander Graham Bell and Thomas Edison promised us a vote after that. And they're finally having it!"

"That's amazing, Mrs. Pepper!" Emmett said. "But how do you know it's happening today?"

Cassandra giggled devilishly. "Bell told me weeks ago. He and Edison have both promised to sponsor me for membership as soon as the Guild changes their charter to allow women."

"You kept this from us? For weeks?" Molly gaped. Keeping secrets was something they'd all gotten better at after three months of being forced to pretend the World's Fair fiasco never happened, but still, this was *big news* for her mother to keep quiet about.

"I wasn't even going to tell you now," Cassandra said. "I wanted to surprise you when you came home from school."

"School?" Molly blurted, wrapping her arms around her mother. "Who cares about school?"

"I do," said Emmett. "Not to, you know, bring down the mood or anything, but . . ." He gestured toward the clock.

"No, Emmett is right," Cassandra said. "As much as I'd love to be there as the results are announced, you two probably shouldn't get caught skipping school right when we've finally gotten the Jäger Society's truancy goons off our back."

Molly scoffed. "And all we had to do to make that happen was save the world."

Cassandra ushered the children toward the door. "The vote is just a formality anyway," she said. "Bell and Edison run the Guild; the others will do what they say. Don't worry, though—as soon as you're home from school, we're closing the shop early and heading straight to the Guild Hall!"

Emmett glanced at a clock behind the counter. "Ugh, the morning bell's in eleven minutes."

"We're fueled by good news!" said Molly. "We'll run fast!"

"Well, actually, we might tire out if we run the entire way," Emmett said. "We should probably alternate. Run the first block, walk the second—no, wait, walk first. Or—are there an odd number of blocks or—"

"I'm running." Molly dashed outside. She didn't know

how she was going to concentrate in class today. Not that she was particularly good at that on a normal day. But today, it was going to be impossible to stop daydreaming about her mother striding up the Guild Hall's golden staircase, about her grand new office with a telephone and electric lights and tools so new they shone, about Alexander Graham Bell fetching her coffee and Thomas Edison humbly pleading for her help on his latest—

Molly stopped. There was a man across the street, a man in a long, dark coat. His bowler hat was tilted down to shade his eyes, but he seemed to be staring right at her. All thoughts of Cassandra's news left Molly's head, replaced by nightmare memories of Ambrose Rector.

Emmett dashed past her, saying, "I thought you said *run* first!"

Molly looked back across the street. The man was gone. She gripped the straps of her bag and ran to catch up, but not before checking over her shoulder one more time.